The Killer on my Doorstep

ALSO BY T.J. BREARTON

THE KILLER ON MY DOORSTEP

T. J. BREARTON

JOFFE BOOKS

Joffe Books, London
www.joffebooks.com

First published in Great Britain in 2026

© T.J. Brearton

Cover art by Nick Castle

ISBN: 978-1-80573-422-2

For Sabine

PROLOGUE

The woman was at the far end of the grocery aisle, her back mostly to me. I could see a sliver of her profile. Someone my age. Fit and trim, wearing dark Lululemon pants and athletic shoes, like she was a runner.

She was motionless, the way people are when they're concentrating. But I didn't see a phone or anything else that might hold her attention.

I continued along the aisle, pushing my cart slowly, sensing something was off. She stayed still as a statue, arm frozen mid-reach for a bottle of purple grape juice. She just couldn't seem to close the deal on it.

No one else in the aisle, only the two of us. I slowed even more, unsure what was happening, uncertain how I should respond.

Just get out of here. For whatever reason — shyness left over from childhood, a sense that I was catching someone in an intimate moment — I almost stopped, turned, and went the other way.

But the closer I got, the longer it went on, the more it felt like something was really wrong. She was just *standing* there. And no, she definitely wasn't on a phone. I could now see her other hand, grasping the handles of a red shopping basket.

Her free hand suddenly went to her chest and clutched her shirt.

Oh no.

She took a couple of deep breaths, shaky, rattling, the way someone sounds when they've just climbed that last flight of stairs. Lungs sucking for oxygen. The basket of groceries tilted first, then dropped, spilling its contents.

A trio of onions rolled away.

I started toward her, moving fast now. I was about to say something — I don't know what — when she began sinking to the floor, as if gravity had suddenly become too much to bear.

I stopped close enough to touch her, hovering, ready. If she collapsed, I could break her fall. Not sure what more I could do than that, though. The CPR course I'd taken in my early twenties felt like a long time ago.

Drops of sweat beaded her hairline and temples. My own heart banged against my ribs, but I remained sort of bent over, waiting. She stayed down on one knee, bracing herself against the dirty white tile.

And then, slowly, she turned her face up to mine.

The air seemed to tighten. Her eyes, a pretty hazel, were otherwise empty as dry wells. She knew I was there — she held up her hand to stop me — but there was no awareness in her gaze, nothing that seemed to understand anything about the moment we were in, no confusion or anxiousness. Only blankness. A cold universe. Frozen in time.

Someone passed by the end of the aisle just a few feet away, breaking the spell. But the older man didn't look at us, only continued on his way.

"Are you okay?" I asked, half whispering.

Still nothing in her eyes. Not looking at me but *through* me. Capacity without comprehension.

A full three-count later, having not even seemed to have heard my voice, she started to stand. She let me take her arm, but it was as if she didn't feel it, didn't react to it or use it. Once she seemed steady enough on her feet, I simply let go.

A moment passed with her looking down at the overturned red basket. She seemed to note the scattered onions, one all the way on the other side of the aisle. Then her gaze wandered up to the rows of juice bottles on the shelves.

I got the impression of a computer rebooting. A machine coming back online. She was remembering who and where she was. Had it been a seizure? Maybe some kind of drug?

And then, abruptly, as if she were in complete command of her body and mind, the woman in the athletic pants and shoes walked away.

Down the aisle she went, out through an unoccupied checkout lane at the front of the store, where she left via the automatic doors that slid closed in her wake.

Just like that.

I stood there, wondering what I'd just witnessed. I glimpsed her through the glass storefront, between the stuck-on signs telling me to *SAVE MORE THAN EVER*, moving among the vehicles in the parking lot.

And then she disappeared from view. Having left the store abruptly, having left behind her basket of unbought groceries — carrots, celery, a small head of broccoli, and those three wayward onions — she was gone.

I ended up bringing it all to the cashier at the front, with a story that I'd found the basket sitting in the aisle. The cashier didn't seem too worried, just set it aside. Then she totaled up my own purchases and went back to looking at her phone.

It was like the whole thing never happened.

PART I:
THE NEW NEIGHBORS

PART I
THE NEW NEIGHBOUR

CHAPTER ONE

Thursday afternoon

The new family moved in ordinarily enough. A U-Haul truck transported the bulk of their furniture, while a pickup truck and a car were stuffed with the rest of their belongings. I was at home in my vegetable garden, which has a good view of the neighboring house. It's just the two homes on this stretch of road outside of town. Across the road is state land, evergreen hills rising toward distant mountains.

Watching as three men began to unload the U-Haul, it struck me how truly bizarre the whole thing was. How people could move into the house next door to you and be completely anonymous. These would be your new neighbors, but you had no say. There was no selection process; it was the luck of the draw, the great lotto of life. In our case, there wasn't even a fence to share. Aside from a short, sparse row of poplars, their yard simply blended with ours.

We had ten acres. I'd never been sure how large the neighboring property was, but both drop down toward a wooded valley in the back that abuts on state land. One might wonder how we could afford a house with so much secluded land. Let's just say the market was a lot kinder seven years ago.

I sowed my late summer seeds — kale, spinach, and carrots — which could tolerate the cooler months to come. For now, it was hot. I considered making lemonade, bringing it over there, saying hello, but decided against it. I'd wait until they had a chance to settle in a little, make them a proper housewarming gift.

I hadn't been close with the previous neighbors. At one time, old Mrs. Marvin had had her own perennials and shrubs and flowers, and you'd see her out there on her hands and knees, digging in the dirt, bony butt in the air. And then one day, she'd stopped. Hospitalized, I eventually heard, though I never knew for what. But she hadn't returned to her perennials.

It was about that time when I started gardening in earnest, as if picking up where she'd left off. While her vegetation remained neglected, ravaged by deer, there I was, building a fence around freshly built raised beds.

Mrs. Marvin was eighty-four when she died. I'm half that, with plenty of years ahead, I hope. But it was as if witnessing her decline got me thinking about my mortality, and this tied in with growing food. Food was life, perhaps. Control. And I liked taking care of things.

Once I'd poked all my seeds into the ground and spent a few more minutes weeding, it was time. My knees were feeling it, my lower back getting tight. I stood carefully and dusted my dirty hands. The garden door squeaked when I pushed it open.

One of the men, wearing a white short-sleeved shirt and brownish work pants, turned and looked my way. He waved, and I waved back. His gaze seemed to linger a moment, as if sizing me up across the distance. Then he went back to moving boxes.

* * *

Though it was only one in the afternoon, I got dinner going. Cooking went more smoothly when I did a little prep work. I chopped onions, carrots, and celery. I minced some of my own parsley and oregano. Together with the chicken thawing in the fridge, we'd have a nice soup. Hot soup on a hot day was good for you, my father always said.

That done, I drifted into my bedroom, where the neighboring house was visible through the window. I don't know what drew me. Natural curiosity, I guess.

The U-Haul truck was gone. The pickup too. But then someone came out of the house and approached the car.

She was dressed smartly casual, in a white T-shirt and short jeans. The distance between us, about a football field, obscured her face as an oval blur. Still, I thought, *pretty*. And a good twenty to thirty pounds lighter than me, I judged. I hated that I was even a little jealous of skinny women, but there you have it.

I squinted, trying to get a better look, but she moved out of view when she ducked into the car.

I stayed there, watching.

Lainey, I chided myself. *Come on.*

But I remained watching for one more second, and the woman stood with an armload of clothes or blankets. When she looked toward my house, I flinched. Like something had flown at my head.

I hadn't seen it right away. But perhaps my eyes had adjusted to the distance.

Or maybe I just hadn't believed it at first.

The last time I'd seen this person was in the middle of the supermarket aisle. Where she had gone through some kind of episode.

* * *

Whatever else happened that afternoon, between one thirty and three thirty, I don't really remember. I grew preoccupied coming up with an explanation for what I'd witnessed in the grocery store, how someone could seem to have gone completely out of their mind one minute and be moving into a new house the next. It was a coincidence too, but that part was easier. Our tiny hamlet of Buxton had less than a thousand people.

Still. It had me going.

When it came time to pick up the girls, I tried to put it all out of my mind. My daughters would have a lot to tell me about their first week of school. Mouths would motor nonstop until bedtime. I didn't want to miss any of it.

The same pickup truck from earlier was returning, coming down the road as I walked to my car. The two-tone truck, with its contrasting gray door and black body, was hard to miss. I got in my car but waited, watching as it pulled into the new neighbor's driveway. Once parked, two little boys hopped out, shouting and full of energy. One took off running around to the back. He looked around eleven or twelve, same age as my eldest daughter.

The second boy was mostly hidden between the two parked vehicles. His head popped up and down as he hopped around like a bunny. But when the woman came out onto the porch, he hurried over and threw his arms around her middle.

That pretty much did it for me. Whatever jitters I had, whatever stories I'd made up in my head to make sense of the grocery store strangeness, this was a loving family. A husband and wife, it seemed, with two boys just about the ages of my own girls. The woman had experienced some kind of spell. She could be diabetic, have low blood sugar, something. I was just glad she was okay.

I continued on my way, turning the vehicle in the wide part of the driveway at the end so I could nose out into the road. It was 55 mph going past our house, and some people would drive like it was the Daytona Speedway, so I always had to be careful.

CHAPTER TWO

"Looks like new people moved in next door?"

"New people?" Charlotte sat bolt upright in her chair at the dinner table, staring at her father. "New people next door?" Charlotte was our resident extrovert. At seven, she had everyone dancing to her beat.

Delia's reaction was more subdued. "Who are they?"

"Just a family that moved in," I said. "Eat your dinner, girls."

They needed constant reminding.

"What about Mrs. Marvin?" Charlotte asked, frowning.

"Well," I said. "Remember when Mrs. Marvin passed away earlier this summer?"

She scrunched up her face. Sometimes it was hard to tell whether Charlotte was actually confused about something or putting on a show. Anything to hook you in, get your attention. She was bound to be our first Instagram influencer.

"Do they have kids?" Delia forked some salad into her mouth, acting casual. Delia loved kids. Highly social, she loved everybody.

"They do have kids, I think. I saw two boys."

"Boys!" Now Charlotte was excited. Boys meant competition and mischief.

"Looks like they're just about your ages too," I said.

"Any idea what they do, or where they're coming from?" Geoff drained the rest of the soup from his bowl.

"No, I have no idea. I didn't talk to them or anything."

"Hmm. Interesting. New neighbors, girls!"

"I think we'll bring them something. Maybe brownies. What do you think?"

The girls were in favor. "Now?" Charlotte asked.

"No, this weekend. Maybe tomorrow afternoon. We'll let them settle in first."

Talk turned to other things. Delia was learning about Mexico in school and had a project to do a biography on a famous Mexican of her choosing. With no input from me or Geoff, she'd chosen Frida Kahlo, the painter. She wanted to watch the biopic starring Salma Hayek for some background, but no way was that happening. "It's a grown-up movie," I told her.

"*Mom*," she complained. "I watch grown-up movies all the time."

"Not like this." In telling Kahlo's story like it was, the film was full of copious drinking and sex.

Eventually, Delia let it go. She was at that age, though, on the verge of becoming a young woman. At times still full of childhood fears, yet smart and capable. The "leave me alone but please tuck me in" stage. We named her after my grandmother, Delia Weston, who'd been one of the first female nutritionists to ever work at Mount Sinai Hospital in New York City. Delia was smart, like she was.

She wanted a phone, of course. Geoff and I were holding out, hoping to make it another three years until she was fourteen. We both knew it was unlikely. Already there were social pressures, and Delia had been working on us for months. She was subtle, crafty, usually bringing it up at bedtime, often with added tears. Many of her classmates played online games together, she said, and talked about it in school. She felt like an outsider whenever they did.

We tried to placate her with a tablet. She could message her friends using our Wi-Fi. She could play games. But waiting for a phone was still tough, and the experts were recommending even older — sixteen! — for social media. Our house might explode with teen angst if we waited that long. You'd find our roof somewhere down by the river.

It was a goal — something to strive for, anyway. My instinct to protect my girls from social exclusion would likely supersede more abstract fears I had of technology. A choice: my daughter losing her mind today, or vague concerns about her self-esteem tomorrow?

Charlotte had a spelling test coming up and we went over the words as she cleared away the dishes. Geoff talked a little about his workday, but only in broad terms — lots of back-to-school sickness going around. He could never reveal any information about specific patients.

Charlotte was in bed by eight. She often talked right up until the moment she fell asleep. On one recent night, I swear she actually fell asleep *in the middle of a sentence*. Charlotte was named after Geoff's grandmother, a homemaker from Maine. As far as I could tell, though, our resident entertainer had little in common with the quiet, dutiful woman with whom she shared a name.

Tonight, though, she went to sleep with much less fanfare. Just a quick story and she was asleep before I even climbed from the bed.

"I think she's coming down with something," I said to Geoff.

He was changing into his sweatpants and a twenty-year-old hoodie, evening wear for watching TV with me. "Yeah, I'm seeing RSV and flu," he said. "Couple cases of COVID."

As we talked, I wandered over to the window. The lights were on at the Marvin house, and I thought I saw someone move past one of the windows.

"I didn't take her temp. Think I should?"

"Did she feel hot?"

"Not especially. I'll do it in the morning."

Geoff finished dressing in his comfy clothes and bent into a stretch.

As I stayed at the window, watching, the lights went out. All at once, the neighbor's house was dark.

"Whoa," I said, and double-checked our lights, which were on.

Geoff neared. "What?"

"All their lights just shut off. Like they lost power."

"Huh. Well, probably not, or we would have. Maybe they're just going to bed."

"They went out all at once. Those are two bedrooms right there, on that end of the house. And the porch light was on, but it went out too. Maybe they — oh."

The lights came back on.

"He's messing around with the breaker box," Geoff said. "Just checking things out. So, cool. New neighbors. You're gonna bring them something, you said?"

I was silent a moment. I'd been wanting to talk to Geoff about what I'd seen that morning, but the girls had been around. Picturing my new neighbor reaching for the grape juice, struck motionless as if receiving instructions from the mothership.

"I think I saw the woman," I said.

"You saw her? What do you mean?"

I gave him the context, then tried to explain how she'd looked to me, the various things that went through my mind in a matter of seconds. "She didn't seem like she was in pain, necessarily. She just like . . . blanked out. Like she was really having some kind of a . . . I don't know."

"Yikes. But she was okay? I mean, she's seemed okay since then?"

"Yeah, she has, I guess. I've only seen her from across the way. I could have gone over and introduced myself this afternoon when they showed up, but it kind of threw me."

"Hmm," he said. "Yeah. And you think . . . maybe she was sick?"

"I don't think so. Not really. More like . . . someone lost in thought, but much more severe. Almost aphasic."

"So what did you do?"

"I didn't really do anything."

"You think she recognized you?"

"What? When?"

"Today. You said you saw them moving in. Someone waved."

"A mover. Not her. Let's just forget it," I said, and walked away.

I suddenly felt grouchy. It felt hard to explain what I'd seen. One of those things that feels profound in the moment but is difficult to convey later.

I started picking up the bedroom, what I did sometimes when I was frustrated and didn't know what to do about it or where to go. As I folded the pair of pants Geoff had sloughed on the floor, I realized my reaction had less to do with the neighbors than my own family. Geoff and I were going through a rough patch, one of those low-grade fights that can last a while, a resolution delayed by other business, never really a good time to talk.

He moved closer and touched my shoulders, started massaging them. "Hey, I know. Things have been tough. The girls just got back into school, it was a busy summer, and you were with them a lot. You don't need to roll out the red carpet for the neighbors or anything. I just—"

"There it goes again," I said when the house went dark a second time.

Geoff looked over my shoulder. "Messing with the breaker, seeing where everything is. You remember that floodlight that used to be on the driveway? Started wigging out, flashing like that? Some of these houses have screwed-up wiring."

"I never saw that happen when the Marvins were there."

"I'd be curious to know what he does. One of the doors to his truck is a different color than the body. Maybe he's an electrician?"

"Because he has a truck with a replaced door?" I asked, attempting levity.

He squeezed my shoulders. "Electricians don't understand cars, honey."

I chuckled, distracted. We fell silent, waiting for the lights to come back on. Nearly a minute passed, and the house was still dark.

Geoff gently pushed past me and got right up to the window, peering out.

Something buzzed against my leg. I pulled out my phone and saw a text from the mom group.

It was from Kimber Hudson, whose son was in the same grade as Charlotte.

Just letting everyone know that Fynn is sick.

"Uh-oh," I said.

"What?" Geoff turned back from the window. I showed him the screen. "Yeah," he said. "Makes sense."

There were already text responses from the group. There were five moms in all. Some did more talking than others; my phone showed each person's initials in a circle, and the bigger the circle, the more prodigious the texter. Kimber's circle was medium-sized. An average texter, like me.

"She says he's got a fever of just over a hundred. No other symptoms yet, just tired."

I left the bedroom and went to the medicine cabinet in the bathroom for the digital thermometer, the kind held just above the skin. Charlotte was breathing softly in her bed. I took two readings and returned the thermometer to the bathroom.

"All good," I said, reentering the bedroom. "Normal temp."

Geoff had moved to the bed and was sitting on its edge, looking at his own phone. "Good."

I went to the window, saw the next-door lights were back on. Messing with the circuit breaker made sense. Time to let it go. If we were going to get in any Netflix shows, it was going to have to start now, before my eyes closed of their own volition. "Come on," I said. "Let's get to it."

And I really thought that would be it. Our new neighbor's fugue at the local grocery store would go down as just one of those weird, unexplained things in life. None of my business, really. Something I'd soon forget all about.

I had no way of knowing what was coming.

CHAPTER THREE

Friday

A beach-day haze suffused the already-warm morning. I sat in one of our wooden Adirondack chairs, low mountain peaks in the near distance, sneaking a cigarette.

"Everything okay?" Geoff sounded worried. I rarely called him at work.

"Everything's fine."

"Girls are okay?"

"Girls are fine; they're at school. I'm sorry to call and worry you."

Those things out of the way, he relaxed a little, though a hint of exasperation lingered in his voice. "What's up?"

"I think I want to go back to work." Best to just come right out with it.

"Oh," Geoff said, as if he'd been expecting worse. "Back to work? Like, restaurant work?"

"Of course not. I mean put my degree to use."

"Okay, right. Sure. I mean, probably that'll affect what you're doing, right? The coaching. The girls will have to get into after-school care . . ."

"I know."

We'd had versions of this conversation before: how much day-care would cost, commuting to an office, buying lunch instead of making it in my own kitchen.

I had a criminal justice degree from Syracuse University, but I hadn't worked since before Delia was born, and my last job wasn't exactly in my field anyway. Bartending had been my way of putting things off; I couldn't decide between specializing in victim advocacy, investigative reporting, or intervention/prevention. I hadn't made the choice, and I'd never gotten back on track. Geoff was a physician's assistant and made enough money to support us. A rare thing, having one income; we were fortunate.

"I know you gave up a lot for us," Geoff said. "For me. You left a lot on the table. And I think you have every right to get back to that. Obviously. Anything you want, we'll make it happen. You know that."

I waited for the "but."

"But, you know, I also think it's possible there's a certain timing to this."

"Timing?"

"Courtney just moved away. You used to do a lot with her. You had someone to talk to more regularly."

"I talk to Kimber. Wendy, Renee, the whole mom group. I see them all the time."

"You know what I mean. The way they can be."

I did. Whatever social penalty outsiders had to pay, Geoff's was waived because he was essentially the local doctor. For me, it didn't seem to matter how much I did for the community, there was always that little bit of daylight between myself and the people who'd lived here their whole lives.

I took a drag of the cigarette, held the phone away so he wouldn't hear the exhalation.

"You there?" Geoff asked.

"Yeah, sorry. Just . . . a bug."

He was right about Courtney — I missed her. She hadn't been like some of the others. She'd been open and warm, even though her family went back generations. But that wasn't why I wanted to go back to work.

I went to every school concert, every parent–teacher meeting, and it was my job to be home with the girls when they were sick, or there was a vacation, a half-day — all of it. My role was to keep the girls' lives in order, keep house, feed and clothe everybody. Maybe it should have felt like enough, but it didn't. I needed some other purpose. An outlet. A pursuit.

Maybe we should get a dog.

"Honey, I have to go. I'm getting paged."

"All right."

"See you tonight. Love you."

"Love you too."

I hung up and, looking around to reassure myself that I was still out of view from the road, and the neighbors, lit another cigarette. Geoff didn't know I'd been smoking for the past month. Not a ton, just two or three a day. Okay, five. Except on weekends, when everyone was home and it was harder to sneak away. I might manage one after the girls went to bed.

The first couple of drags felt good, as they usually did, and justifiably devious. I closed my eyes and felt the warm sun burning through the haze. It was going to be a hot one, with temperatures in the mid-nineties.

I knew smoking was bad, but it took the edge off. And if I was being totally honest, I liked that I didn't snack as much.

I was halfway through the cigarette when I heard a noise: someone knocking at the front door.

"Hello?" A man's voice.

I quickly put the cigarette out and waved away the smoke, dropping the butt in the can I hid behind the wood bin. Package deliveries rarely required a signature, but maybe Geoff had ordered propane for the stove? Or someone was running for office? Local elections were coming up in the fall. But something told me that wasn't it.

Perhaps I was still on alert from the grocery store incident, but I rounded the corner of the house with my heart going a little faster than normal. And I was right. Standing on my porch was my new neighbor.

"Oh," he said, seeing me. "Hi. Hope I'm not bothering you."

He was handsome. That was the first thing I noticed. The kind of man that embodied the old term my mother used to use — *good stock*. Dark hair wavy and full, a little shaggy around the ears. Expressive eyebrows arching to a point.

"Oh, no, you're fine." I walked up the small incline toward the porch in khaki shorts and a tank top, sports bra underneath, probably looking like a middle-aged housewife. Which I was. My hair was loose and frizzy. I hadn't touched up the scattered gray in almost a month.

He'd been standing with the screen door open, knocking on the main door. Now he let it go, and it slapped shut with a bang, making him jump.

"Sorry. It does that."

"Powerful spring," he said, examining it. Then he gave me a sheepish grin as he took the two steps off the small porch. "I'm Eric Scheller. Just moved in next door."

I considered, lightning-quick, acting like I hadn't noticed the move-in. "Sure, we saw you yesterday. The U-Haul."

"Right, duh, yeah. I guess we were pretty obvious."

"I'm Elaine," I said, and we shook. His grip was warm and dry, not too lax, not too firm. His eyes were light blue, almost icy, the way they caught the late morning sun. "Elaine Barrister."

"Nice to meet you." He let go of my hand. "Sorry to just show up like this. I saw the vehicle in the driveway . . . I thought maybe someone might be home."

"It's no problem. Yeah, I'm usually home during the day. I was just . . . getting some air."

Those eyes might have danced a little. Had he smelled the cigarette from around the corner? "It's beautiful out. Hot, though. And the mercury is still climbing."

"Going to be in the nineties again," I agreed. "Summer seems to be hanging in there."

"Right." He smiled fully, showing teeth.

The way we were positioned, though, with him still slightly uphill from me, made me uncomfortable. I moved, putting myself between him and the porch. He seemed to interpret this as needing to get to the point. "Anyway, I just wanted to say hello and introduce myself. Formally. More than a distant wave. So, hello."

"Hello," I said again, smiling. Too much smiling? Maybe. Then I thought of his wife, standing there in the supermarket aisle, eyes like olive pits, and my expression faded.

"How is everything so far? I haven't been over there in years. Was the move-in okay?" Rambling a little.

"Yeah, smooth sailing. Did have a little trouble figuring out some of the power in that place. The electrical work is spaghetti inside those walls. You turn on the switch for one room and a light comes on in another one."

"No . . . really?" I forced myself to stop thinking about their flickering lights, lest he read it on my face.

"Yeah. I had to test everything a few times. I think we over-loaded a circuit in the kitchen. Anyway, did you know the previous neighbors?" His eyes widened and his mouth hung open. "Oh God, did I just insult somebody?"

"Oh, no, no. I didn't know them all that well. Just that they lived there for years and years before we moved in. She was old, Mrs. Marvin. I doubt she did any wiring. Or her husband before her. He was the school principal for a long time. I don't think he did electrical work."

"Okay." Eric Scheller's face was open, accepting this.

"Where are you moving from?"

Suddenly there was a catch in his gaze, like a guard had gone up. "Um, not far. Just down in Tannersville."

"Oh, okay. Big transition," I said, making a joke.

"Yeah, big transition."

Conversations are largely unconscious. Body language, tone of voice. When he changed the subject, it seemed cumbersome and obvious.

"That's a great view."

I looked behind me at the gently rising mountains. "Yeah, we love it. Those trees, though . . . Geoff, my husband, he's been planning for years to cut some of those down."

"I could see that, yeah. So, it's you and your husband and . . . ?"

"Two girls. We have two daughters. Delia and Charlotte."

"Those are beautiful names. We have two boys. Jasper and Mack. Short for Mackenzie."

"Also great names. How old are they?"

As we continued to discuss our children and their similarities, I took him in a bit more. He was about my age, maybe a couple of years younger, and fit. He wore canvas-type shorts, carpenter-style with a loop for a hammer. In the pocket of his tattered retro short-sleeved dress shirt was a square object that could only be a pack of cigarettes. His nails were trim and clean. His hiking boots were scuffed and worn, but high-quality. No white tube socks sticking out; if he was wearing socks, they were ankle-cut.

"How are the ticks?" he asked.

It took me a second; I'd gotten mentally sidetracked. "They're bad, honestly. Charlotte actually had Lyme disease last year."

His face opened with concern. "Oh, no."

"We caught it early enough and knocked it out with a course of doxycycline."

He nodded. "We gave that to Mack too, after he had one of those halos. You know? The red halo around the bite site?"

"I do. They say you can still be infected even if that doesn't show up."

"Right."

He studied the yard like he might spot some of the nearly microscopic bugs crawling through my lawn. And he'd have words with them if necessary.

I liked him immediately.

"I keep it mowed down to the nub," I said about the lawn.

"Oh yeah? You're the groundskeeper?"

"Only after I talked my husband into letting me do it. We've got one of those serious riding mowers. We do what we can for prevention. If the girls are going near the woods, I have them wear long pants, tucked into their socks, all of that." I continued to talk, half convinced he was interested, half suspecting he was just making conversation. Studying me, almost. "Some of the tick repellents seem to work, but it's hard to know. And you've got to spray them all the time."

He shook his head in dismay. "They're coming further and further north as everything gets warmer too."

I nodded, wondering if the conversation was headed toward global warming, but Eric Scheller just shook his head and mumbled about it being a shame, fearing that kids playing outside and enjoying themselves could lead to things like Lyme, when being out in nature was what they needed more of these days.

"My girls are very excited," I said, returning to the original subject. "We planned on bringing you something this weekend, a welcome-to-the-neighborhood treat."

"Oh, yes please. They'd love to meet you and your girls. Your family."

"Is there anything anyone can't eat? Any allergies, aversion to certain things, anything like that?"

My question wasn't designed to draw out information on his wife, but that would be a bonus.

"We're scavengers," he said. It might've been a slightly odd thing to say if he didn't flash that movie-star grin at me again. "We're opportunists who accept all welcome-to-the-neighborhood treats."

"All right, great. It's settled."

The encounter reaching its inertia, he started to back away, and then he raised his hand. "It was nice to meet you, Elaine."

"Lainey. And you too . . . Eric."

Still smiling, he turned and walked back across the conjoined yards between our homes.

CHAPTER FOUR

Tannersville, I thought. Just thirty miles south. You took the winding, mountainous Buxton Falls Road, which got its name from the cascading waterfall you passed on the way. Or you could drive east for a while, take the interstate and then drive back west, but it didn't save any time. Most people took the back road: forty-five minutes.

Not a very big move, no. Probably work-related, if I had to guess. Eric hadn't said. He'd just smiled his *I know I'm good-looking* smile. A version of Ray Lamontagne in his prime.

That twinkle in his eye, I couldn't get past it.

"Screw it," I said. The first Google hit for *Eric Scheller Tannersville* was a farm property insurance agent on LinkedIn. The Tannersville part didn't actually apply, since this guy lived in the Midwest. There was an Eric Scheller running for a seat on the Hamilton Beach School Board, and a *David* Eric Scheller who had died in Lancaster, Pennsylvania, in 1883 according to Find-a-grave.com. (What a morbid website that was.)

Nothing was showing up that seemed like my guy. But I was only guessing at the last name. When I dropped the *c*, I got a hit that made more sense. Eric Sheller, attorney at law, Tannersville. His picture was a professional headshot in which he looked far less rugged. Squeaky clean in a suit and tie, almost like a different person. The hit was also for LinkedIn, but this was him. My new neighbor. A lawyer from the next town over.

I deflated a little at that. Not that I had anything against lawyers. He just looked so normal in his picture. A professional person with a career. One that involved lots of sitting and talking.

Maybe I was a little embarrassed too. Recalling how he'd looked at me when I'd said I was "getting some air." Like he not only smelled the traces of cigarette but was trained to recognize deceit.

Setting my phone on the counter, I pushed it away. I'd liked him, but now I wondered. A woman had freaked out in the supermarket and then the next day her husband shows up at my door. He was nice, but maybe flirty? Overly convivial? And they'd only moved such a relatively short distance.

When Delia came home from school, the first thing she would want to do was make brownies and cart them next door. I could convince her that Saturday afternoon was the more appropriate, even optimal, time for brownies. She wouldn't like it, but it would buy me a little time, let me talk to Geoff. Maybe I was overreacting, maybe not.

I walked outside then, into air so hot it burned, and looked past the oaks in our yard, across grass browned and brittle from long days with no rain.

The Sheller house wavered in the heat. Sweat popped up on my skin as I stood there, the blazing tarmac of the driveway beneath my feet, the sun at its peak and raining down fire. No sign of activity from the new neighbors. But the car was back in the driveway. A Subaru, instantly recognizable. In the time I'd gone inside, put the groceries away, and spent a few minutes Googling on my phone, Mrs. Sheller — whatever her first name was — had returned home.

What was she doing right now? Was she on the phone with her doctor? Maybe her cardiologist? Was her episode at the grocery store something that happened on a regular basis or was it a one-off? Was it so unusual that she'd remained in shock, temporarily unable to act?

I wondered if she'd even blacked out, had no memory of it. She'd looked at me with such mute incomprehension, like she'd suddenly returned to her body from elsewhere.

Maybe it was some kind of New Age meditation. A trance induced by her shaman therapist.

Maybe the sun was baking my brain.

CHAPTER FIVE

"He rented an office in the Parker building," Geoff said, still wearing his scrubs from work. He munched some potato chips at the kitchen island, meaning he was hungry for dinner.

I dumped steaming pasta into a colander in the sink. The girls were in the playroom, their school stuff scattered about the entryway. "Who told you that?"

"Mae."

Mae was a nurse at the clinic where Geoff worked.

The Parker building was on the north end of town, part of what constituted our "business district." I didn't know lawyers rented space there, but why not. And there was at least one therapist and a chiropractor. I did the math: Mae's sister was the chiropractor, who'd likely told Mae, who'd told my husband.

"So, you were just talking about the neighbors to her?"

Geoff cleared his throat suddenly, like a chip fragment had gotten stuck. "She asked me, actually. She said her, ah . . . sister told her about this guy who'd rented the space. She wondered if it was my new neighbor."

Small town, so naturally everyone mostly knew what was going on. But I also detected some jealousy in my husband. Mae's sister was young, single, her interest piqued by the mysterious newcomer.

"Huh," I said, thinking about Sheller's blue eyes. I had yet to tell Geoff about my afternoon encounter. For one, the girls were home. Even though they were in the other room, they had a way of showing up in the middle of adult conversations at precisely the wrong moment.

For another, something else was on my mind.

"You and Mae were just talking about all of this at work?"

"We took a walk at lunch. I wanted to stretch my legs."

"My God, it was so hot."

"It was, yeah. But we just needed to get out." Geoff loaded another chip into his mouth and crunched down on it. For some reason, the chewing sounded extra loud. I was a little irritated, but I couldn't put my finger on why. Maybe because I'd wanted to talk to him about this morning, but now I felt reserved.

"Any more thoughts about working?" he asked.

I wondered if he was eager to change the subject.

"Not really. You're right, it's sort of the same thing. I could work for the county maybe in advocacy or intervention, but the starting pay is low. Anything else and . . . this isn't really the area to do it."

He nodded, like he already knew this, and had been patiently waiting for me to remember it for myself.

Having returned the pasta to the pot, I poured in the homemade pesto. We harvested a lot of basil and used it to make pesto in the blender. I added some sliced cherry tomatoes and gave it all a stir.

We spent dinner listening to the girls. Mostly to Charlotte, who'd been pushed on the playground by another girl, Riley. The push was hard enough that Charlotte fell. We asked if she told one of the aides about it, and she had. Charlotte's stories often began with her being the victim of some wrongdoing, and while pushing was always wrong, a little more investigation revealed that she and her two best friends hadn't included Riley in their game, which led to Riley getting aggressive.

"It's not your fault, honey," I told Charlotte. "But I think it's also important to understand that Riley might've had hurt feelings for not being able to play the game with you and your friends."

"But she's so rough!" Charlotte exclaimed. "We *try* to play with her, but she's always so mean, and she wants us to do everything she says."

"I know," I said. "I understand. Maybe just do your best and try to make sure she feels included, though." I leaned in to smell the basil in the pesto. The pine nuts.

"We *try* to," Charlotte repeated, on the verge of getting emotional.

I caught Geoff's gaze at the table. I raised my eyebrows, signaling him, a mostly unconscious act. He turned to Charlotte. "Sometimes people like Riley don't know how to handle their feelings," he said. "They get mean because they're feeling hurt." I got the sudden sense he knew something about Riley, maybe about her family. Geoff was tuned in to the community in ways I wasn't. The ways I wished I was.

It was all in his glance — *Riley is having problems at home.*

We left it at that.

"Did either of you see the new boys at school today? Their names are Jasper and Mack."

"I did," Delia said. "Jasper is in my class."

A little thrill shot through me at that bit of news. "Really? Oh wow, cool. So, he was there today?"

She nodded and forked in some pasta. "Mm-hmm."

"Was he nice?"

She shrugged, then swallowed. "Yeah. He was nice."

On the other hand, Charlotte hadn't met Mack. It was possible he was in a different class, or a different grade even. Delia wiped her mouth with a napkin, carefully dabbing the corners. (Our eldest daughter has adult table manners.) "So, are we going to make the brownies?"

Both girls awaited my answer. I gave them my spiel about waiting until Saturday, a better time for delivering brownies, and dealt with the disappointed groans and frowns and listened to their best arguments for doing it now. By this point, Geoff was looking at his phone.

After dinner, he cleaned up. That was our routine: I cooked and he did the dishes. Normally, I might move on to something else, like bringing up the laundry to fold, or getting the girls into the shower. But it was Friday night, and I was ready to talk. I brought out the wireless speaker and put on some easy listening, just a little extra sound cover. Getting near him at the sink, I said, "He came over."

"Who came over?"

"Eric Sheller."

"Really? Huh. What did he want?"

"Just to say hello. He asked about the girls, and we just chatted."

"Sounds like he was doing recon. I bet the wife recognized you."

Geoff gave voice to my suspicions. I thought about the quiet spaces during my small talk with Eric. "Maybe," I said. "It's possible she doesn't even remember it. But . . . did Mae know her name? Eric's wife?"

"Naomi. She might be a grant writer. She likes to trail run. Um . . . that's about all I remember."

I thought about the athletic clothes she'd been wearing. The shoes. That she'd been damp with sweat.

I went through it again with Geoff, including how she looked at me without seeing me. I dug into his gaze, waiting for any sign that she'd followed that episode with a trip to the health center, but he betrayed nothing. Done with the dishes, he dried off his hands and went out to the garage. Geoff had had a Volkswagen Beetle since I'd first met him. It ran less than half the time, but he liked to work on it.

That weekend was going to be busy, beginning with a soccer game in the morning. I ran a load of soccer socks and made Charlotte hunt for her shin guards.

Naomi, I thought, feeling the connection a name could bring. I still couldn't say what had happened to her. Even though Geoff couldn't tell me anything private, I just didn't think she'd had a medical emergency. People didn't walk away from a heart attack or a stroke. It was more likely something mental. She just seemed to switch off for a second.

Like the Marvin house going dark.

CHAPTER SIX

The evening moved on, and Geoff eventually returned inside. We played games with the girls for a bit — Rack-O and matching. Delia won the matching game easily, twice, which upset competitive Charlotte. But Charlotte, gifted in math for her age, creamed us all with Rack-O, even though it was as much luck as it was handling numbers, and Geoff and I both made some on-purpose mistakes.

Is it right to let your kid win because it upsets them so much to lose? Or is it better to let them face defeat and suffer the fallout? I could never decide. But after Charlotte's day getting pushed by Riley, Geoff and I were both thinking she needed a win.

* * *

When the kids went for their TV time and Geoff got into the shower, I opened my phone and checked the mom group.

As it turned out, another girl had been bullied by Riley that day. Wendy's daughter. The largest circle contained Wendy's initials — she was the most active communicator in the group — and she held forth about Riley. Riley did more than push her daughter. She punched her in the back and called her a "skank."

Second-graders, using such words. Good grief. Though I suppose it wasn't any worse than in my day. I had a girl in elementary school who sometimes waited for me on the path home through the woods to heckle me with nasty names. Imagine kids today taking paths through the woods. But we used to do it. We'd walk to and from school, cutting through a small swath of forest to shorten the trip.

Stacy Meyer, the girl who had it in for me all the way up until middle school when her family moved away (thank God), always seemed to be there the days I walked that route alone. She called me "fat ass" and, every once in a while, felt the need to yank my backpack loose and kick it.

I sympathized with Wendy, but for some reason I withheld that Charlotte had also been bullied. I didn't know why. Normally I was frank with the group; it usually seemed like the best policy. Just not this time.

Instead, I found myself texting about other matters.

Hey, we have new neighbors. Their boys are Jasper and Mack Sheller. Sixth grade and third or fourth.

Wendy was the first to react. I waited a moment, watching the three little wiggling dots.

Hopefully they're not bullies.

Still stuck on the Riley situation. Understandable. Another one of the moms, Theresa, popped up.

Ohhh that's cool. We have so many girls. Nice to get some boys in the crew! Lol. Who are the parents?

Naomi and Eric Sheller, I wrote. Immediately, I worried I was somehow oversharing. But it was normal to gossip about newcomers in our little town, wasn't it? So why did I suddenly feel guilty?

Because I had an ulterior motive: I wanted more information. But the mom group hadn't heard of the Shellers yet, or their sons.

They mostly asked *me* questions, and after a few minutes I set the phone away. Delia came into the kitchen, wanting to use my iPad to play *Roblox*. I straightened from the kitchen island and got her set up.

* * *

A flicker of light caught my eye. I stood at our bed, turning down the sheets. Geoff and I had just watched one of the new crime shows we liked.

"What is it now?" I said, going to the window.

The Sheller house was dark, but not completely. Light glowed from somewhere deep within. As I stood watching, I thought I saw movement near the back. The Marvins had built a nice deck there, replete with tiki-torch-style lights.

Geoff came into the room, his electric toothbrush buzzing. He tossed something on the bed. My iPad. "Just wrestled that away from Delia," he told me through a toothpaste-filled mouth.

I'd forgotten about getting her off the device. "Sorry."

He left again, buzzing his way back to the bathroom.

I stepped closer to the window, thinking I could make out two shapes, people outside.

I had a pair of binoculars somewhere, didn't I? Hurrying down the hall past the bathroom — so as not to be snagged by Geoff or either of the girls — I flicked the basement light on as I went down the stairs. In the back of the space were our boxes and bags for camping. Geoff grew up camping around the Adirondacks with his family, and we went once or twice each summer. I thought the binoculars were in the "box-o-fun," as Geoff called it. I was right.

I put the lid back on the plastic tote and hurried back upstairs. Feeling a little ridiculous, I waited as Delia walked by, whining to her father that she hadn't gotten her full amount of iPad time because Char kept distracting her and wanting to use it.

Stupid iPads, I thought. *Stupid screens.*

I almost closed the bedroom door but didn't. I'd rather hear Geoff coming. It wasn't radically nosy what I was doing, but still.

I peered across the conjoined lawns with the binoculars pressed to the window. The two people were still out back. It was the Shellers. Eric was gesturing with his arms, flipping his hands in the air. The tiki lights illuminated him well enough to see the stress on his face. Naomi Sheller, meanwhile, seemed detached, like a child getting lectured. Whatever he was saying wasn't getting through, because he only seemed to get more incensed. Finally, he seemed to give up, just lowered his head, shook it as if in disbelief. Naomi stayed mostly subdued at first, then grew animated, feisty. They were in the middle of a full-on argument. A doozy, by the look of it.

Before the guilt was too much to bear and I put away the binoculars, Naomi went inside. I saw the door slam a split second before I actually heard it from across the distance. Eric stayed behind, standing motionless. Then he dug for something in his pocket, shook out a cigarette from a pack, and popped it in his mouth. *I knew it!* He cupped his hands against the breeze and lit it. I watched him drag and inhale, the image triggering my own desire.

"Same thing?"

I jumped. Geoff had been so quiet coming up behind me. I'd been entranced.

I almost tried to hide the binoculars, but that would be even worse. "I thought so. I saw a light, but it was just their back deck. I got these from downstairs just to make sure everything was okay."

Geoff went over to the bed, again not really paying attention. "Girls are ready for you."

"Okay."

Before leaving the window, I took one more look. Eric Sheller was still there, puffing his cigarette. Moments later, he mashed it out. I thought he was about to go inside when he suddenly spun on one of the upright lights and smashed it with his fist.

CHAPTER SEVEN

I wasn't going to tell anybody in the mom group about the grocery store incident. I'd done enough thinking about the people next door, enough spying, to embarrass myself in my own mind. The last thing I wanted was to embarrass anyone else.

Plus, for years, I'd been the new kid on the block. Now the Shellers were the new people, and I felt protective. Once gossip started about an unstable woman in town, Naomi Sheller might struggle to shake off that reputation.

We weren't the only ones to have moved to the area in the past seven years, of course. I was aware of other families that showed up. But their kids were younger, or they didn't have any. My social life revolved around my girls and their activities. Maybe that was part of why I was yearning for work, to have colleagues and work friends. Like my husband and his "work wife" Mae.

It was Saturday morning, which meant soccer. A home game against Dewitt, a school three times larger. Their players looked like Olympians to me, eating raw beef and breaking wild horses on their family farms.

We were going to get crushed.

The kids fanned out onto the field and Wendy warmed them up. I was glad I'd opted for shorts and a tank top as I hustled the bag of balls from Renee's big truck over to the field. Renee was in the mom group, though her kids were grown. She'd lived in the city for a while, and now had a big spread just outside of town.

I didn't mind my role on the coaching crew. Renee came up with the drills, Wendy was good at barking orders, and I was there to make sure everyone had equipment and water. I also tended to any twisted ankles.

I disseminated the soccer balls, and our players started their passing drills. Fynn, Kimber's son, liked to bounce the ball on his knee. He seemed okay for a kid who'd been sick just two days ago. Charlotte wanted to do whatever Fynn could do and so was bouncing a ball on her knee too.

Wendy blew the whistle, rallying the young athletes into a huddle. Wendy had been born here, and aside from four years of college in Rochester, had lived here her whole life. Theresa, mother of Cooper, the other star player besides Fynn, was from Plattsburgh, but she'd been here since childhood. Cara Cormack, who came to the games despite having no kids (she was just twenty-four), was a Buxton sports hero who'd been on a reality survival show and had become a local celebrity.

My friend Courtney Whitmer was also from here. Outgoing by nature, she'd been the first to really welcome Geoff and me to the area. Her gregariousness was like a social lubricant. You'd stand there as she effused over some funny story, and you'd meet the people who were also listening in. A regular Mr. Miyagi, binding you to the community when you didn't even realize it.

Geoff had developed his own circle of mostly older, monied families like the Cotswolds, who owned the one local restaurant, and Folger Hemlock, a widower who lived all alone in a big house overlooking the town. But Courtney had made that first crucial introduction for us, connecting me to Wendy and Renee. Renee was on the youth commission board and Wendy was the head coach of the grades-one-to-two soccer team. When they needed an extra hand the year Delia was in second grade and on the team, I volunteered. Four years later, I was still doing it. And now Charlotte was playing.

With the huddle over, the refs took the field and the kids got into position. Charlotte played halfback, which suited her boundless energy. She was such a promising athlete, standing there in her pink socks and Buxton Tigers gold-and-green jersey. Somehow the clashing colors worked.

For the most part, we'd settled in, but there were nevertheless moments, little things, when I was reminded that Geoff and I were transplants. A school board meeting about a proposed new wing? I'd stood and said we should welcome anything that would provide opportunities for the kids, and was given scornful looks. I wasn't from here, so who was I to support something bound to raise taxes? Or the "Buxton Day" parade. There was literally a float for lifelong residents only. I'd been sitting on it with some other parents, not knowing, and a local had kindly asked me to get off.

Maybe it's just the nature of people, I don't know. Community pride isn't a bad thing. But after a rootless childhood, this was the longest I'd lived anywhere, and I'd have been lying if I'd said I didn't want to fit in.

For a time, Geoff and I tried a bit of "high society." We went to a few birthday parties, holiday events, and fundraisers organized by some of the wealthier people in town. But I didn't feel right there either. As if I'd been granted a day pass to the world of the upper class, but I'd never have full membership.

So, yeah, I was protective of the Shellers. I didn't know whether they had money or not, but they seemed about our speed. They'd showed their humanness — possible panic attacks and backyard arguments. Maybe it was because they weren't local that I felt kindred. And you didn't want anything sticking on you your first week in town, so I kept what I'd seen and heard to myself.

* * *

Buxton had a tradition. After the first soccer game of every season, we had a picnic. It was just about noon, the sun screaming down, the day bright blue, the kids flush from the soccer game (Dewitt had creamed us 6–1), but no one refused the barbequed chicken, corn on the cob, and three-legged races.

A huge gathering with friends and other family members taking part. The playground adjoining the athletic field had a pavilion with several picnic tables, so there was shade. I sat with Kimber and Theresa. Everyone was drinking water — twice as much as normal, even the parents.

We talked about the game and other surface topics. Tucked into the shade, people on their phones, Kimber quietly said, "Look at them."

I followed her gaze to the kids, but of course I was drawn to my own girls. Delia and Charlotte played so differently. Delia was calmer. I watched as she helped two other girls with the rope tied around their ankles for the three-legged race.

Charlotte, meanwhile, played four square on the edge of the pavement. She had the red ball in her hand and was explaining something to all the others, making faces and laughing and wiggling her little body. They were listening and cracking up, riveted. I could hear her voice even if I couldn't discern the words. Whatever she was saying, she was killing it.

"They're so young," Kimber said, "just having fun, but they also have these complex social lives. They're forming who they'll be as adults right in front of our eyes."

I glanced at Kimber, who continued to wear that bemused grin. Something brewed behind her eyes. "My mother thought social acceptance was everything," she went on, confirming my hunch. "If I wasn't doing well in school, if I wasn't keeping up with piano, that was one thing. But if I got in trouble for bad behavior? That was a major issue."

"Sure," Theresa said.

"We would pass notes back and forth in Physics. It was fourth period, just before lunch. This one girl didn't like it. She had it in for us, you know what I mean? She was this real troubled kid. All the problems. Divorced parents who ignored her, let her do whatever she wanted. No guidance, no supervision. You know how women are hardly ever killers? It's always men? She'd be the type to buck that trend someday."

I checked if anyone else was listening in, but we had the table at the end of the pavilion, the others occupied by people invested in their own conversation and activities.

Theresa responded, "Women can be psycho-bitches, that's true. They kill themselves, they kill their boyfriend, or their husband's mistress. But they don't go out and kill random people. Usually."

"Unless there's some intimate betrayal," I said. Surprised as I was by the turn in conversation, this was actually something I knew a little bit about, having studied it for my degree.

"Exactly," Kimber said. "She could've been someone like that," she said about the girl from her school days. "But it's not like it would've just happened in a vacuum. She was an a-hole to people, and so they, in turn, shunned her, ostracized her. I think that's what happens. Social isolation is terrible. And yet kids do it like it's nothing."

It made me think of Riley, the girl who'd been troubling Charlotte. Riley wasn't here, wasn't on the soccer team, and her parents weren't very active in the community. I thought they lived in one of the single-wide trailers east of town, but I wasn't sure.

"Who we are, how we protect ourselves, the guards we keep up, all of that." Kimber waved at the day: the kids playing various games and sweating. The younger ones trying their luck at corn-hole or getting ready for the race. The teenagers lingering at the edge of the field by the tree line, both aloof and constantly checking for who might be watching. "It's all happening right now," Kimber said wistfully.

"Aww, Kim," Theresa said.

It sounded almost like Kimber was describing internal family systems, something else I'd learned as a criminal justice major/psychology minor. Sometimes called "parts therapy," IFS was about the way trauma, shame, and other difficult emotions could form both "protector" and "exile" parts of our personalities. The "exile" was the subpersonality that bore guilt, shame, and hurt, while the "protector" was the part that worked to mitigate those emotions, to shield the exile part from pain.

"You're so outgoing," Theresa said to Kimber. "You're the most outgoing one of us!"

"That's my take-no-shit personality." She laughed then, suddenly, perhaps to break the tension. I was interested in the subject almost in a clinical way. But Kimber had a personal stake. And maybe I did too. Thinking of Stacy, that girl who waited for me on the wooded trail. Thinking, too, of Naomi Sheller. Realizing that what I'd witnessed in the grocery store could have been some kind of trauma response.

Of course, I thought suddenly. Guilt, fear, even grief. I could have witnessed some crack in her armor, some sign of a breakdown to come. Equally, it could've been an echo of her recent past.

I pictured Eric Sheller smashing the light outside the house.

He'd been exasperated; she'd been mostly shut down. Afraid? Avoidant? Traumatized?

We fell quiet, giving the children our full attention again. Delia had finished helping the kids and the three-legged race was about to begin. Wendy blew her whistle — a single ear-piercing shriek

— and the kids took off. Four pairs of them. The families cheered and hollered. Kimber stood up, suddenly smiling brightly, clapping for her son, for all of them. Some parents, I noticed, took it all a bit too seriously, faces red and neck cords bulging as they yelled like their kid was in the Kentucky Derby.

The leading pair toppled, and this at least elicited laughter and cheers of encouragement. The next to fall was the pair trailing — no hope for them. The poor kids were the boy–girl team Delia had been helping, the boy with eyeglasses thick as the Hubble telescope.

It was the third-place pair that never fell, took the lead, and won it. Theresa's daughter Cooper was one of the two girls, and Theresa raced over to hug her.

Delia made her way to me more slowly. Older, more self-conscious. Her hair clung to her forehead in sweaty strands. When she reached the table, I wordlessly handed her my bottle of water. She drank for a full five seconds before setting it back on the table and wiping her mouth.

"Good job, Delia," Kimber said.

"Thanks." Delia faced me next. "Mom, can we take brownies over to the new neighbors now?"

CHAPTER EIGHT

At last, some clouds were knuckling together over the western ridge of mountains, signaling a potential break in the heat, although not promising anything. The summer rainstorms often failed to dissipate the humidity as expected, merely thickening the air to a hot cloth.

I steeled myself for the trip next door. I knew why I was so concerned Naomi Sheller would recognize me. We didn't know each other, yet I'd been a witness to a private, perhaps even intimate moment in her life. Multiple moments, now, but the grocery store especially. Like someone who'd blacked out at the party after humiliating herself.

Naomi had done nothing to be embarrassed about, of course. Any embarrassment to be had was mine. For not knowing quite how to handle it. Because of my own "protector" part, perhaps, attempting to shield me from the shame of having Stacy Meyer call me fat ass while kicking my backpack into the dirt and me doing nothing about it. Even in adulthood, I avoided that hurt as best as I could.

Both cars were in the driveway at the Sheller house, though no sign of anyone outdoors. Busy unpacking, I supposed. It rose up in me to make another excuse — *let's give them a little more time to settle in* — but that was just procrastinating. We'd say a quick hello, drop off the brownies, and be on our way.

* * *

As we approached the house, I felt a tension band cinching tighter around my chest. But the girls ran ahead, and I couldn't stop them. Charlotte yelled after Delia to slow down, and then as soon as Delia did, Charlotte raced past her. They'd both showered and Charlotte had traded in her soccer jersey for a T-shirt with ponies on it.

Just another day, I told myself.

Charlotte sprinted up the incline to the house, Delia on her heels. "You cheated!"

"I did not!"

"Girls," I called. "Stop it."

Charlotte arrived first, bouncing up onto the Sheller porch and practically crashing into their front door. Delia pressed the doorbell as she recovered. "Aww, Deeeelia!" Charlotte was about to have a meltdown. It wasn't enough to arrive first. No, she wanted the doorbell privilege too.

"Girls!"

Charlotte pressed the doorbell anyway, right after. I hustled to get there just as the door opened. Eric Sheller wore white jeans splattered with various paint colors. "Hi," he said to the girls. "You must be our new neighbors."

"I'm Charlotte! Are your sons here?"

"They are, they are. And you must be Delia."

"Hello."

Impressive memory. I stepped up onto the porch. "Hello. We come bearing gifts."

"As promised. Oh, that's so nice of you." The faded black T-shirt he wore read *TOOL*, with more paint smears. "Brownies? Oh boy, I can practically taste them. Did you girls make those?"

"We did," Charlotte said. "I made the whole batch."

"No, you didn't," Delia corrected. "Mom and I did most of it. You just kept licking the batter out of the bowl."

"Oh, I understand that." Eric Sheller raised his eyes to mine. "What a kind thing to do. We're painting. Redoing Mack's room, giving it some new life. I'm happy for you to come in, just watch where you step."

"That's all right, we don't want to get in the way."

Commotion in the background. Familiar arguing, only with young male voices. The older boy, Jasper, approached from behind his father.

"Hi," Charlotte initiated.

Delia turned shy, brushing up against me.

"Are you the older boy or the younger boy?" Charlotte asked Jasper.

"I'm older. Two years older."

"You're eighteen *months* older," said the second boy, Mack, appearing. Not only was there paint on his clothes, but on his face. It was a perfect mirror image of my girls; I recognized the same older/younger dynamic.

Eric reached for the brownies. "Here, let me take those. Come on in, please."

I thought to resist again; with the ice broken, it would be even harder to leave. But Eric's demeanor was sincere; he wasn't just being polite. It might be rude if I refused.

"Okay. Just for a minute. But we really don't want to get in your way." *Or meet your wife, if I can help it . . .*

Ridiculous. Immature thinking. Like my exile was in control.

With Eric having taken the plate of brownies — it was a large oval plate, one from my grandmother, the brownies wrapped in cellophane — I stepped inside.

The strong tang of paint hit me, and construction, some sawdust in the air. But beneath it, a familiar scent: Mrs. Marvin's house had held an odor not terribly unpleasant but vaguely digestive, the smell of a home with a nearly shut-in person. I suddenly found myself thinking about where she died. I knew she'd passed in the house. I'd never sought details, but in her bed, most likely.

"Naomi!" Eric's call for his wife gave me a minor shock. But he quickly smoothed it over. "These really look great," he said about the brownies. "Let me just go put them down." He walked deeper into the house. There was no foyer. The front door opened to the living room, similar to our house, then it was open-plan to the kitchen near the back. He weaved his way around a pile of paint cans over a sheet on the floor and set the brownies on one of the counters. Moving boxes crowded both rooms, most of them closed. Furniture, too, that hadn't been placed yet. A twin mattress leaned against the wall, the unassembled twin bed next to it. Shelves, chairs, everything jammed into the space.

The kids were chattering away, mostly Charlotte and Mack. Delia and Jasper were more reserved, gauging one another from a slight distance. "Why don't you play soccer?" Charlotte asked Mack, and the boy looked at his father for an answer.

"Just didn't get to the forms in time," Eric said. "Next year, though."

"There was a party," Charlotte said. "It was our first game and then we did races."

"Oh yeah?" Eric smiled politely.

The band around my chest cinched a little tighter. "I'm sorry. I should have invited you and your family. It's not just for soccer players."

"Oh no, not at all." Eric gestured at his surroundings. "We're up to our eyeballs here."

"Can I show her my room?" Mack asked.

Eric glanced at me for approval.

"Just be a good girl." I was in it now, no turning back.

"She might get some paint on her," Eric warned.

"That's okay."

"We wanted to do this before moving in, but it just didn't work out. So now we're sort of suspended, living out of boxes until we get it done. Mack's room, and I'm doing the bathroom and the hallway." He called out again, this time with a gentler tone. "Hey, honey? Can you come out here?"

I wanted to politely redirect him, but put my arm around Delia instead, who remained beside me. Eric regarded her. "So what grade are you in? Fifth?"

"Sixth," she said.

"Wow, Jasper's in sixth too."

"I've seen him," Delia said. "He's in Mrs. Cluckey's class."

"That's just my homeroom," Jasper said.

"I know."

With these facts established, the skepticism between them seemed to dissipate.

"Mack is in fourth grade," Eric said. "Charlotte is in . . . ?"

"Second."

And there the parity ended.

A female voice echoed down the hall, and it sent a little electric shock up my spine. I controlled my breathing and listened as Naomi, out of sight, introduced herself to Charlotte and talked about Mack's room a second before continuing her approach.

This was it. The moment of truth.

"Hello," the woman said, entering. She picked her way past the boxes and furniture, meeting my gaze as she did. When she was close enough, she shook my hand. Her eyes, that Cognac hazel I remembered from the store, held me whole, with no hint of recognition or embarrassment. "I'm Naomi."

"Hi. Lainey."

"Nice to meet you, Lainey. I'm sorry I haven't come by sooner. I know Eric stopped over, and I meant to say hello myself, but it's just been one thing after another."

"Not at all. Totally understand. We know what it's like. I mean, we moved a few years ago, but I remember it like it was yesterday. You never realize how much you have until you move, right? And then it's like, 'Where did I get all this stuff?'"

My relief that Naomi didn't recognize me had charged me up, and now I was rambling, offering clichés and possible offense by suggesting they were overly material.

Naomi just smiled pleasantly, and Eric gestured to the kitchen and said, "They brought brownies."

"That's so nice of you. Thank you."

A silence developed, unexpected. Things had been flowing along, now we were all just standing there, Naomi seeming to look everywhere but at me or her husband.

"Yeah," Eric said, "moving is really crazy. Like I said, we wanted to get to the painting first, get up here and get it done, but life happens while you're making other plans. Right?"

"That's right." I looked between them, noticing that Naomi wasn't wearing paint clothes like he was. Instead, she was in gray sweatpants and a dark-blue Calvin Klein tank top. Her reddish hair was tied up in a ponytail. She was even prettier than I remembered, even more fit. Taut across the belly, perky breasts. Even in sweatpants, I could tell she had a runner's figure.

Charlotte's laughter — a cackle, really — reached us from the other room. My youngest daughter was already perfectly at home. Jasper hadn't said anything else to Delia, instead pulling out his phone. Before Delia started coveting it, I began our exit.

"Well, anything you need, don't hesitate to let us know," I said. "You know, if your power goes out again or anything." It was sort of a joke, but when Naomi smiled, it was perfunctory, not reaching her eyes.

"That's very nice of you," she said. "Thank you." And she fell silent again. Not one for small talk, I thought. And more than pretty, really; she could be a model with the way her looks managed to outshine her husband's.

"Okay — Charlotte? Come on, honey. The Shellers have work to do."

Neither of them challenged this.

Charlotte did, though. "Ohhh," she whined from the other room. "Can I stay?"

"Charlotte, get out here right now." It was maybe just the slightest bit harsh from me. But Eric showed a sympathetic grin.

"Come on, young lady." She shuffled her feet and slumped her shoulders, as if going slow might get me to reverse the decision. "We'll see them again another time."

"Yeah," Eric said. "Once we get up and running, we'd love to have you over. Maybe we can do dinner. I plan to get the grill going on the back deck."

He squeezed past us in order to open the door, and I ushered both of the girls outside and into the fresh air. The day seemed especially bright, as if it had been darker in their house than I'd realized.

I turned back to Naomi. "Nice to meet you."

She was staring into space. A split second later, though, she looked at me, her slack face turning into a polite smile again, and she held up a hand. "Mm-hmm. You too."

"Thanks again for the brownies," Eric said as we pushed off the porch. He lingered in the doorway. "And please don't give a second thought to today. We're just happy to be here and to be getting started. Grateful to have such nice new neighbors."

Mack crowded in at his side. "Bye," he said to Charlotte.

"Bye," Charlotte said, maudlin, as if it was the last time they'd be together for years.

Delia, on the other hand, was already on her way back home; she'd slipped past, silent and quick as a cat.

I saw Jasper inside the house, just sort of standing there in the dusky light.

Eric and I broke eye contact, and I started back with Charlotte. As I crossed the large lawn connecting our homes, my mind began to replay every moment of the encounter. The way the house was weirdly closed off. How they hadn't offered any kind of tour. How they were painting in the gloom.

Probably they were in the middle of a fight. Few things were as stressful as moving. So, if there was ever a time for marital discord, this was it. Maybe that was what I'd heard in Eric's voice when he'd called for Naomi. Tension. Volatility. Like things between them were still difficult.

That could be it; that could be all. The rest was none of my business.

But as I walked back to my house, my girls running ahead, I'd be lying if I said I didn't feel dread. Like Naomi Sheller was a prisoner in her own home.

CHAPTER NINE

I took the girls to the pool most every Sunday, almost a ritual. While our area boasted lovely rivers and lakes, the rocky shores and stinging bugs could make outdoor swimming a challenge. Our school didn't have a pool, but the school in Tannersville did. A big one, competition-sized.

Delia was already at the top of the four-tier program, a strong swimmer who could dive and retrieve bricks off the bottom. In the second tier, Charlotte worked on floating and strokes. I was proud of them both — swimming was not part of my girlhood, and I still felt knock-kneed and awkward in the water.

Geoff and I had no interest pushing the girls into things they didn't like, or turning our lost dreams into their achievements. But we were unified in raising strong, capable women. Something about the full-body exercise, the confidence-building that came with mastering another medium, seemed to make it one of the best activities for them.

Tiers one and two ran concurrently, then three and four. It meant Delia had to wait while Charlotte swam, then vice versa. But the sessions were only a half-hour and went by fast.

I sat in a folding chair along the pool edge, watching the girls, talking with the other mothers there. None of my personal mom group was around. They all worked and liked to keep their weekends open.

It was a good time to get in some reading. The humidity, the echoey sounds, formed a kind of white noise helping me sink into a story. Police procedurals tended to pique my curiosity the most, which made sense given the focus of my schooling, but I tried just about anything. From horror to romantasy — if it was good, it was good. The current read was a psychological thriller.

The mom group talked about forming a book club, but it had yet to come to pass. At least, I couldn't remember where we stood. Kimber and I often traded reads. She was into nonfiction, subjects like history and women's struggles. Theresa preferred the big, splashy commercial hits like *The Hunger Games* or anything by Colleen Hoover. Renee might've been into more literary fiction, since she'd been an English teacher in New York, albeit retiring early. I couldn't say what Wendy's reading habits were.

Delia had her own book — *My Side of the Mountain* — and sat reading beside me while Charlotte followed the swimming instructor's commands, periodically checking to see if I was watching. "Hi, honey," I called, and waved. Reverberating voices and splashing water in the cavernous room swallowed my words. I sank back into my story.

* * *

Later, I helped Charlotte peel out of her bathing suit and sent her to the shower to rinse off. She still needed my help — or preferred it, really — while Delia was independent. With everyone dechlorinated and back in street clothes, we headed to the car.

The clouds were still hanging in, no rain yet. Muggy. I turned on the AC once I got the car started. The girls chattered as I pulled out of the parking space.

"What's the difference between dolphins and porpoises?" Delia asked.

"Porpoises are longer and skinnier," Charlotte said quickly.

"No," Delia corrected, "*dolphins* are longer and skinnier. And they have longer snouts, and their dorsal fins are more curved."

"*Snots?*" Charlotte asked. "They have longer *snots?*"

"You heard what I said."

"What does a dolphin say when it's confused?"

"I don't know." Delia sounded morose. She'd been interested in trivia; her sister wanted jokes.

"Can you please be more Pacific?"

Delia groaned. "You don't even know what that means."

The parking lot was busy as the other families worked their way out to the road. It took us a few minutes. The girls sensed opportunity and pestered me for ice cream.

"It's not even noon yet. We haven't had lunch."

But they wore me down, as they usually did, and before long, we were pulling into the Stewart's convenience store and gas station, which offered ice cream year-round. We sat in one of the booths by the front windows. As the girls ate with their usual gusto, I took out my phone.

Now that we were back in service, a text from Geoff had come through:

Crazy busy, backed up for at least an hour. Maybe two. Sorry.

Too bad. Dinner would have to wait a little. But that was all right: I could feed the kids early and Geoff and I might have a moment to ourselves. I felt a twinge of jealousy, though. Mae was working today.

I found myself eyeing the girls' ice creams, particularly Charlotte's Peanut Butter Everything, imagining the sweet, nutty flavor on my tongue. Maybe just a lick, to help keep it from dripping. Even in a convenience store like this, with so much air conditioning you started to feel like refrigerated beef, ice cream still managed to run . . .

"Mommm," she whined.

"Just a little maintenance, honey. Don't worry, there's still enough to put you in a dairy coma."

"A dairy *what*?"

I smiled and looked out the window. My baby girl wasn't the only one with jokes. In fact, I had a dolphin one of my own I was about to spring on them when a truck pulled up to one of the fuel pumps outside.

Black, with a gray door.

I sat up a little straighter in the booth.

The driver got out; it was Eric Sheller all right.

What are the odds? I thought at first. But the Shellers had moved from here. What was he doing back? Still getting stuff from the old house? Or maybe his prior law office?

He walked around the front of the vehicle and stepped behind the pump. He worked the pay terminal, then started to fill up.

He was dressed similarly to the last two times, just a simple T-shirt and blue jeans. Seeing him produced conflicting emotions. I'd liked him when he came over. I was usually a good judge of character. But his wife was so strange, and their relationship just gave off bad vibes. While I'd mostly forgotten about them for the last twenty-four hours, thoughts about Naomi being trapped returned.

Eric replaced the spigot and returned to the driver's side door. I hadn't noticed anyone else inside the truck when he'd first pulled up. For one thing, the windshield mostly reflected the ominous sky. For another, I'd been focused on him.

But as the truck rolled forward, I saw a woman in the passenger seat. She faced my general direction, and I saw her clearly.

It wasn't Naomi Sheller.

This woman's hair was darker, her features more rounded. She was around the same age as Eric's wife, maybe even a little younger. I'd never seen her before.

She flipped down the visor then, applying lipstick in the small mirror there.

As I stared, Charlotte said something to me about her ice cream that I didn't really hear. "Just a second, honey," I whispered, barely audible.

At that same moment, Eric Sheller looked over.

"Shit," I said, and ducked.

"Mom!" Charlotte yelled.

Delia, more perceptive: "What, Mom? Is something the matter?"

"Sorry." I couldn't stay hunched like this for very long.

"Mom, what are you doing?" Delia asked.

"She said the S-H word!" Charlotte sounded more delighted than mortified.

"I just dropped something," I lied in a strained voice. Bent over like this, I was running out of air. I slowly rolled back upright, daring to look out the window.

The truck had left the pumps and was stopped at the edge of the gas station lot, left blinker on to make the turn. If Eric Sheller had seen me, he wasn't sticking around to make sure I'd seen *him*. The truck turned onto the street and got up to speed, racing away.

CHAPTER TEN

It was a client.

Eric Sheller was a lawyer, after all.

But what lawyer drives clients around in their pickup truck? And what lawyer dresses in a white shirt and jeans?

He's having an affair.

Well, that was a heavy assumption, one I had no right to make. I saw Eric with a strange woman, yes, but I'd been inside a shop, looking out through the glass at a truck maybe twenty yards away, and at barely enough of an angle to see inside.

The way she'd been applying makeup, though . . .

The whole thing had the look and feel of a date. Or something personal, at least. A woman aiming to make a good impression.

In such a public place, though? In the very town he'd just left?

They acted like they had nothing to hide, so maybe they didn't.

The whole thing just seemed odd, at best. Married men didn't typically drive around with other women in the cab of their trucks. She'd been a little younger too, and attractive.

It could be his sister.

Sure, I thought, as I drove back home to Buxton, it could be that. Could be a cousin too, or a colleague. I knew nothing about him. Not even what kind of lawyer he was. Only what Mae had told Geoff, that he'd rented a space at the Parker building.

Speaking of my husband and the head nurse on staff, perhaps I was just projecting my own insecurities. I was jealous of Mae. Not in any major way, but enough that it bothered me how much time my husband spent with her. That they took walks together. Maybe I needed to talk to Geoff about that, tell him how I felt. It could've been fueling the distance between us.

I wondered whether I should also tell him about seeing Eric with this other woman. Geoff might think I was being nosy again, but I'd been minding my own business. I hadn't been following anyone. I hadn't asked for this.

* * *

Confetti blasted. Celebratory symbols and emojis peppered my phone screen.

> *Congratulations!!*
> *Congrats, girrrrrll*
> *Wishing you all the happiness!*

I was making the girls' food and my phone had been rattling away on the counter. I finally picked it up, assaulted with a barrage of texts I'd missed.

> *You two are going to be a POWER COUPLE!*

A little back-scrolling and I saw a photo of a sparkling ring on a young woman's finger. Cara Cormack, the high school athlete turned reality star, was getting married. While I hardly knew her, she was a favorite of the group, sort of an "honorary mom."

Another picture showed her and the fiancé. I'd seen him once at one of the practices in August. He wore a baseball cap pulled low then, but here his face was fully exposed and handsome. I heard he worked for a regional contractor and that he showered Cara with trips and gifts.

I sent a flurry of exclamation points, the customary *OMG* and *Congrats* and *Wishing you both all the best*. When I set the phone back on the counter, it might've been a little too hard. It made a clattering thud.

Something out the window caught my attention: Eric's truck pulling into the driveway. I moved closer for a moment and watched as he got out.

He looked alone. He walked around to the back of the truck and opened the tailgate, where he slid out a duffel bag, small and light blue, and then a backpack, which he slung over his shoulder. He wore different clothes. A different shirt, at least — a gray tank top.

He hurried inside.

* * *

Geoff was late coming home, as he'd predicted. It had been a long weekend for both of us. The girls bickered most of the evening, and at bedtime, Charlotte wailed about feeling cold. I found her warm to the touch and with a fever — 102. Geoff told me the virus was still going around.

Great.

We ate a late meal together mostly in silence, with Geoff looking at his phone. The morning, seeing Eric with the strange woman, felt distant now and maybe even a bit silly.

I'd harvested butternut squash from the garden, cooked it with wild rice, chicken, and sorrel. Also, a fresh salad with some of the last tomatoes of the season — a cherry variety called "chocolate sprinkles." I hoped Geoff would notice the meal, but he remained preoccupied.

When he did finally ask about my day, I gave him a generic response. "Oh, good, you know. Char was definitely not herself.

They're always a bit at each other's throats by Sunday night, but she had a fever, so she's exhausted. And meanwhile, Delia just wants to be online with her friends, or to have someone over."

"Yeah. It's normal, I guess. She's a sixth-grader now. A middle-schooler."

He wasn't telling me anything I didn't already know, and his honey-it's-all right tone burrowed right under my skin. I took my dish to the sink.

Geoff and I had met somewhat later in life. I was already thirty-one and several years into bartending, my bachelor's degree gathering dust. He was eight years older. He'd come into the restaurant on his friend's birthday. He approached me about a cake when he couldn't find his server. After dinner, he and his friends ended up closing the bar.

Geoff was the designated driver and spent most of that night chatting with me while nursing club sodas. He confessed he was divorced three years from a seven-year marriage. I remember how him being almost forty seemed so much older, and worldly in a way. He had just that hint of gray in his beard.

He'd recently started working as a physician's assistant for a small health center forty minutes away. "There's really nothing there, though, nothing to do," he said. "My friends are here."

He planned on coming back to the restaurant, wanted to know my shifts. Three days later, he showed up alone in a striped dress shirt, eyes clear, hopeful but confident.

I wasn't the type to just jump into bed with someone, but I did that night. And soon — as in, a couple of months — Delia was conceived. Geoff proposed right away. He'd been planning to already, he'd said. He called me an amazing woman. Said that he loved my humor, my "grit," and my inquisitive nature. He got down on one knee and said he wanted to spend the rest of his life with me.

Romantic, sweet, and all fairly quick. A blur, really. One day I'd been working in the restaurant, hanging out with friends and wondering about the rest of my life. The next, I was expecting a child and getting married.

"That's how it happens sometimes," my mom had said. "And it strikes me that his previous marriage, no kids . . . Maybe she couldn't? And so maybe his wanting to be a father, start a family, that's not a bad thing."

Mom tended to see the best in people. She had gone to college too, something that put her a little ahead of her time. With a degree in history, she taught at a university for a while but struggled to find new work each time we had to move. She'd ended up getting kind of quiet. While Geoff's mom seemed to revel in her role as wife and mother, it didn't fit my mom in the same way.

Maybe he'd been in a hurry; maybe I had too. But Geoff and I didn't really get a proper romance. Not a lot of proving ground. We'd known we were compatible. We'd felt it and tacitly decided that was enough. For the most part, it was true.

It was also true I'd been feeling lonely for some time now. Getting quiet myself. Uneasy, gaining weight. Not always able to meet my own eyes in the mirror.

I left Geoff in the kitchen as he did the dishes. He wouldn't likely notice I was gone. Or he'd notice, but he wouldn't think anything was wrong. I wasn't trying to play games with him, but I did hope that something would change — that tonight wouldn't have us playing out the same script, the same pattern: I give him the silent treatment for an hour before he finally looks at me with widened eyes and a slack mouth, going, "Honey? What's wrong?"

You notice the habits of your marriage fairly early on. You notice that things don't change, that your spouse doesn't change. You have the same arguments, and you seek solutions but wind up pretty much right back where you started.

It could be depressing; it could make you feel doomed. Like everyone was just living out some role, helpless to do much of anything about it.

I needed a cigarette.

I snuck outside, mixed feelings that Geoff wouldn't notice that either. I checked on the Sheller place. Dark but for one window at the back. A steady soft light glowing, but nothing flickering. No lights going on and off. No one arguing outside by the tiki lights.

I thought again of Eric smashing that one light with his hand.

Was that me? Was I getting frustrated, repressing too much? I'd told Geoff I wanted to work, but had I given up on the idea too easily? I thought of myself as a well-balanced person, emotionally stable, but perhaps I was hiding from something.

I resolved to change that. And I would start by talking to Geoff. I'd be straight with him, tell him how his relationship with Mae made me feel. Tell him how I thought — despite all of my self-corrections — our neighbors were weird and something was going on.

But I never got the chance.

Streaking down the road toward me was a vehicle with flashing lights.

As I watched, cigarette forgotten between my fingers, the police car slowed and turned into the Shellers' driveway.

CHAPTER ELEVEN

The first police vehicle was joined by a second.

A third whizzed past the end of my driveway, coming from the other direction.

We didn't have that many cops in our local department. Not on duty at once, anyway. Two of the vehicles had a yellow stripe down the side. That meant state police. The other was county.

I stood for a moment in a kind of trance. Hearing voices, the occasional burst of static. Watching as several figures made their way to the door. And then they went inside. I disposed of my cigarette just as Geoff stepped outside.

"Jesus. What's going on?"

"I don't know. They just got there."

"I saw the lights." He joined me. "Where were you?"

He had to have been in the bedroom, since it was the only place to see the neighbors from inside. Since I hadn't been there with him, he was wondering how I knew.

"I was out here." I must've said it in a certain way, because he didn't ask a follow-up question. Plus, we were distracted.

"No ambulance, at least," Geoff said.

I started toward the Shellers' house then, cautious, as if I might catch whatever was happening. At the same time, my heart went out. Those two boys. And poor Naomi. Whatever was going on, ambulance or not, it probably wasn't good.

I strained to listen, but there was nothing but the rumbles of the many engines. Voices inside? Faint, muffled, barely there. At least no one was screaming.

My phone vibrated, startling me. I'd nearly forgotten I was holding it.

The mom group. Wendy told me that Martin, her husband, had just gotten a call to go over to the Shellers. She knew because she kept a scanner whenever he was on shift. Wanted to know if I knew anything.

I texted back, *Don't know for sure. Just lots of police. I'm outside now.*

I tucked the phone under my arm as I hugged myself. I dared to take a couple more steps, nearing the halfway point between our two homes. A warm breeze swished through, stirring the grass, carrying the moldering scents of late summer. Traces of cop car exhaust.

Geoff squinted in all the bright flashing lights.

"No sirens either."

"Silent run," I said. "Could be a home invasion call, could be they just don't want to be disruptive for whatever reason."

We were whispering. The girls were out of range, the people next door out of range, but still.

My phone buzzed in my armpit. Then again. I checked it. Wendy had more questions, but I still didn't have any answers.

Geoff pulled a deep breath. "They . . . oh, here we go."

People were coming out now. A pair of state troopers, identifiable by the silhouettes of their wide-brimmed hats in the porch light. I suddenly felt self-conscious, exposed. But we were standing beside the oak tree, away from the light of our house. Anyone looking would really have to squint or shine a light to see us. Plus, what we were doing was normal.

The troopers returned to their vehicle. Wasting no time, they roared off, lights going again. Seconds later, more troopers exited the house and got into their car, pulled out, and also left.

"All going the same direction," I observed.

The last cops to come out didn't drive away. Flashlights snapped on and the police started circling the house, moving toward the tree line.

"Oh, Geoff," I said under my breath.

"Maybe we should go back inside."

But my feet didn't move, and one of the beams of light landed on us.

"It's okay," I said to Geoff.

A lone cop approached. Bit of a gut and no hat.

"Folks? Hello?"

"Hi," I said, and started toward him. It was Martin, Wendy's husband.

"You folks seen your neighbor tonight? Naomi Sheller? She come by your place or anything?"

"No," I said. I glanced back at Geoff, not because I expected him to say differently, but to let him speak for himself. My husband shook his head. "No, we haven't seen her."

"What's going on?" I asked. "Is everything all right?"

Martin stopped a few feet away, looked over his shoulder, taking stock. Then he turned back to us.

"Eric Sheller called 911. His wife is missing. We're looking for her."

PART II:
THE CURSED TOWN

CHAPTER TWELVE

It went on all night.

I got up twice to check on Charlotte, each time stopping at the window.

Police cars, lights.

The second time, I never went back to sleep.

My phone had been going off at all hours, Wendy keeping me updated.

She was going running at Blueberry Hills.
They're looking there now.

Blueberry Hills was a series of woodland trails through the neighboring foothills. I could hear a helicopter in that direction. At least one, maybe two.

Geoff stirred. "Is that, ah . . . ?"

"Naomi Sheller was jogging," I said. "Trail jogging before dinner. Eric called the police when she didn't come home, didn't answer her phone, nothing."

He went up there, Wendy's texts informed me. *To see if he could find her.*

Geoff's eyes were puffy from sleep, hair sticking up. He wore those striped pajamas you sometimes see on TV dads. In that moment, I saw his age.

"Jesus," he said. "I hope something didn't happen. She didn't fall, something like that."

I agreed, even as I kept picturing her standing in the grocery store aisle, reaching for the juice, her brain switched off. The strange woman in Eric Sheller's truck putting on lipstick like she was going out somewhere special. I would have told Deputy Martin about the woman if he'd asked, or the argument in the backyard. Because what they said in countless cop movies was true in criminal justice: every detail mattered. But after checking if we'd seen Naomi that night, or had any idea where she might've gone, Martin had returned to the Sheller house.

Geoff swung his legs out of bed and came to the window. I looked back through Wendy's messages.

> *He couldn't find her so he came back home and called the cops.*
> *Martin says he's a wreck.*
> *They searched the house just to be sure.*

That was when they'd gone out with the flashlights, I figured.

Geoff stared across the distance, pushing the small drapes aside. The girls would be up soon. I needed coffee. Like it or not, it was Monday, and we all had things to do and places to be.

My phone jittered in my hand.

I didn't look at it at first. Something about this one felt different. Like when a phone rings and you know who it is before checking.

Geoff noticed and glanced down at my hand. His expression mirrored how I felt.

I slowly looked at the text.

CHAPTER THIRTEEN

They found her.

No other messages. Just that one, from Wendy, coming through at 6.54 a.m.

I started typing out my response, needing more.

But Geoff was tapping me. Looking out the window again.

Slowly, as if in a dream, I stepped closer. I peered through the glass as the police, all of them gone except the one trooper who'd remained through the night, came screaming back. Their lights were going, and this time their sirens were too.

Let the world now know, they seemed to say. *Let it be known to all that something has happened.*

My heart throbbed in my throat as they turned into the Shellers' driveway. In front of the house where old Mrs. Marvin had withered away in her bed, no more gardening, no more bony rump in the air or hands in the dirt. We were here, and then we were gone, and none of us could wrap our minds around it either.

When the police exited the cars, I hoped to see Naomi with them. In her jogging clothes, hair tied back and a bit mussed with a couple of leaves sticking out. Because she'd been trail-running and fell and broke an ankle. There would be a smudge on one cheekbone, another scrape on her elbow. But even a little shaken, she would be back home now. Reunited with her children, her husband. All together in their new house.

Only, Naomi Sheller did not emerge from the back of any of the police cars. Police alone did, and they hurried forward, going two-by-two up the stairs and into the house.

"Mommy?"

Charlotte stood in the doorway, rubbing her eyes and coughing. Holding her favorite stuffy, a floppy rabbit.

"Honey," I said, unable to keep the alarm from my own voice. "Stay there."

Geoff gave me a funny look. The situation warranted special care, sure, but it wasn't like Charlotte was in any danger, and I made it sound like she was. Because for the first time since this whole thing began, the first time since I'd seen the moving truck pull in the driveway, I was scared.

Geoff went to her. She held the rabbit by one arm, the rest of its limp pinkish-yellow body dragging on the floor. He scooped our daughter up, saying, "Mommy's going to be with you in a minute. How did you sleep?"

"What's all the siren noise?"

"Oh, it's nothing, we'll talk about it in a little bit." They moved together down the hallway, Geoff asking her what she dreamed about before they faded out of earshot.

I drifted closer to the window again, drawn like a moth to a porch light. Sirens blared, and vehicle lights flashed, and troopers posted up outside as if waiting for something.

And then Eric Sheller appeared. Flanked by two beefy state troopers and another one following behind. I could read the agony on his face from here as they walked him out.

One of his sons — Jasper, I think — came to the door, looking like he was yelling and crying. A female trooper took him gently but firmly in her arms.

Eric turned back to his son. The way Jasper suddenly stopped yelling, I imagined a devastated father doing his best to say something consoling.

It's going to be all right.

Maybe that's what he said. What I hoped he said.

Everything's going to be all right.

But then they put him in the police car.

CHAPTER FOURTEEN

The rest of the morning was a blur. Information came sporadically. I tended to Charlotte, home from school, feeding her tomato soup and lots of liquids.

What I knew by midday: Naomi Sheller had been found some twenty, thirty yards from one of the many interwoven hiking trails. A state trooper had spotted her by her lavender running shorts. Before a search team was even assembled or a K-9 unit dispatched, troopers and EMTs had rushed her to the local hospital.

She'd been pronounced dead right about the time Charlotte appeared in our bedroom door. Just as more police were escorting Eric Sheller to the hospital, the emergency room doctor was already calling it.

I lost track of how many times I composed a text to Wendy Baker in my head. *Has anyone said cause of death? What was the condition of her body? Were there signs she fell?*

I knew that whatever the police had now would be need-to-know only, and a medical examiner would have to rule the cause of death.

Were there signs of foul play? Something else I couldn't ask Wendy. Something she couldn't answer even if I did.

But I kept thinking of the argument.

The grocery store episode.

The other woman.

Everything.

I'd already considered that Naomi could be a victim of abuse. But I only had circumstantial things. Random moments that didn't add up to evidence of anything.

Couples argued. Geoff and I might've even had an episode or two within view of the Marvin house, raised voices, gesturing. What if Mrs. Marvin had seen us?

And the woman in Eric's truck could've been anyone. A sister, a friend, a client. He hadn't exactly been hiding her.

By evening, I'd tried to put it as much out of mind as possible and resume normal living.

Which was not possible, really. Charlotte's fever had broken, her energy back with a vengeance. Even though she'd missed school, she insisted on soccer practice. We coaches agreed it was best to proceed as normally as possible, so I put her in her shin guards and shorts, and she only coughed in my face twice as I laced up her cleats. Probably still contagious, but she'd be outside. Most of the other kids had already gotten it.

I passed out the soccer balls and Wendy led the drills. We constantly snuck looks at each other. Soon, we huddled to discuss the Shellers. Soccer parents on the sidelines did too. The whole town did, because how could they not? Buxton was a thousand people, give or take. The entire county was only ten or twelve thousand; two hundred square miles that were less populated than most cities. The news was on everyone's mind.

"He was in the woods," Renee said to me at one point as we rolled soccer balls toward the kids, who then dribbled them toward the goal and took a shot. "He doesn't even have an alibi."

"I know," I said, remembering Wendy's text.

Eric Sheller had gone into the woods, yes. Something that made perfect sense if his story was true and he feared for his wife when she'd not come home for supper or answered calls. But it also worked well if he'd needed an excuse. His sons would have noticed him gone and told the police at some point, so now he had a sensible reason.

But it risked suspicion.

"I heard she was in rough shape," Renee said. "God, how awful."

I still hadn't heard anything about her condition and wondered how Renee knew, but before I could ask, Wendy blew the whistle.

"All right guys, time for cooldown."

The kids started to fall in, but there were always stragglers, and my job included rounding them up. Wendy liked everyone to stretch at the end of practice. It provided a good opportunity to talk with them, and their focus was generally good since they'd just had so much exercise. I had a little speech I gave when Wendy was done with her skills critique.

"Okay," I said. "Good job today, everybody. Good job doing your best and being your best."

Some of their little faces turned up to me, pink-cheeked, still breathing hard from the exertion. Charlotte sat between a couple of boys, chatting with them both, giggling. All three still doing the butterfly stretch, which we'd come out of a minute ago. "Charlotte Barrister? Ellie Saltamach? Jace McMahon? Guys?" When I had their attention, I continued, "What do we say about good behavior?"

I received scattered replies. Some kids were always more eager than others. Charlotte's voice came from somewhere in the middle. "It matters even when no one is watching."

"That's right. When you're out there on the field and you're being a good team player, when you're being respectful of the other team, and everyone is watching, that's good. But it also matters when you're off by yourself, dragging the ball bag to the shed. Or when you're doing your homework, and you could have the computer do it for you, but you don't. Right?"

I noticed Renee watching me, an amused smile on her face. She winked and faced the kids.

"So," I concluded, "let's remember to be good sports on and off the field, and do your best even when no one is — what?"

"Watching!" they yelled.

Chaos ensued after that, kids running to their parents. People said their goodbyes, vehicles started up. I found myself clocking the young Cara hugging Gary Latrelle, her new fiancé, him in rugged jeans and logging boots despite the heat.

Life went on.

"They look happy," Renee said. She was coming out of the shed, dusting off her hands. The soccer field had an area Wendy's husband, Martin, would flood in the wintertime to make an ice rink. The shed served as a warming hut during the colder months, and sports equipment storage year-round. There was a crude bathroom in there, and I could smell the bubble-gum-flavored soap on her hands.

I watched Cara and Gary get into his 1960s classic car.

"Ugh," Renee said, sighing. She moved closer to me, lowering her voice. "Cara's such a good egg. I hope he treats her right." The big key ring Renee always wore lay against her hip. She was a funny woman, at once salt-of-the-earth and someone who corrected the kids' grammar. Like an old-fashioned schoolmarm.

I waited, figuring there was more.

"Supposedly he's sober," she said. "But he's got a reputation as a bit of a partier. He enlisted after high school, but then failed out of Basic. Some medical condition. He came back kind of aimless, got into the . . . well, I don't know."

"What?"

"You know, out at the bars, getting into mischief. He would've had a DWI if Martin hadn't intervened."

My gaze switched across the field to Wendy, piling her boys into her minivan. If Martin was here, I hadn't seen him. Wendy looked over at us and waved. Wendy was perpetually energetic, heavily involved with the school, a born-and-bred local. Renee put on a big smile and waved back, yelling, "G'night!"

She resumed her low tone. "But like I said, he's supposed to be out of that life, so let's hope it sticks."

I watched the blue classic car grumble down the access road away from the field. Even from here, Cara looked happy. I wished them all the best.

"Young love," I said, and Renee sort of snort-laughed.

"All right," she said. "Night."

Charlotte played with some of the last kids still running around in the buggy evening. A mini-Wendy, in a way. Even recovering from a cold, she was a windup toy who could go for hours and never tire, matched by a mere handful of other kids, most of them boys. Fynn Hudson was out there now with her, charging back and forth on the field. Kimber stood by, patiently waiting.

I called to Charlotte as I walked toward my car, parked beside Wendy's minivan. Wendy had just gotten in, but she rolled down her window as I approached. She glanced at her phone, then looked at me, and I could see it in her eyes. News on Naomi.

I got close enough so she could whisper. Her three kids were in the back, chattering away, but she was still careful they didn't overhear.

"It's bad," she said.

I braced myself.

"I'm not supposed to say anything but . . . it's blunt force trauma to the head."

I put my hand to my mouth briefly, then said, "That's the primary cause of death?"

"Looking like it."

I thought about it. Medical examiners could come back with a preliminary cause of death fairly quickly, usually within a day or so, if I remembered my schooling. But a full report with detailed findings could take a lot longer — days to weeks.

"Did they rule on the manner of death yet?" I asked.

"You think homicide?"

"I don't know. Or natural, accident, suicide . . . undetermined?"

"Pending."

Thinking, I said, "It's possible she fell, hit her head, was disoriented, then wandered off into the woods, right?"

Wendy nodded, but her eyes said otherwise. "Sure. But her clothing was ripped. She had defensive wounds." She looked back to check on her kids. "I think she was attacked."

CHAPTER FIFTEEN

Tuesday

I think she was attacked.

Wendy's last words stayed with me. Getting the children up and out the door the next day, seeing Geoff off to work — I felt like I was on autopilot. Like I'd found some new gear in my life where I could speak and move and get things done and be completely somewhere else in my mind. Maybe I'd never really had to do it before. Or maybe I'd caught what Charlotte had.

Outside, after everyone was gone, I went into the garden and weeded for a while. I liked the feeling of my hands in the dirt, the satisfaction of ripping out the crabgrass and dandelions. Usually, by midsummer, I let weeds be weeds. But this morning I needed some way to channel my energy. When weeding wasn't enough, I took a cigarette from my pack hidden above the side door to the house, lit up, and walked into view of the Sheller house.

The pickup truck with the gray door was there, as was the Subaru. Plus, more vehicles too, ones I didn't recognize. Family, I supposed. For the boys' sake, I hoped. They'd just lost their mother, and while their father was still with them, it was good for him to have help.

Did I think Jasper and Mack Sheller were in danger? I didn't
know. But as I stood there smoking, I found myself replaying the
afternoon in Tannersville. The woman in the cab of Eric Sheller's
truck putting on her lipstick in the mirror, smacking her lips
together. Eric pumping gas. He'd looked at me. At least, before
getting back in his truck and leaving, he'd gazed in my direction.
Sitting there with my two daughters, mid-lick of my daughter's
ice cream cone, staring back.

The more I ruminated, the more I felt sure Eric Sheller had
seen me. Perhaps, more importantly, that he had seen me see *him*.

If I worried about anything, it was that.

My phone buzzed with a text from Wendy.

Are you going to the memorial?

Wow, I thought, *that was fast.* I hadn't heard.

There's a memorial even with the ongoing investigation?

I watched the three lines wiggle on screen.

*Her body is staying with the medical examiner. It's just the
service.*

I waited through more undulating dots.

Her family wanted it right away.

I exhaled. Looked back across the yards at the Sheller house.

I'd met Naomi only once — that she was aware of, anyway.
And while Eric and I had exchanged a few pleasantries, we were
essentially strangers.

But I thought of my daughters. How they would feel, what
they would think about what I did in response to this. And I made
my decision.

* * *

Wednesday

I wore a simple black dress I hadn't put on since my father died, six years before. None of the mom group was there that I saw. Just me, the neighbor. Even if we hadn't really known each other, our neighbors' presence meant something to my girls. I needed to model the behavior I preached — it was a good thing to pay respects. And this was what I wanted more of in my life: community. Offering my support.

The funeral home sat on the main road through the small downtown area. The Catholic church across the street seemed uninvolved. I was handed a pamphlet out front that described a simple, nonreligious service for family and friends. Naomi's picture showed her smiling in a way I'd never seen in person, just as beautiful, but less severe. I realized that, not without reason, I'd formed a hard opinion of the woman as unhappy, perhaps trapped. But here she looked joyful and free, wearing a simple summer dress while posing in front of a blossoming tree.

The person who handed me the pamphlet stood at the end of a canopied walkway rising to the front door, at the end of a line of mourners. Eric stood there with his two sons. He greeted people, giving and receiving hugs. The boys were expressionless, blinking up at the procession of people. Each wore a short-sleeved button-down shirt and a tie. Mack's shirt was blue, Jasper's white. Simple black pants. Like Amish kids.

Eric had shed his dark suit coat and rolled up his white sleeves. Glancing to my right, I saw a man standing near the sidewalk on the edge of the lawn. He blew out smoke then stamped his cigarette out on the ground. He seemed to be watching the queue of people. I didn't recognize him.

We edged closer and I thought of what I was going to say. *I'm so sorry for your loss.* There were reasons people stuck to the traditional sentiment. No point trying to reinvent the wheel during such a momentous time. Say you're sorry and move on.

An older woman embraced Eric, and I could see his face over her shoulder, his eyes shut tight. A trembling smile formed as they held onto each other.

I looked away. The man on the sidewalk had his back to me now as he talked with someone else. Martin Baker. Martin wore jeans and a black shirt that looked like silk. Too flashy for a funeral and doing a lot of work, straining against his barrel chest.

My guess was that most of the people attending had come up from Tannersville. Wendy said the funeral was at the insistence of Naomi's family, and I tried picking them out. But I didn't know what they looked like.

A big man with large hands shook with Eric next, and Eric nodded and mouthed *thank you.*

Now I was just three people away.

I looked at the boys again, distracted by a couple of other kids their age. Mack even smiled and playfully punched one of them. I couldn't imagine what life would be like for Naomi's sons now. What would it be like for my own girls if I died? Not that I was so special life couldn't go on. But losing a parent had to be one of the worst things that could happen to a child. To go through life without your mother? My heart broke for them.

"Ma'am?"

Someone behind me was trying to be polite when I failed to move forward. It was my turn.

"Sorry."

As I stepped toward Eric Sheller, he smiled at me.

"Oh wow, thank you for coming."

"Mr. Sheller . . . I am so sorry for your loss. I'm just . . . If there's anything I can do, please don't hesitate to ask."

"Thank you," he said. His eyes were that bright blue, but red around the edges from crying, dark underneath.

"We're right next door," I said. I couldn't seem to stop talking. "I can cook, I can take the boys, anything."

He started to respond, then stopped. Something shifted in his demeanor and now he seemed to search me, the light in his eyes quivering with emotion.

"Thank you again," he said at last, and the moment passed. I moved on, stepping up onto the porch to where the boys were.

They each studied me in their own way. I wasn't sure Mack remembered me. But Jasper, almost my height, seemed to know who I was.

"Jasper," I said, taking his hand. "I'm so sorry."

"Did Delia come?"

"Oh, sorry, honey. She's in school."

He didn't respond, just turned his face toward the line, ready for the next person. A chain of mourners on this long, horribly sad day in his young life. Jasper, at eleven, and Mack, at nine, were old enough they'd likely never forget it.

I wanted to say more. I wanted to take them into a giant hug and tell them I could mother them, if they needed, for a time. That I could take away their horrible pain and make life normal for them again, which they deserved.

But of course, I didn't, and I couldn't, and so finally I moved on.

* * *

No casket. Just that same picture of Naomi, looking bright and carefree, this one framed and propped on an easel. Nice flower arrangements all around. A lectern nearby. I found a seat near the middle of the room. Basic metal chairs with seat cushions, arranged classroom-style. I still couldn't figure out who was who;

they were nearly all unfamiliar faces. But the people nearest the front, I supposed, were immediately family. I had a rear-side view of them. A woman around my age wiped her eyes with a wadded Kleenex. A man sat next to her with a straight back, his arm around her.

As more people filed in, I glimpsed a couple of faces I recognized after all. Wendy and I made eye contact and traded reassuring smiles. Renee De George was there, wearing black, talking somberly with a cluster of people standing in the corner by a water cooler. As I watched, she filled a paper cup. She seemed to realize I was there and watched me for a moment before she drank.

Eric and his sons approached the framed picture together. A boy on each side, Eric's arms across their shoulders. He might've said something. Then Jasper shrugged his father's arm off. Eric seemed to reprimand him quietly.

Jasper responded loud enough that I could hear his voice, but not discern his words. It could have been a moan. I wondered if it was harder or easier that their mother's body wasn't here. Probably harder. To only have a picture to say goodbye to. To know she was somewhere in a cold room after being poked and prodded by investigators.

Had it been a full autopsy? Was a tox report pending? It suddenly struck me that all this time, I'd barely considered drugs being involved. But her extremely unusual behavior in the grocery store, the way she'd seemed so detached when I'd visited her home, it was back on the table. She very much could have been someone struggling with an addiction.

Jasper continued to act unhappy. His father tried drawing him in again, but Jasper yanked away this time. I heard someone gasp.

He backed away from the picture of his dead mother and stumbled as he turned, fell to one knee. I got to my feet, moving as if to go to him, help him. But others were closer, and a man

I didn't know caught Jasper in his arms and held him as the boy collapsed and wept.

* * *

I didn't care how hot it was — the fresh air was amazing. I took a deep lungful of it through my nose. But I couldn't linger on the funeral home porch, since people were coming out behind me. As I descended the stairs, two men approached.

Deputy Martin said, "Hi Elaine, how you doing?"

"Okay. How are you?"

I kept walking, and Martin fell into step with me. So did the man with him.

"This is Investigator Bo Smith," Martin said, indicating the bald man to his left. "He's with the state police."

I kept going until we reached the sidewalk, then stopped for what seemed like an unavoidable introduction. Smith smiled wide and shook my hand. He had a dry, hard grip and his breath smelled like mint gum. "Mrs. Barrister."

He must've seen me glance toward the funeral home because his smile faded quickly. "Sorry if this is an inconvenient time. I'd planned to call you and your husband — Geoff, is it? — and ask if I could see you both. But you ended up here."

He smiled, and I could see one of his teeth was capped silver. A state police investigator at the funeral made sense, especially if there was an open death investigation. But approaching me like this out in the open felt inappropriate. I just wanted to get into my car and go home. Eric and his sons were going to step out of the funeral home at any moment and see me standing there, talking with police. They might know who he was, even if the rest of the people coming out and walking to their cars didn't.

Smith slipped me a business card. "Okay if I come by the house tonight?"

I stuck it in my small purse. "Of course."

"It'll only take a minute. Just routine, a couple of quick questions. Seeing as how you live right next door to the Shellers. Then I'll be on my way, and we can put this awful tragedy behind us."

He gave me cop eyes, unreadable, and then that smile again, silver tooth winking in the back.

CHAPTER SIXTEEN

"Dinner!"

The girls arrived slowly, rarely interested in actual meals while always hungry for snacks and dessert. Unless the meals consisted of pizza. Or chicken wings.

Delia slumped into her chair as I spooned mashed potatoes onto her plate. The real kind, from our own garden, peeled and boiled, along with burgers from Kimber's farm. A simple but pleasing dinner for a busy and sad day.

"You okay, honey?"

"Mm-hmm."

Geoff came in from the bedroom, having changed out of his PA scrubs into a pair of sweats and an Ithaca College T-shirt. He'd completed all his schooling at Ithaca, including his master's in PA Studies. After passing his certifying exam and obtaining his state license, Buxton's community health center had snatched him up. "What's going on?" He pulled out a chair. "You okay?"

"It's nothing," Delia said.

Sometimes our eldest daughter really made you work for it.

Her sister bounded into the room. And Charlotte had no problem holding forth. "Riley said someone died," she said as she climbed into her seat.

Geoff and I connected. In that second or two, we somehow communicated that he would field it.

"Who did she say died?" he asked Charlotte as I distributed the burgers.

"She said Mack's mom died and Mack's dad went to jail."

"No," I interjected. "Mack's dad didn't go to jail." I realized I'd forgotten the green beans on the stove and went for them.

Geoff asked Charlotte, "Did Riley say how she thought Mrs. Sheller died?"

"She said she was attacked by a bear."

"Hmm."

I came back and spooned the beans.

"Is that true?" Charlotte asked.

"No," Geoff said. "She wasn't attacked by a bear, honey."

"Then what happened?"

"Well, we don't know."

I sat at the end of the table opposite Geoff. "The police do an investigation for this sort of thing," I said, "to try and figure out what happened."

"She might have fallen and hit her head," Charlotte said.

Geoff gave me a look like he doubted that explanation.

"We just don't know," I told Charlotte.

Delia was still slumped, holding her head up with one hand, pushing her fork in and out of her potatoes with the other. She wasn't talking. Just Charlotte.

"So, Mack's father didn't kill her?"

"My goodness, Char. We don't know."

"When will we know?" It was Delia, finally joining in.

"Well, that's tough to say. They have to gather all the forensic evidence."

Charlotte had the ketchup bottle and was holding it upside down over her burger like a pile driver. She squeezed and the ketchup jettisoned out. She kept going as it covered her entire burger. She'd lost interest in the conversation.

Geoff took the bottle away from her. Charlotte relished what came next — pushing the bun down on top of the burger so all that ketchup oozed out the sides. The bright red of it made me think of blood at the scene. I had no way of knowing, but blunt force trauma could've caused a lot of blood. I thought of Naomi lying there in the woods alone. Her picture on the easel in the funeral home, her elder son pulling away from his father, collapsing from the grief.

We ate for a few seconds in silence until Charlotte started talking about a boy who'd been hit in the stomach during four square and had to sit out the rest of the game. Someone else had burned themselves on the slide. "It was so hot, Mom. Treeny just burned her legs. Like, burned her *butt*."

I put my hand on Delia's, gently encouraging her to eat. She finally did — I knew she was hungry — and then she started to open up. Kids had talked about the Shellers in the middle school too. But she was less preoccupied with the details. She had other worries on her mind.

"What if you died and Dad had to go to jail? Or if both of you died? Like, when you go on dates, you drive somewhere and get killed in a car accident? Or the house burns and me and Charlotte get out because we're small, but you and Dad can't?"

"Oh, honey." I got up and held her while she sat in the chair, and Geoff joined us. Charlotte clambered out of her seat, scurried around the table, and threw her arms around the group.

We were like that when someone knocked on the door.

* * *

Bo Smith was in the same clothes from earlier, pleated slacks and a white short-sleeved button-down with a blue tie. The shirt had darkened around the armpits. With him was a short, slight woman who said her name was Investigator Cojuangco. She pronounced it *Koh-wahng-koh* and spoke with an accent.

Once we'd all tolerated the girls asking a million questions, we shooed them off and sat in the living room. I hastily cleaned up the toys, dishes, and stuffed animals. Geoff apologized for the mess.

"Not at all," Cojuangco said warmly in her Spanish or Filipino accent. "It's life."

"We'll be quick, like I promised," Smith said, getting down to business.

I took my seat beside Geoff. A burble of cartoon voices came from Delia's room, the girls now watching a show on her tablet.

Smith said, "So, as you both obviously know, Naomi Sheller died on Sunday. Given the circumstances, an investigation has been opened. Have either of you heard anything about her cause of death?"

He seemed to divide his gaze equally between Geoff and me.

Geoff shook his head and said no, which surprised me a little. With the investigators both now watching me, I answered, "I heard it was blunt force trauma."

Smith studied me. "Who told you that?"

"I'm not sure where I heard it." Lying went against my principles. But so did throwing other people under the bus. "It was at soccer on Monday night. Lots of people were talking about it, and someone said blunt force trauma."

"And why did you take them at their word?"

"Sir, I didn't say that. I just said I heard."

Cojuangco cleared her throat. Smith closed his mouth before saying anything else. He scribbled something in the notebook open on his knee instead. Probably that I had an attitude. I didn't mean to, but his approaching me at the memorial still didn't sit right with me.

"Mrs. Sheller experienced an injury leading to physiologic changes that resulted in her death," Cojuangco said. "The manner of death is something we're still determining." The statement felt directed at everyone in the room. "An investigation is normal following an incident like this. And in this case, Mr. Sheller has been explicit in wanting us to pursue it to the fullest. Which of course we would do anyway."

"Mr. Sheller wants . . . ?" Geoff didn't seem to know how to finish. But I understood: he was surprised they weren't already treating Sheller as a suspect. Maybe they didn't have enough evidence. Or maybe he was innocent.

Smith jumped back in. "So just as background for us, can you confirm some of the following information?"

"Sure," Geoff said.

But this was going to be more about me.

"The Shellers moved into the home on Thursday of last week. Did you see them move in?"

Geoff looked over and I nodded. "I did. Yes, I was outside in the garden, and I noticed them. There was a moving truck, it looked like two movers, and the family."

"Any interaction other than that?"

"Mr. Sheller came over and introduced himself."

"When was that?"

"The next day. So, last Friday."

"He came over and knocked on the door?"

"I was . . . outside."

"In the garden?"

I inhaled sharply and held it. Three sets of eyes keyed in on me now. So I'd been smoking. What of it? Was it relevant? Would it help them find out what happened to Naomi Sheller?

"I was on my way back inside and encountered Mr. Sheller on the porch. We spoke."

They waited for me to elaborate.

"We just said hello, talked about our kids. Their names. The school. And then the next day we brought over a housewarming gift. I had . . ." *I had been debating it,* I almost said. *Given what I'd seen in the grocery story last Thursday morning.*

"I hadn't been sure what I was going to make, but the girls insisted on brownies," I said instead.

Cojuangco smiled, straight teeth shining white. Smith moved on. "Anything else? How did you find everything when you dropped in for the housewarming gift?"

"They were busy, moving in, painting. I observed that Naomi Sheller was . . . She seemed stressed out. She was quiet. She had a sort of . . . She was stiff. Which, I don't know if it means anything."

"Everything is helpful," Cojuangco said. It was a well-worn line, but coming from her it rang true.

"I should tell you that I also saw Naomi Sheller in the grocery store the morning they moved in. It's possible they stayed in the house the night before and we just didn't notice. Or maybe she was just in town early for groceries. But she was there. Thursday morning. In the juice aisle."

Smith and Cojuangco perked right up, Smith leaning in a little, his notebook balanced on his knee, pen hovering.

"I didn't even know who she was. I just saw a woman who was . . . She seemed to be having an episode. It could have been mental or physical, I don't know. Geoff and I have discussed it, and from what I saw, it could have been a lot of things."

"Can you describe it?"

I did the best I could, finding that the more I revisited that scene in my mind, the less certain I felt about any interpretation. People didn't tend to walk away from medical emergencies, no — and yet the way she'd clutched her chest and dropped to one knee definitely suggested a physical problem.

But then that period of stasis, just reaching out for the juice, still as a statue . . . The startling lack of humanity in her eyes when she looked up at me afterward. Those all seemed like some kind of mental problem, like a response to trauma, perhaps even a potential psychosis.

But I was neither a pathologist nor a psychiatrist, so I stuck to the facts, describing what I'd witnessed and not what I thought.

"And no one else saw this . . . event?" Smith asked.

"I saw one man walking by at the end of the aisle. I'm not sure he was aware of it, though."

"Can you describe him?"

I did, though it seemed a strange line of inquiry. Even if they were being thorough, did they doubt what I was saying happened? Or did they just want someone else's take?

Smith jotted more notes. When he finished, he leaned toward Cojuangco and spoke quietly in her ear. She nodded. She pulled a manila envelope out of her bag, placed it on her lap, and opened the flap. She removed a photograph and showed it to us.

My throat closed up.

"Do either of you recognize this person?" Cojuangco asked.

Smith gave us his full attention again.

Geoff glanced at me, and when I didn't speak, said, "No. I don't know her."

"I recognize her," I said. The words felt thick in my mouth. I wondered if they could all hear the tom-tom beat of my heart.

"Where do you know her from?" Smith asked.

"I saw her this past Sunday, in Tannersville."

"What were you doing there?"

"Who is she? Is she . . . ?"

"Mrs. Barrister?"

"I was there for the girls' swim lessons. We were stopped at the Stewart's Shop coming back to have ice cream and I saw her." I could feel Geoff watching me. "She was in Eric Sheller's truck. With him."

CHAPTER SEVENTEEN

Geoff was giving me the silent treatment. We lay in bed, both of us on our phones, not talking. He was obviously upset I hadn't told him about seeing the woman in Tannersville, and I didn't know what to say. I'd had opportunities. I just hadn't wanted to, for reasons I didn't quite understand yet.

For the mom group, life went on. Cara's wedding wasn't happening until the spring, but there was plenty to plan for and think about — dressing the bride and her bridesmaids, the ceremony and reception, the honeymoon. Half a dozen women living vicariously through their younger, unmarried, childless friend. It made me think of myths about virgin sacrifices. *Clash of the Titans*.

The book club idea had also resurfaced. Theresa's daughter wanted to read one of the newest, ultra-popular series about dragons, romance, and power upheavals. She wanted to know if anyone had read it, if it was appropriate for children. *Hard no*, Cara wrote. *Not for kids. Maybe in high school.*

And that was why we needed some sort of club, Theresa said. Even if it was just on Facebook and not necessarily in person. To keep people informed about what was good for kids and what wasn't. What was overhyped and what was worth it. There was so much to choose from.

But adult fare too, Renee insisted. She didn't come right out and say it, but I could read her distaste for modern genre fiction.

We've tried this, Wendy warned. *We can never agree on a book!*

And, she reasoned, we each had to read it by a certain point, understand it enough to intelligently discuss, all while enduring some combination of kids, jobs, and marriages. Getting through a book on time with the mental bandwidth to comprehend it was no small task.

Geoff sighed.

"Honey," I said.

"Mm-hmm."

"I didn't say anything to you about seeing that woman because it felt . . . I guess it felt silly." I propped up on my elbow and faced him. "I didn't know who she was. And you've been so busy at work that—"

"Please don't blame my job."

"I'm not blaming anything. I just mean I didn't want to bother you with it. I didn't even know what it was. I was just . . . waiting. And then everything happened so fast."

But there was more.

"To be perfectly honest, I thought you'd wonder why I cared. That you'd ask why I was so interested in our neighbors. And . . . I don't know. They just got my attention right away. Well, obviously Naomi did. But then . . ."

"And you saw them argue?"

I'd also told Smith and Cojuangco that I'd seen some kind of altercation Friday night. Watching out our bedroom window, half expecting their lights to be flickering again, that heated conversation on the back deck.

We both just breathed for a moment. Geoff avoided eye contact.

"Do you think they know who the woman is?"

"They asked about her," Geoff answered, irritated. "Obviously they know who she is. For all we know, she's someone he's sleeping with."

"Have you heard anything? About what might have been wrong with Naomi before she died?"

"I've been up to my eyeballs with patients. I've seen half the town with the viruses going around. Folger Hemlock was rushed to the emergency room. You know who I mean?"

I did. "Top of the hill. Friends of the Whitmers."

"Right. He's in his eighties. Wife died from Alzheimer's about five years ago."

My friend Courtney had come from a bit of money; her parents were loaded. I'd heard about the Hemlocks through her. The well-to-do in the area mostly stuck to their own; you didn't see them at the local grocery store or at the picnic following the first soccer game of the season. Buxton was a microcosm of the wealth gap, I supposed — many of the few wealthy families lived up on Pine Ridge, a long, wooded drive that, in certain spots, overlooked the town from a distance.

"Is he okay?" I asked.

"He's old. He's had COVID, and now this RSV that's still circulating. It's taken a toll on him."

"I'm sorry to hear it."

"Yeah."

I rolled onto my back and gazed up at the ceiling, thinking about the way Eric Sheller had seemed so naturally charming, almost guileless. I supposed anyone could cheat. But was he also a murderer?

He'd been at the scene of Naomi's death — he'd even told his sons he was going to look for her. Why tell his sons if his intention had been to kill her? It could have started as another argument, of course, and escalated into murder.

But then to just leave her there? It took the police less than an hour to find her. She'd been within view of the hiking trail.

"What type of condition could someone have that wouldn't show up right away in an autopsy? Something that might take a little while?"

For a moment Geoff didn't move, then he joined me in staring up at the ceiling, as if the call of medical prognostication was too good for him to stay angry. "Aortic stenosis. Heart valve failure. It would be odd that she wasn't treating it. If she was, they'd have that information. But it might be challenging to determine that posthumously."

"Maybe they already did."

"I don't know why they wouldn't be forthcoming with it. Why show us a picture of a woman her husband was with, but not talk about her heart condition? Heart disease is the leading cause of death for women in the United States. A-fib, stenosis, coronary artery disease . . . but this is a woman barely in her forties. Fit, seemed to have a good BMI, healthy all around."

For a moment, I wondered how he knew so much about her to describe her like that when, to my knowledge, he'd never met her in person. But then, I'd been talking about her for days and could have put those descriptors in his mind.

"Maybe all the more reason she didn't know she had a problem," I said. "She's such an unlikely candidate that she just doesn't consider it. Never gets it checked."

He considered it silently.

"But now we're really just speculating," I said. "Could've been a lot of things, right?" I yawned, feeling more relaxed myself. The fight between us — if you could call it that — seemed to have dissipated. Either that, or I was just exhausted. A fatigue like vapors behind my eyes.

"Could've had an aortic aneurysm," Geoff said. "She falls over in pain with the rupture, gets scraped up, disoriented. Stumbles into the woods, her sense of direction gone, wanders off the trail, falls again, hits her head." He rolled over to face me. "But that's something they'd likely see. That's internal bleeding. If they cut her open. Which . . . I don't know."

I faced him too. At last, we were connected. I stroked his cheek. "I'm sorry I didn't tell you that I saw Eric Sheller with a woman in a parking lot in the town where he used to live."

It was an apology that simultaneously made my case: the whole thing had seemed silly. Geoff countenanced it well. He was a good sport, and I loved him. When I gave him a kiss, he kissed back.

We returned to our supine positions. Then I reached for my bedside lamp and shut it. He clicked his off a couple of seconds later.

Just there in the dark, the two of us.

"What a couple of days," he said.

"I know." I worried about those boys. And my own kids. Charlotte was still so young. But Delia was feeling the effects. It had taken a good while to ease her mind tonight. And even then, she'd fallen asleep clinging to one of her old teddy bears, one almost forgotten but rediscovered again.

On the edge of falling asleep myself, I thought of Courtney. Wondering what she'd make of all of this.

But she was way out west somewhere, going from place to place. Free.

CHAPTER EIGHTEEN

Thursday afternoon, one week since the grocery store

"Where's Charlotte?"

Delia didn't know.

It was after school, and I was chopping carrots for dinner. Not paying attention, I slipped and sliced the tip of my finger. "Shit," I muttered, going to the sink. Unlike me to do that, since my father taught me early to always curl my fingers when using the knife so an errant blade would hit fingernail instead of flesh.

"Can you check her room for me?"

"Uh-huh."

Delia was reading at the dining room table. Lately she'd been sticking close to me, not wanting me out of her sight.

"Charrrlllottte!"

My own personal megaphone. Delia checked the room and came back. Not in there.

"Bathroom?"

"Nope."

I wrapped my cut finger with a paper towel. Holding some pressure, I went down the hallway even though Delia had just been. Sometimes Charlotte liked to hide. "Charlotte? Honey, no playing games. I need you to come out right now."

I looked behind the door, in the closet. Under the bed. Pushed open the bathroom door and found the room empty. I went through all the hiding places, including the clothes hampers. "Charlotte, I'm serious!" She wasn't in my bedroom either.

Though she was generally too scared to go down to the basement alone, I still looked. After checking the washer and dryer, the narrow space behind the dry goods shelves, I gave up. Back upstairs, I went out the front door, Delia right behind me.

"Charlotte, honey, it's Mommy! Answer me!"

The garage was separate from the house, and Geoff usually kept it locked. But it was open today, redolent of oil and gas, the Beetle sitting with the back propped open, exposing the rear engine. A greasy red rag hung from the bumper.

"Charlotte!" Back outside, I yelled as loud as I could. It's not like there was anyone to disturb. Just us, out here on the edge of town.

And the Shellers.

I looked there now, not seeing anyone outside. The extra vehicles were gone too. The place was in a state of transition — walls being painted, furniture piled in the center of rooms. Not somewhere to have a funeral reception.

An SUV tore by on the road. Someone going too fast as usual. No reason to think Charlotte would have crossed the road; there was nothing but woods on the other side.

I took a deep breath and looked down at Delia, who seemed to know what was next.

We started across the connecting lawns to the Shellers' place. By the time I reached their property line, I was jogging.

* * *

Maybe I knocked on the door too loud. But when Eric opened up, he looked a little taken aback.

"Sorry to bother you," I said, a bit out of breath. "Is there any chance Charlotte is here?"

"Charlotte?"

"My daughter. I'm sorry to just barge over here. We just can't find her and—"

"Are you okay?" His eyes locked on my hand. The blood from my cut finger had soaked through the paper towel.

"I'm okay, it's nothing. We can't find Charlotte and I thought I'd check over here."

"Right. My gosh. Let me call the boys and see. I haven't seen her, but maybe they know." He turned away to shout into the house. "Jasper! Mack! Can you come out here, guys?" When he faced me again, I noticed the darkness around his eyes had deepened since the memorial. "When's the last time you saw her?"

"Just a little while ago. Ten, fifteen minutes, maybe. I was making dinner. I thought she was right in the other room, on her tablet. Maybe she . . ." I started to turn, suddenly rethinking all the places I'd looked, considered that I might've missed something. But Eric's eldest son approached from the back rooms.

"She's with Mack," Jasper said. He stood beside his father and looked at Delia. "Hi."

"Hi."

"Where are they?" Eric asked his son. He started calling for Mack again.

"They're not in here." Jasper looked paler too. Like he'd aged a few years with his mother's passing, the poor kid.

"Well, where are they?"

"I don't know."

I could see Eric ready to push a little. He faced me instead. "I'm sorry. I didn't know she was over here."

I looked at Delia. I needed to turn away from the grief in Eric's face, regroup. "Let's look," I said to her, and she nodded.

We started around the house, calling Charlotte's name. Jasper came running past, then stopped ahead of us to tie his shoe. "Maybe the valley." He seemed invigorated by the prospect of adventure.

Eric joined us and I asked if he usually let the boys down in the valley.

"Just once. Well, they were with me. We went to check it out. It's tough going."

We moved to the back edge of the yard, where the woods started and the ground sloped steeply down into the wide ravine. Jasper bounded ahead, even as Eric cautioned him to slow down.

"Charlotte!"

"Mack!"

A breeze stirred the trees. In late summer, the vegetation was thick, and I wondered if they'd be able to hear us. "Should we have checked the house?" I wondered aloud.

"Jasper would've known." Eric grabbed a handful of ferns to steady himself. "I'm really sorry. I had no idea."

"It's o—"

I didn't finish because Eric pulled the ferns out by the roots as he slid down the embankment. Digging in his heels, clawing against the earth, he brought himself to a stop.

"Are you all right?"

He nodded. "Don't go that way."

Jasper was ahead of us, but saw what happened. "This way. You have to zigzag back and forth like this."

"Delia," I said when she started to follow. "Stay here, please."

"Mom . . ."

"Stay up here in case she comes back, okay? Right there, where you can watch me and watch for her at the same time, okay?"

She didn't like it, even looked like she might cry, but she said, "Okay," and stayed put. I made my way down carefully, both

Eric and I following Jasper's lead, switching back and forth every couple of yards. What were we going to find down here? My mind started playing out awful scenarios.

But before we got halfway down the embankment, Charlotte and Mack appeared on the level ground below, looking up at us.

"What are you guys doing?" Charlotte called. "Coming down to play?"

* * *

Emerging from the woods again ten minutes later, the yard seemed extra tidy. The whole world felt more orderly than the thick underbrush, clawing branches, and steep terrain. I was too winded to be angry at Charlotte right now, too glad she was all right to be upset. Instead, we let the kids go inside to play for a minute, and Eric produced a pack of cigarettes and shook two out.

I waved it off.

He looked apologetic. "I thought I smelled it the other day."

"You did. I just . . ." My labored breathing spoke for itself.

He put one back in the pack. "Probably for the best. I should too." But he flicked the lighter and inhaled.

As we fell into a semi-comfortable silence, I wondered if he was in shock. If maybe I was, even, to be standing here with a man who might've killed his own wife. He looked like he'd lost weight. I was about to make an excuse to gather the girls and leave when Eric said, "Thanks."

I hesitated, not knowing what was coming next.

"I don't know. For being normal."

I wasn't sure how to respond to that. Had he seen the unmarked trooper car at my house yesterday? While he'd been ostensibly grieving with friends and family members, I'd been telling the cops about the woman I'd seen in his truck. Did he know? I'd felt sure he'd spotted me, but he wasn't acting like it. Unless it was a ploy to draw me in.

I remained at a loss for words, again thinking I needed to get the girls and get the hell home.

"It was all over so fast," Eric said. "Just . . . God, just a couple of days ago Naomi was here, in this house. Going out for her pre-dinner run. And now she's gone. And there's already been a funeral. Well, memorial. And it's over. It just makes no sense."

I tried not to blatantly analyze him. "It did seem fast," I ended up saying, more about the memorial — and instantly regretted it.

"Yeah, I just . . . Was it? I don't know what happened. I went into a kind of autopilot. I think I thought, if I just do this, go make the arrangements, get it all done, it'll be over, and then life will go back to normal. Like it wasn't even about her. Like I would come home afterward, and she would be sitting there, and we would talk about it."

I thought Wendy said Naomi's family had been the ones to push for a timely service, but I kept quiet about that too.

"The police have talked to me multiple times. Why did I go to the woods? Did she have any medical conditions? They want to see if I change my story. I have nothing to change. They wanted to do an autopsy. I said, 'Okay.' I let them swab me — buccal swab in my mouth. I'm a lawyer. I don't usually do criminal work, but I know plenty about due process. I couldn't for a second do anything but cooperate. She was my wife. And she was here one second, in our house, and she went out for a run, and then she was . . . then she was . . ." Eric bent forward, unable to finish as a sob wracked him.

Not knowing what else to do, I looked around to see if the kids were watching. I could hear them inside, voices coming at a normal volume, mainly Charlotte's. I put my hand on Eric's back as he cried. After another moment, he straightened, wiping his eyes and sniffing. "Sorry. I don't know what that was. Being in the woods I think, just now, it . . . She . . . I went in looking for her, you know? I couldn't find her. I must've just missed her. What if I could have . . . Oh God, what if I could have helped her and I didn't . . ."

Another bout of emotion gripped him. He tried to fight it, but the tears came anyway. When it was over, he said, "I haven't really done that. I didn't want to lose it in front of the boys. I mean, it's okay that they see me have emotions, to show them, but I just . . . It's just that, you know . . ."

"I understand."

He faced me then, eyes shining, pink with emotion. "I didn't have anything to do with what happened to her."

Did she have a medical condition? The words were on the tip of my tongue, but I just couldn't.

Instead, I stood there with him a moment longer, in painful, grief-soaked silence.

"I didn't have anything to do with it," he repeated, almost to himself. "I tried to find her. I loved her more than anything. Through everything."

He took a cleansing breath, seemed to focus. "Somebody did this to her."

This was all so sudden — his emotion, this whole confessional moment — that I found it hard to speak. "Do you have any idea who?"

He looked at me then, and what I saw in his eyes I'd never forget. He had an idea. Or maybe thought he did. At the very least, there was a story there, just beneath the surface, that I obviously knew nothing about.

He blinked, and it all seemed to clear. Then he gave a slight shake of his head. "Elaine, I'm so sorry. You didn't ask for any of this."

"It's okay. I told you, I . . . I'm here."

"Well, please, then. You can help me with all of this food. We have so much and it's going to spoil."

"You should freeze it."

"Yeah. Yeah, that's a good idea. Let me at least get you something to drink."

He started around the house and I followed. "It's okay," I said. "I think we'll just . . ."

He stopped and looked at me, his face soft, and he nodded again. "Of course," he said. "Absolutely."

And after a few minutes of wrangling kids — mostly Charlotte — we were backing out the front door. I literally had a hold of her shirt to keep her from scurrying away. I wasn't going to let her out of my sight ever again.

"Bye," Jasper said to Delia.

"Bye," Delia said.

"Tell Dr. Geoff we said hi," Jasper said.

It caught me by surprise.

"Dr. Geoff." The boy looked at me. "Isn't he your husband?"

"He is . . ."

Eric explained, "Naomi took the boys for their well-child visit — you know, their physical — a couple days before we moved in, since it was required for school. And we wanted to establish a primary here in town."

"Bye," Mack said this time, then turned and ran deeper into the house.

Jasper followed him, and Eric saw us the rest of the way out the door. Then I took both girls, holding each by the hand now, back to our house, struck by everything that had just happened. The raw emotion of it.

And thinking about how my husband had met Naomi Sheller and never told me. Not even after she died.

CHAPTER NINETEEN

Saturday

I focused on our lives. On housework. I spent time job-hunting. I soaked in a long bath. But the Sheller business never cleared completely. I thought about it day and night.

The moms wanted to throw an engagement party for Cara Cormack. Nothing formal, more of a family affair. Renee had volunteered to host, naturally, since she had a huge place between Buxton and Tannersville that would accommodate guests from both places. It was set for Saturday, following the soccer game. Kimber would provide food from her farm, and Renee had all the other accommodations. Plenty of space, extra tables and chairs, huge yards for the kids to run around.

By 11 a.m. that morning, they were doing just that. Spirits were high coming off of a rare win (a Dewitt rematch, no less!), the kids still sweaty in their jerseys as they goofed around on the big De George property. They ate hot dogs and burgers and Rice Krispie treats and didn't bother us for a while. It gave us time to moon over Cara and congratulate her officially, in person.

"You didn't have to do this, Renee," she gushed. "You're so thoughtful. All of you."

I remembered Renee confessing her doubts about Gary. Maybe the impromptu party was a way to dispel any bad juju. To support Cara, but to also show Gary that Cara had friends who cared about her. That if he messed with her, he messed with all of us.

When Gary showed up in his royal-blue classic car, it was an hour into the festivities. We'd eaten and were enjoying the panoramic views from Renee's wraparound porch. It sparked further thoughts about the Shellers. I imagined Naomi here with us, what might've been. I would've asked her to come. Her sons could've been out there running circles around the house with the rest of the children. With Charlotte and Delia. They'd seemed such ready-made friends.

I wondered which of the mom group might be thinking about her too. But studying their faces, I doubted anyone was. She was in the background, already fading from collective memory.

Gary brought a couple of men with him who might've been his cousins. They hung back by the parking area as he climbed up onto the porch with a wry smile. He was in slim jeans, faded and only a little ripped. He wore the usual thick-soled logging boots and a white T-shirt that showed his young, muscular physique.

"Hey, everybody!"

Cara jumped up, almost squeaking with glee, and threw her arms around him. "Thanks for coming, babe."

The kids came tearing through, breaking the moment. Renee shooed them off the porch. The men by the car smoked and smiled from a distance.

"You want something to eat?" Cara was already putting a plate together for him. She was definitely a darling. I liked her tomboy haircut, the bangs in her eyes, her muscly arms. I still hadn't seen her reality show appearance, but apparently she'd come in third and seemed fine with it.

Gary took the plate of food, wiggling his eyebrows. "Thanks, babe."

"What about your uncles?"

Uncles, then, not cousins. Young for uncles. Gary said they'd like some too, and waved them up onto the porch. Soon everyone was eating and chatting in smaller groups, half a dozen conversations going at once. For a moment, it all felt quaint. All of us together on the rambling porch of this huge farmhouse overlooking a sparkling Lake Champlain. Multiple tables covered in red-checked tablecloths. Rich, salty smells of barbequed meat on a grill. Birdsong and insects chittering, the shriek of children's voices in the near distance.

"Kids!" Renee called. "Stay out of the barn, okay?"

"Okay!" a couple of them yelled as they ran past.

"I keep it locked," she explained. "But kids have a way. There's a hay loft in there, trapdoor for grain. You don't want kids messing around."

The property fascinated me. Like many homes in the region, it had a past, once a full, working farm. The big red gambrel barn, a smaller foaling shed, a butcher shop, a tenant house. "Is this really all yours, Renee?"

"It's still technically my parents'. But they're only here part-time. And it's all left to me and my brother Dale. He's way out west, though, doing his thing. This place goes back to the Revolutionary War. Can you believe it?"

I studied the hayfields beyond the cluster of buildings. Lakefront with stairs descending a steep embankment to the water below.

Kimber started talking about the rise and fall of small farms. How big agribusiness had put small farm owners out of business. But these days, people wanted local. "And we want resilient communities," she said. "Our county feeds itself from its own farms more than any other in the state."

"Is that right?" Renee asked. "Well, I don't know if I could ever get this place going again as a working dairy farm."

"Even vegetables. Be a market gardener!"

"For now, I do what I can with haying and just the upkeep."

I never thought about my own horticultural efforts in the context of the region. So many people were farming and growing food in the area, a true renaissance, and I didn't know much about it. "Renee, how did you wind up back here? You grew up here, right?"

"I did. Right here. It's in the Tannersville school district, so that's where I graduated. I actually went to Cornell, then Columbia and got my master's. Started teaching in the city."

"And you were married?" I glanced around at the others, looking for a barometer, if I was prying, or if it was common knowledge and I was acting like an outsider. But the other women were just eating and listening.

"I was married," Renee said. "He passed. Life wasn't the same there, so I came back here."

"I'm sorry for your loss."

She nodded and smiled appropriately. "A lot of people return here. You see what's out there in the world and you realize — the wide-open spaces, the fresh air, the small-town community? That's where it's at."

The talk continued about who'd returned here from the larger world, who'd never left. I kept listening, but I couldn't help picking up on the next table over, Cara and Gary. Cara laughed about something while Gary and his uncles grinned. One of them started toward the front door.

Renee stopped talking and looked.

"Bathroom?" the man asked. He resembled Gary, a little, through the mouth and jaw.

Renee pointed. "Through the kitchen and first door on your left."

He went inside. The air felt heavy for a second. Renee seemed to be looking at Gary, her expression betraying her continued distrust.

And then Gary did something you usually only see in movies — he swept Cara off her feet into a giant bear hug. And this time, she did squeal. He kissed her while she kicked her feet out behind her.

"Save it for the wedding," Wendy said, grinning.

"I'll have plenty to last my whole life," Gary said. And he kissed her again.

* * *

I helped clean up. The Charlotte-is-missing scare had left a psychic mark, and I stayed aware of where she was at nearly all times. Every few seconds, I would spy her, red-faced and running from one place to another, hear her laughter, shouting important kid things at other kids, who shouted back.

"So," Theresa said. She held a stack of paper plates she was about to shove into a garbage bag. "How are things over there?"

I had to look in her eyes to intuit her meaning. It was the first time anyone in the group had mentioned the Shellers for days. "Good. It's been quiet."

"He's probably not working, is he?"

"I don't think so. I don't know, though." The question struck me as a little odd.

"And the boys haven't been in school."

"No. They definitely haven't."

Theresa shook her head in dismay. "God, what a thing. I just can't imagine it. I mean, has he said anything to you? Like, what about the investigation? Is there any sign of anything?"

Wendy stood nearby, overhearing us. "Martin thinks they're going to nail him. Soon."

"What are they waiting for?" Theresa's question was genuine.

"They want a proper arrest warrant," Wendy answered. "Something that's going to stick and keep him in jail. With enough evidence, the judge will set a high bail. He could be a danger to society." She looked at me. "Are you doing okay with it?"

I nodded, weirded out at being asked. Eric's emotions still felt close.

"Why are they so sure he did it?" Theresa asked.

"Trust me," Wendy said. "Let's just say people were aware that they were having problems. For a long time." She spoke in a whisper. "I think he was having an affair, and she was going to leave him. Take half of everything, or more. Take the boys."

"Jeez," Theresa said. "So, he follows her into the woods . . . ?"

Wendy shrugged. "No divorce, but a nice, big life-insurance payout."

"They know for sure he was having an affair? Or I guess you can't say . . ."

"He was seen with another woman."

Heat rose to my face. I suddenly looked for something to do and started gathering up the cutlery. Renee's cool hand landed on mine. Her eyes, marble gray, regarded me levelly. "I've got it," she said.

"I don't mind."

"Just let me." She put the last few used forks and knives in the small tub she carried.

Wendy didn't give any indication she knew I'd spoken to the police about the other woman. Theresa just seemed to be following wherever the story went. "Wow," she said. "Our own murder mystery here in the Adirondacks. It's like a book. Hey — are we going to do this book club or what? I think it would be great."

"Oh God, not this again," said Kimber.

As the topic of discussion shifted to the merits and demerits of the unkillable book club idea, I checked for Charlotte. Just a couple of steps away from the porch I found her, charging toward me, eyes bright and face flushed.

"Mom," she said. "We can't get into a building."

"The barn is locked."

"It's not the barn."

"Well, honey, if you can't get into a building — any building — it means you're not supposed to."

She slumped her shoulders. I could tell she was tiring; she looked like she was about to cry or pitch a fit.

"Honey, I actually think it's time to go."

"Noooo . . ."

Here comes the tantrum.

"Mom, I don't want to. I want to stay!"

"You're tired, honey. You were up early, you played soccer — you played so hard — and you've been going nonstop." I checked my phone. Not quite 4 p.m. But good enough. I just wanted to be home, back with Geoff and Delia. People seemed to be clearing out anyway. I hadn't seen Cara or Gary since the porch. This whole thing was supposedly for them, and they were off somewhere. Probably making out.

"I don't want to go!" Charlotte yelled, and she turned and ran. Straight into the arms of Wendy, who was behind us.

"Gotcha!"

Charlotte started to protest, but this was her coach. "Your mom is right. You're one of my best players, and it's important you get some downtime too, okay?"

Charlotte turned to mush. "Okay."

Renee and Theresa watched from the porch, smiling approvingly. Then they entered through the front door, Renee carrying the tub, Theresa the garbage bag stuffed with plates.

Wendy handed Charlotte to me.

"You sure everything is okay?"

"I think so. Why?"

She only looked at me, her own face red from the heat. Maybe she *did* know I'd spoken to the police. Maybe she was worried about me. But this wasn't some murder mystery novel. This was real life, and Eric Sheller wasn't going to hurt me because I'd done my duty as a civilian. At least, I didn't think so.

Wendy broke eye contact and smiled at Charlotte one more time.

"All right," I said. "Have a good evening."

"You too." She stepped onto the porch and went inside.

I got Charlotte into the car without too much trouble. Coach Wendy's mollifying effect on her was wearing off as we drove away, Renee's brick house fading in the mirrors. "I wish we could have stayed," Charlotte said, slouching.

"Listen to me, young lady. If I tell you we're going to go home, we're going to go home. That's it. I don't want any whining, I don't want any complaining, and I certainly won't tolerate any disobedience. Do you hear me?"

My words came out loud, maybe a little louder than intended, and I could see the impact. Charlotte's eyes widened, her shoulders up. "Yes," she said softly.

"What?"

"Yes, Mom," she said, louder.

"Good. Thank you."

We drove home.

* * *

I pulled in the driveway and killed the engine, instantly aware of a helicopter thudding close by. *Oh God, what now?* But I knew the sound, the pitch of the rotors, different from the search helicopters

115

last weekend. Life-Flight took critical patients from our hospital to other trauma centers and had a distinctive fluttering sound. It wasn't searching for someone; it was taking someone to a bigger hospital.

My phone started buzzing like a swarm of hornets. A dozen texts from the mom group, I saw, all coming in now that I was back in service range.

"What is going on?" I asked aloud.

Terrible car accident, Wendy had written. *He's barely holding on.*

Oh my God, Theresa had written. *What is happening?!?*

CHAPTER TWENTY

They're rushging him to burlngton

Rushing him to Burlington, I understood. The nearest city with a Level 1 trauma center. That was the Life-Flight helicopter I'd heard moments ago.

I scrolled to figure out who she was talking about, even as the texts kept coming in.

Gary.

There it was. Gary Latrelle. He'd been at the engagement party an hour ago, grinning and *aw-shucks*-ing, picking Cara up off the ground. Now, he'd been in some kind of terrible accident.

"Mom?"

"Undo your seat belt, honey. Go ahead and go inside. I'll be right there."

"Are you still mad at me?"

"No, honey."

"I'm sorry I wanted to stay. It's just that I wanted to keep playing because—"

"I know, Char. It's okay. Just head inside, please. Daddy and Delia are in there."

"Yes, Mom," she murmured.

The texts popped up fast and furious, typos aplenty. Gary had left Renee's place not long after I did. He'd been able to stay only a short while because of work. Cara was upset, wishing he'd taken the time off, but the party had been somewhat last-minute, and there would be more formal events to come. Cara had stayed at Renee's and Gary had left. En route to his job, he went off the road.

Buxton Falls Road. Notorious for its many accidents. Twisting through the woods, winding and undulating. People got too comfortable and took it too fast. You could expect multiple accidents every winter. It was only autumn now, but Gary had gone off a sharp curve and collided with a tree.

He went right through the windefilf

Wendy was barely typing coherently, but *windshield* was the only thing that made any sense.

Gary Latrelle had hit a tree and was launched through the windshield.

In critical condition now, Wendy wrote.

A separate text chain included Cara. I scrolled through the texts. No details or speculation about the outcome, just support. *Are you okay? What can we do?*

She had yet to respond.

Theresa was right to ask, *What is happening?!?* She didn't need to elaborate; we all knew what she meant. Two tragic events in a short period of time. In an area where nothing much ever happened, and probably wouldn't for a long while. I didn't believe in curses, but it was starting to feel like we'd been getting away with too much for too long. Someone had crossed some Rubicon, opened a box they weren't supposed to, and now we were all in trouble. No one was safe.

But that was just emotion. Bad things happened without patterns.

The texts stopped. I looked up, realizing I was still in the car. The past few minutes had felt like a wild ride.

I forced myself out of the car, went inside, and packed Charlotte away in her room with snacks and her tablet. It was really dinnertime, but we'd eaten a late lunch at the De George place, and I needed a break. Maybe Geoff would run out for takeout. There wasn't much where we lived, just Chinese and pizza, but I'd be up for anything if it meant I didn't have to cook.

"What's up?" He gave me a worried look from the couch, where he'd been poking at his own phone. "You okay?"

I told him everything. The party, the accident. The way Cara and Gary were such happy young lovers. I even talked about how I'd yelled at Charlotte.

Somewhere in the midst of it, I started crying. I didn't know Cara that well, but I knew that spark of life she had. That spark she shared with Gary — who cared if it was infatuation? Life was short. Maybe they could make it together; they'd had a fifty–fifty chance, at least. I'd been cheering them on.

On top of what had just happened with the Shellers, the way Eric nearly collapsed in his backyard, it was just too much grief to handle, patterns or not. I folded into Geoff's arms, and he held me as I cried against his shoulder.

CHAPTER TWENTY-ONE

Two days later

"Faulty brakes," Wendy said.

Sunday had come and gone. Monday meant soccer practice. I could hardly believe we were all here. People were dying on hiking trails and crashing into trees. The idea that life continued no matter what just felt surreal.

We stood on the sidelines while the players did their laps, warming up. Blissfully unaware of the horrors around them, for the most part.

"Faulty?" Renee asked.

"Martin said something like 'perforations at the pressure points.' It could be wear and tear, could be something else." Wendy watched the kids closely as she spoke, pinching the whistle that hung around her neck. Always ready to pounce if they goofed off too much.

Renee shook her head. "Gary knows cars too well. If it was leaking brake fluid, he would have known it."

Wendy blew the whistle. "Hey! Dalton Hubble! Stay in formation, buddy."

The kid shouted back, maybe something about a dead bird in the grass. The rest of them moved around it like a river around a rock. Some slowed to look, two stopped. Wendy blew the whistle again. "Sorry," she said. Then, "It might not leak that much, but when you put pressure on it — when you brake hard, like coming up on one of those sharp corners on Falls Road — then the line snaps, the fluid gushes out. The next curve you take, there's no hydraulic pressure. Martin said it looked like he tried to pull the emergency brake, but by then it was too late."

Kimber and Theresa joined us. Cara was in Burlington at the hospital, where Gary was still in critical condition. It wasn't looking good.

Renee said, "If the fluid was low, the car would warn him. Cars have brake pressure warning lights. If he was ignoring it . . ."

I glanced at the nearby parked cars. Renee's massive old Ford truck. Kimber's brand-new Hyundai Ioniq. "Probably not a car like his," I said, remembering the royal-blue classic car. "It was a 1963 Plymouth Savoy. I'm pretty sure there's no brake pressure warning light for those."

Renee's look begged for an answer.

"Geoff is into classic cars," I said. "He's talked about them so much over the years, I guess I've picked up a thing or two."

She seemed impressed, pooching out her lips and raising her eyebrows, like, *Get a load of you!*

The kids had completed their lap, not knowing what to do next. Wendy hit the whistle once more. "All right, people, let's line up in two groups facing the goal! And if you touched that bird, wash your hands!"

* * *

After practice, some of the moms wanted to drive over to Burlington and check on Cara. We debated who would watch whose kids if necessary. My name came up, and I said sure, of course I would help. Apparently, no one considered I might like to make the trip too. Understandable, but it still stung.

"Mom?" Charlotte tugged on my short pantleg with one hand, rubbing her eye with the other, face streaked with dirt. "I'm hungry."

"Oh, my poor love." I picked her up and she felt so light to me, like papier mâché. "Where's your sister?"

"Over there."

We went together and retrieved Delia, off by herself reading a book, then trooped back to our car. By the time we got there, the other moms had all left except for Kimber, who saw me and waved. Maybe I was overthinking, but it seemed conciliatory, like she felt bad I was being left behind. No one asked me to watch their kid either. Deciding to let it all go, I waved back, packed the girls into the car, and drove home.

* * *

I was staring over at the Shellers' house when Geoff came into the bedroom and slowly walked up behind me.

"I hate how I feel," I said.

"How?"

"Like I'm being selfish. All this going on, and I'm fixating on the stupid mom group. I don't really know Cara. They do. Wendy used to babysit for her. They know each other, they're comfortable with each other in times of crisis, and that's okay. I just want to be part of this community. And I want to help people."

"You want to be seen for who you are," Geoff said.

In the hour prior, I'd put the girls to bed a little early, took a shower and shaved my legs, pulled out my best Havana Nights sleepwear. Then I'd sort of lost myself in a trance, fixed on the Sheller house's one lighted window. When Geoff slid his hand up the back of my nightie and nuzzled my neck, it wasn't exactly unexpected. I needed this.

I leaned back and closed my eyes as he kissed my neck some more. His hand went between my legs from behind. I mumbled, "It's all going to be okay. Tell me."

"It's all going to be okay," he said, his breath warm in my ear.

As his fingers pressed gently and he pulled me in tighter, my mind slipped. For a moment, I wondered what Eric Sheller was doing right now. I pictured him sitting alone at his dining room table, looking at the empty seat his wife used to occupy at dinner.

I forced myself to snap out of it. To be in the moment.

Geoff cupped my breast, thumb against the nipple. He worked both hands over me as I leaned further against him, reached up and grabbed the back of his neck. "Lock the door," I whispered.

"Already did."

But as he brought me to the bed and I lay down in front of him, I couldn't help but think of the cold, un-slept-in side of Eric Sheller's own bed. That he would never make love to his wife again.

Did he regret what he'd done with that woman in Tannersville? Who was she?

* * *

My phone moved on the bedside table. First, I looked at Geoff, who was asleep. I checked the door, which we'd unlocked and opened since we'd finished our rendezvous. The house quietly breathed. It was almost 1 a.m. I must've dozed off.

One message from two minutes ago; it must've been the reminder that woke me up.

The text was from Cara.

He's gone.

I sat up slowly and swung my legs out of bed. I was going to get up, but to do what? Where was I going to go?

I remained perched on the side of the bed, staring at the phone. No one had responded yet. I hesitated, but Cara was a friend. Even if I hadn't known her as a baby, or a local sports star, the social politics didn't matter; she was hurting. I started to type a response when one of the moms beat me to it.

Oh God Cara honey I'm so sorry

I waited again. What was Renee doing up at this hour? But then I remembered Gary had died driving on his way to work from her house. Maybe she thought that if she hadn't thrown the little impromptu engagement party, he might still be alive. She could be sleepless with guilt.

I stretched out on the bed again, holding the phone over me. Wendy was next:

Cara, my deepest condolences. Such a tragedy. He will be so missed.

And Theresa, moments later. Didn't anybody sleep? I guessed not, given the circumstances.

Cara, if there's anything I can do, I wrote, *please don't hesitate to ask.*

And that about covered it. What else could you say? What else could you do? It was times like these that control felt like such an illusion. A daydream we had when things were going mostly our way.

We believed we were in charge. Until, suddenly, we weren't.

I thought of my dad moving us from one place to another, six schools in five years. How I'd never really been able to settle in anywhere, make any lifelong friends. This was the longest I'd ever been in any one place — seven years — and until now it had all felt like a normal life. The kind the whole world crowded around, hopeful for a happy marriage, kids, a decent place to live.

I got up and went to the window. As if to remind myself of what real suffering was.

The Sheller house was dark.

Naomi Sheller's death might've been natural, but the police didn't seem to think so. And now a young man had been in a terrible car accident, questions raised about his brake lines. Theresa was right: what was happening in Buxton?

I'm not sure how long I lay in bed, but I stirred again when I thought I heard a car door slam. Once more, I slipped to the window and watched as headlights blinked on in the Sheller driveway. A vehicle, the pickup truck, I thought, backed into the road. The lights swept my house and then the truck got up to speed. The engine noise passed and faded.

It was well after midnight. Where was he going? Had he left his boys?

I crawled back into bed and checked my phone one last time.

Cara hadn't responded to any of us. There was just that one message from her.

He's gone.

Nothing added up. On the surface, these were random tragedies. The universe reminding us what was in charge: chaos.

And yet I had this nagging suspicion that everything since seeing Naomi Sheller in the juice aisle was connected. That somehow, her death and Gary's death were linked.

PART III:
THE BOOKS

CHAPTER TWENTY-TWO

Tuesday

"There's a package on the stoop," Geoff said as he left for work. He set it inside the door. It was about the size of a small toaster. I hadn't ordered anything recently that I could remember.

After getting the girls off to school, I brought the box deeper into the kitchen. It weighed a couple of pounds. It was addressed to me. The return address was Cozy Time Bookshop in Buffalo, New York.

I took a knife from the kitchen drawer and split the tape. With everything that had been going on lately, I used the knife to flip back one of the flaps so I could peer in from a distance.

Something colorful, like a picture.

I leaned closer. Not a picture, per se. A book cover.

"Okay," I said, relaxing. Not just one book, but three books. Packed in nicely with a little bit of brown paper filling in the gaps around the edges.

I set them on the table and looked in the box to see if there was anything else — a receipt, proof of purchase, something — but that was it. Three books stacked on my table.

Paperbacks. Looking gently used.

I left for a moment, got myself a cup of coffee from the percolator. I had multiple things on my to-do list that morning, including a deep clean of the kitchen, which I'd been neglecting for weeks. And you'll forgive me if I was a little distracted from my date with my husband the night before. It was a good one. No analysis, nothing that needed to be said, just a bit of tension between us dispelled by physical connection.

I'd been awakened by Eric Sheller driving away from his house in the middle of the night, but so what? Maybe he'd gone out for ice cream. His truck was there this morning. No sirens, no mom group gossip. The phone was still.

Sipping my coffee, I laid out the books on the table.

They had to be books for the book club idea. That's all I could think of. I'd missed some text or conversation where things had been decided at last.

I picked up the first one: *The Family Next Door* by Bonnie Harper.

It was only then, book in my hand, coffee cup to my lips, that I actually grasped the title.

I set the mug down and turned the book over to read the back blurb.

> *New residents of an idyllic suburban neighborhood seem like the perfect family. But a series of bizarre events threatens to shatter the facade and unravel the dark secrets of the small community, a terrifying truth that involves nearly everyone . . .*

"What?"

There was no one home, but if a situation warranted talking to oneself, this was it. I kept turning the book over, flipped some pages and did a little skimming. I hadn't fully expected it, but of course the characters all had different names than the people in Buxton. The family next door was called the Fullers, and it was set in California. I felt strangely relieved.

I picked up the next book, *Her Perfect Fiancé*.

And the blurb spelled it out:

A young woman is thrilled when her handsome rich boy-friend asks her to marry him, but will his past come back to haunt her?

"Okay," I said. "Okay now, what the fuck?"

Feeling increasingly surreal, I went to the last one.

The Housekeeper.

Hmm. These housemaid/housekeeper books were everywhere these days; I'd read one or two myself. This one sounded right along the same lines: a young housekeeper goes to work for a wealthy family whose lives are full of secrets, and she sees things she's not supposed to see. But I didn't know any housekeepers, and I hadn't heard anything happening along those lines.

Setting the books side by side, I thought about it. Two out of three of them were striking coincidences, eerily similar to things that had just happened. Was it someone messing around? Someone's poor-taste practical joke?

If so, there was a problem. Gary had just died the night before, while these books would have been ordered at least a few days ago.

To be sure, I looked over the package more closely. I'd cut through the sticker with UPC symbols and QR codes. But my address was clearly marked and the Cozy Time return address in the top-left corner. It was shipped through USPS. No shipment date, though. No dates of any kind. Was that normal? I'd never really studied a shipping label before.

Another thing was the timing. Mail came at eleven, not this early in the morning. I thought of Eric Sheller driving off the night before. I'd been asleep before he returned. Had he dropped off a package at my front door?

We didn't have any cameras. Didn't even have a dog. Someone could have left it, and I'd have no idea.

But it did have the shipping label . . .

I was going in circles.

"It must've been on the porch last night and I just didn't see it," I said to myself. The girls and I often came in the side entrance off the carport when we returned from soccer. I'd missed it.

Regardless of how the books got here, they clearly meant something. Whoever sent or delivered them was certainly admitting their knowledge of recent events, perhaps even confessing their involvement. Either way, they connected the tragedies, just like I'd feared.

I wondered if Gary had been responsible for what happened to Naomi Sheller. If maybe Eric cut his brake lines in response. But these were just guesses.

I was seconds away from calling Geoff, calling Courtney, calling *someone* to tell them what was happening, but then the plot of the third book registered, and everything slowed back to normal speed. I didn't know any "housekeepers." Certainly not any live-in ones.

They had to exist, though, even in a more working-class region like ours. I checked each book for the copyright date and publisher information. Three different publishers, each released in the past few years, more or less current with the times. I googled the name of the bookshop in Buffalo, called the number. While it rang, the urge to smoke a cigarette hit sudden and strong.

"Hello, it's Cozy!" a young voice said.

"Hi . . . I'm calling from Buxton, New York? I just received a package from your store with three books. I was wondering, if

I give you my name and address, can you tell me possibly who ordered these?"

"Um . . . sure! We get orders online, mostly. I can give you an email, but that's probably about it. Unless the person came into the store. But even then, we don't ask for any personal or identifying information."

"Sure, I understand." I gave her my name and address and waited while she checked the computer.

"Okay, got it. So, that was an Amazon order. We actually don't get any identifying information at all for the purchaser. Just where to send them. Order came in Thursday, and they shipped on Friday. And that was to you!"

I thought about it. "Is that odd? Usually if you're ordering books secondhand on Amazon, they're from various third-party sellers. Why did they all come from you?"

"Oh. Well, we have a very good reputation. And we have an enormous used section. We're the biggest in the state. We're called Cozy, but we're three floors!"

So, the buyer made sure to get each of these titles from the same place. Why? Maybe so they'd all arrive together. Anonymously.

After assuring her that everything was fine, that yes, I was happy with my books, I thanked the young woman and hung up.

I went straight outside to my secret stash above the side door, shook out a cigarette, and lit it.

It was another scorcher, going to be ninety by noon. For this time of year, now going on mid-September, it was unusual but not unheard of. We'd had heat late into the summer before. Last year, we had a green Christmas, a bit of a disappointment for the girls.

Smoking, I felt the familiar mix of relief and guilt. Relief that the nicotine provided, guilt that I was still hooked. And probably getting more hooked with each nail in the coffin. But this was background to the books sitting on my table in the house. I got my phone out again and texted the mom group.

> *Hey, did someone send me books as part of the book club thing? If so, I just got them!*

I hit send and felt an instant pang of regret. If the books had come as part of a club, I was admitting I missed some crucial decision that had been made. What if I was supposed to decide which one? Or had I agreed, explicitly or implicitly, to read all three?

If it wasn't part of that — and I was leaning toward not — now I was just going to seem batty. I'd get asked questions I didn't have any answers for.

It was midday, but no one responded. Wendy and Theresa, of course, worked at the school. Kimber was always busy with the farm. And even though Renee was retired, she kept active on various boards and took care of her property.

On a whim, I called Courtney. I couldn't remember the last time we'd spoken on the phone. Since before she left, possibly. Had I even heard her voice in the six months since she and her family had picked up and left, or had it just been texts and Instagram? I was preparing to leave a message when she picked up.

"Lainey? Oh my God. Is that you? How are you?"

Ebullient as ever, the sound of Courtney's voice immediately made me smile. This had been the right choice. I stripped the cigarette and put it in the hidden can under the porch while I responded, "How are *you?* How is everything? How are Dave and the kids?"

"Oh my God, great. Yellowstone is amazing. Just got here last week."

I'd seen some of the pics online. "How is it?"

"Incredible. We're staying at this place, Mammoth Station. It's like a movie. You walk out on the deck, and you can see the mountain goats on the cliffs overlooking the Boiling River. It's not literally boiling, but it's a thermal river. You get in and it's like a Jacuzzi."

"That sounds fantastic."

Things were good with the boys, she said. She was home-schooling them while Dave worked, things going well with all of that. "Traveling was great, but I'm glad we're here. The RV was cramped. We spent a lot of time outside! Anyway, how are *you?* Oh my God, I heard that someone died while jogging? What the heck is going on back there?"

"That's just the beginning . . ."

I gave her the whole story, omitting nothing, including the fight I'd likely witnessed and the other woman in Tannersville. When I got to Gary Latrelle succumbing to injuries from his car accident, Courtney said, "Get the fuck out of here."

"No. It's crazy. And get this — they think it was his brake lines."

"Brake lines? Like, cut brake lines?"

"They said wear and tear."

But it got me thinking, remembering Wendy's description — "perforations at the pressure points." I suppose if you wanted to sabotage someone's brake lines, that would be the way to do it. They'd wear down until they snapped, looking like wear and tear.

"The thing is, he knows a lot about cars," I said. "And Falls Road always has accidents."

"True. But doesn't he live off Falls Road? Or at least he used to. If someone had messed with his brakes, they could have done it when the vehicle was sitting in his driveway."

"I don't know," I said. I hadn't decided how I felt about Gary's accident. Mostly just sad.

I told her about the books.

"Oh my God, Lainey! You're making me want to come back. Things were never this interesting when I was there!"

"I wish you would come back. It's gotten a little weird around here."

"It's always been weird around there." Some of the good humor left her voice. In the ensuing silence, I realized she never had any intention of returning to Buxton. My attempt to requisition her was pure selfishness. I wanted Courtney to be happy.

I could still use her vast knowledge of the area though. "Do you know anyone around here who has a live-in housekeeper? Or even a housekeeper at all?"

"Well, there's Bee. She's been cleaning houses since I was a little girl. But she goes from place to place. Um, there was another, younger woman named Margaret Ptolemy. With a P-t. She worked at a bed-and-breakfast for years and then went out on her own. She does the thing where you fold the toilet paper into a little triangle at the end? People love that. Those are the only two I know of. But it's possible there are some live-ins. I can ask around if you—"

"Oh no. You don't have to worry about any of this. I just . . . you know. It was all hitting me, and I wanted to hear your voice. It's good to talk to you."

"It's good to talk to you too."

I heard someone calling "Mom!" in the background. Courtney muffled the phone and said something to one of her kids. Then, "So how are the girls? How is Geoff?"

"Everybody's good . . . Court, listen. I don't want to keep you talking."

"Oh no, it's—"

"I miss you guys and wish you all the best. Let's talk again soon, okay?"

"Oh, Lainey." Courtney sounded wistful. And then her voice dropped to just above a whisper. "You need anything, you call me, okay? And listen — this is probably all just bad luck. Bad things happen. It'll all blow over and life will go back to normal. But if anything else . . . I don't know. I'm going to text you a number, okay? And if you need to, you call it. Tell her I told you to."

"What?" I suddenly felt like I was in some movie; Courtney was being very cloak-and-dagger. Probably my nerves.

"Put it in your back pocket. It's just someone who might be able to help you. I do have to go. Magnus has something stuck in his foot."

"Good luck. Thank you, Courtney, I . . ."

"Love you, girl."

"Love you too."

And she hung up.

CHAPTER TWENTY-THREE

Wednesday

At soccer the next night, I realized it had been almost two weeks since I'd seen Naomi Sheller in the grocery store. Some months, getting a new haircut was a major event. So far, September was like living in an alternate reality.

I tried to focus on soccer, but I kept zoning out. Wendy asked if I was okay.

"Yeah, sorry."

We had a scrimmage at the end of practice — kids versus adults, something we liked to do for fun. The parents got into it. Renee wasn't exactly fast on her feet, but she could boot the ball halfway down the field. She looked like a giant among the kids. Wendy was nimbler, a former athlete herself. Cara would've loved to have been here — she'd played with us in the past — but looking around I didn't see her c—

"Oh! I'm so sorry, sweetie."

I'd collided with one of the kids while seeking to steal the ball from her. She'd gone down, skidded a little in the grass.

"Here, let me help you up."

"It's okay, Coach Lainey." There was a grass stain on her knee, but otherwise no damage done that I could see. People clapped as she got back to her feet.

Wendy was looking at me again. I wiped sweat from my eyes. Looking over the spectating parents, everyone seemed to understand and were ready to move on. But I thought I saw some worried faces, someone shaking their head in dismay.

I excused myself and went into the small sports hut, closed myself in its dingy bathroom, shivering with the idea that I could've just hurt one of the children. It was an accident, but it woke me up. I was preoccupied and not fully present.

I had to talk myself back onto the field, but I needed to finish out the practice. The scrimmage was nearly over. Parents no longer stared, and the little girl I'd run into was out sprinting for the ball like nothing happened. The event seemed to be behind us. I stayed engaged, playing right up to the final whistle, everyone pumped up with good vibes. The kids won, of course, 3–2. (Wink-wink.)

I gathered the equipment and dragged it all into the sports shed. Dusting off my hands, I took stock of who was still around. Kimber wasn't, and her son Fynn hadn't been there either. Theresa was getting in her car. Wendy left before saying goodbye. It wasn't unusual, but it felt poignant.

The moms' group had eventually replied about the books the day before, and no one admitted to sending them. It was as I'd feared, and my situation was more bizarre than people wanted to think about — or maybe had the mental bandwidth to think about in their busy lives, especially with all that had happened.

I'd ended up confiding in Wendy separately that I thought the books were too close to be coincidence. I asked her if she would mention it to Martin and she said she would, but as she tore off in her minivan, I wasn't so sure.

"Mom? You ready?"

Charlotte guzzled water from her Nalgene bottle. Dirt across both of her knees. Pink cheeks and wild hair. We were the last ones; I hadn't even seen Renee slip away, nor heard the jangling of her key ring.

"Yeah, baby. Let's go."

Anyway, I had business cards from both investigators. Cojuangco seemed warmer and more open-minded. I'd try her first.

But once we were home and I had a minute outside with a cigarette, Cojuangco didn't pick up.

Investigator Smith answered on the second ring, though, like he'd been waiting by the phone. "Mrs. Barrister," he said. "What can I do for you?"

I'd spent at least five minutes rehearsing what I was going to say and now it all went right out of my head. Only the bare facts remained. I got right to the point: "I've received something in the mail I find very strange."

"Tell me."

I paced the dark yard as I explained.

He took a beat. "Who are they from?"

I told him about calling the bookstore.

"And when did they arrive, did you say?"

"I saw them this morning, but they could have been there before that. The night before was the engagement party, and I'd just gotten the news . . ."

"About Gary Latrelle."

"Yes."

"You were at that engagement party?"

"I was."

"How did it go?"

"It was fine," I said, after a pause. My mind chased several thoughts. Tell him what Renee said? Tell him about the severed brake lines rumor? No, I was calling about the books. "One of the books is literally called *Her Perfect Fiancé*."

I took a drag while I waited for his reaction. I was in plain view of the road, but screw it. I didn't care who might see me.

"Have you read it?"

"Since it arrived? No. Well, some of it."

"Anything you read that was . . . especially pertinent?"

"Well, those two premises. And they're all the same genre . . . Do you know what a domestic thriller is?"

"About domestic abuse, you mean?"

"It can be, but not necessarily. One book is about a family that moves in next door to the main character. It's set in California, but it's very similar to what I just went through. With new neighbors who seem odd. Little things that cause suspicion, then there's a major event . . ."

I pinched the bridge of my nose, tried to slow my breathing, to fight the tightness that had appeared in my chest. I was trying to explain something that I understood on an intuitive, gut level. I'd read these types of books; I knew how they tended to follow similar formulas. Tropes they tended to deploy, things you could count on happening. Even if the details were different between books, those tropes were the same. But try explaining that to a police officer who'd probably never thought twice about it.

"Do you remember that I saw Mrs. Sheller in the grocery store?"

"Yes. I remember you telling me you did."

"And then Mr. Sheller with the other woman . . ."

I paused, giving him space to say anything about her he hadn't been willing to the other day. But he only said, "Yes."

"The way my husband and I were curious about them," I hurried on. "The odd things I witnessed, and then what happened to Mrs. Sheller — that's exactly what happens in those kinds of books."

"But the details are different, you said. The location, the characters. Does a woman die in the woods?"

"No. The main character is wheelchair-bound and watches everything out her window. She realizes the wife next door is leading a double life. I haven't read it all, just skimmed. But I think in the end, the woman in the wheelchair turns out to be unreliable . . . Are you still there?"

"Yes, absolutely. Who did you say the author was?"

"Bonnie Harper."

"Is she still alive?"

It was an interesting question. "I think so. I don't know. I don't recognize her name. But one of the other authors is familiar."

"Which one?"

"C.M. Draper. The fiancé book. A woman with a dark past meets a young man. Someone went missing years ago and was never found. It turns out that he's part of this cold case . . . Maybe I should slow down. Are you taking notes?"

"You said the author . . . ?"

"C.M. Draper. I've read him before." It was over a decade earlier; Geoff and I had only been briefly married and I was pregnant with Delia. The book had been unremarkable, but the name stood out. When I saw it in the box, I checked the basement and found my old copy of his other book.

The third author, Jessica Corrie, was unfamiliar.

Bonnie Harper was San Francisco-based, Draper lived in Florida, and Corrie was English.

"The fiancé is caught up in this possible crime syndicate, and the main character, she's about to marry into it . . . Her father thinks she's making a huge mistake and being taken advantage of, but it turns out she sort of wants it."

I made an effort to slow my pace. I was needlessly trying to get Smith to see connections that I myself wasn't fully sure of. The overarching similarities themselves were too big to pass off as mere coincidence. Surely, he at least saw that. *You can stop drilling, you've hit oil,* my father used to tell me when I was adamant about something.

"Well," Smith said. "What do you think about all of it?"

I licked my lips and took a breath. "I think it's meaningful. That's all I can say. Someone sent me these books. All these things have happened. If it was a joke, even in bad taste, I think someone would have owned up by now. Or I would know. We've been talking about a book club, but no one who—"

"A book club?"

"It's not official. We just talk about it. Or maybe they started one and didn't tell me."

"Okay . . . Who?"

I named everyone in the mom group, because as far as I could remember, they'd all been included in the conversation about it at one point or another. Wendy, Renee, Kimber, Theresa, Cara, and me. Six of us. I pictured each of them now, Renee in her overalls, badmouthing Gary. Wendy giving me the stink-eye as I helped the fallen player back to her feet. Kimber talking about her childhood. Theresa being, well . . . Theresa. Cara's major life tragedy. *He's gone.*

I realized Smith wasn't speaking. I got the sense he was gathering his thoughts. "You have the books now?"

"Yes. Inside. Should I . . . ?"

"No, no, that's fine. Leave them and I'll come by to have a look. Is tomorrow morning all right? Have to be a little later, like around ten."

It seemed like a long way off. And these books had to mean something.

"In the meantime," he said, "can you give me all the titles and authors again, one by one? I want to write them down and do a little bit of research."

The tightness in my chest unraveled. He was taking it seriously. I knew it was a bit left-field, but it had to be more than coincidence. Why I was sent these books was hard to parse though. Why me?

A question came out before I could stop it. "Has anyone else received anything?"

"No, actually. Nothing like this."

Maybe because I was an outsider of sorts? I was neighbors with the Shellers, yes. But I only knew Cara a little bit and had never met Gary Latrelle before Saturday. What was my role supposed to be in all of this?

We talked a little bit more, with the investigator making further promises to look into it, and that he would come by the next day. By the time I hung up though, my relief was waning. I knew the books meant something, and Smith had taken it seriously — at least I thought so — but there had been an undercurrent of skepticism. Like maybe I was just some ditzy housewife who read too much.

I sat there looking at the third book. *The Housekeeper.* And I thought at it, *What about you? What is your significance? What's going to happen next in this insane town?*

CHAPTER TWENTY-FOUR

That night, I watched the Sheller house from my bedroom window. I'd been eyeing the place all week. Maybe I was waiting to see if Eric took another mysterious midnight run. Or if the lights flickered. Or if there was any sign of those boys. What was it like inside a house suddenly empty of its wife and mother? I pictured quiet meals, morose routines; boys brushing their teeth while staring off into the distance, a father speaking in low tones as he ushered them to bed. Each crying softly to himself in the dark.

Eric hadn't set foot in his office at the Parker building since he'd rented it, Geoff said (intel from Mae and her sister). And the boys hadn't been back to school yet, something I'd confirmed through the girls. So, what were they doing over there?

Geoff entered the bedroom. I saw his reflection over my shoulder.

"All good?" I asked.

"Just when I was about to call it quits, I found a tiny one in her closet."

A spider. Maybe it was all the late-summer heat, but the bugs had been bad this year, and getting into the house. Geoff just spent twenty minutes scouring Delia's room. Spiders, ants, flies, stinkbugs — anything that skittered or crawled, flew or buzzed. Her fear of insects had metastasized from typical to phobic.

"Was it a big one?"

"No, just a little one." He grabbed a tissue from the box on my dresser and walked out of the room.

Delia stood further down the hallway, leaning against the wall, arms drawn in.

"Okay, here we go. Bug-killing time!" Geoff crushed the spider up in the tissue and took it to the bathroom. She dared to venture to the doorway to witness him flush it down the toilet. "I banish thee," he cried, "to the eternal sewer for all spiders!"

"There could be more," she said as Geoff dusted his hands. No matter how small, it validated her fears. At any given moment, things lurked and crawled in her room.

"Yeah, but there's not."

"They could be hiding."

The three of us gathered in the hallway outside the bathroom. "Honey, I just spent twenty minutes in there. And I'm good at what I do."

"You can't get them all."

Geoff looked at me, out of moves.

"Come on," I said, putting my arm around her shoulder.

I managed to coax her into her bed, where she lay with covers pulled up to her chin. The pink canopy was gone, removed when she'd found a stinkbug in one of the corners, twitching its long antennae. Now she eyed the ceiling, scanned the walls.

"Sometimes I imagine there's so many of them that they swarm me and I can't breathe," she whispered.

"That's not possible, honey," I said.

"Yes, it is."

"Well, if it's possible, it's the most remote possibility you can imagine. Like a hundred million to one."

"But still possible."

I leaned down and looked into her big brown eyes. "Delia, we can't worry about every random, remote thing that could happen.

146

We'd spend our lives afraid. You're full of joy and creativity. You're a good and kind friend, a wonderful big sister, and my amazing daughter. And you're strong. You have in you everything you need; you don't have to be afraid. You need to trust yourself. Okay?"

After a moment: "Okay."

I kissed her forehead. But in the bedroom moments later, Geoff whispered his concerns that she might need to see somebody. That she needed help with this. That *we* did.

"I think it's normal," I said. "It's acute right now, but it's peaking."

"I hope so."

I wondered how convinced I was by my own words. Every morning lately was the same thing: the typical preteen ran off to school without so much as a look back, while Delia clutched me around the waist and buried her face in my sternum. "I love you, Mom. Please be careful today."

"I will," I always told her. And that morning I'd added, "I plan to vacuum under the couch, but I'll take extra care not to have it fall on me."

"Ha-ha," she'd said, giving me a flat look.

Watching her walk into the school, I thought about control. I didn't have any, and neither did she, not about the big things. This was maybe something she was starting to process on a gut level. She'd indirectly witnessed what could happen. That anybody could, at any moment, be struck by terrible tragedy. In a way, her response was completely rational.

Of course, her fears of Geoff and I getting hurt — getting into a car accident, one of the scenarios she'd dreaded — had come up before Gary Latrelle's Plymouth Savoy nosedived off curvy Buxton Falls Road. So maybe it was just her age, just that time in her life when childhood began giving way to adulthood.

Gary hadn't been much older than she was. A decade or so. With one funeral only a week past, another one was already coming up. Geoff thought it might take a while longer than usual because of the condition of the body. "Unless they end up going closed casket," he'd said. I turned toward him now in bed, but he'd fallen asleep.

So.

What could I control? I told Investigator Smith about the books, yes. I checked with the bookstore, asked the mom group, talked to my husband and my best friend about it. But I wasn't out of options.

The Family Next Door. Her Perfect Fiancé. The Housekeeper. In bed with my tablet, I went from one to the next. Clinical, scanning for clues. Was there anything about prescient preteen girls? Anything about doctor-husbands spending questionable amounts of time with coworkers?

No.

No plot detail revealed a connection, just those thematic similarities. The fiancé keeping secrets. A rich family riven by drama and conflict. Perfect neighbors with their hidden lives.

What didn't I know about the Shellers? Signs pointed to Eric as an abuser, yet I just didn't get that feeling. Gary Latrelle was a working-class kid, yet he'd had enough money to buy a vintage car and take his lover on expensive trips.

I sighed, feeling overwhelmed.

There were no CliffsNotes for these books, but I found summaries online. Reviews on bookseller sites and blogs. I read up on the authors too. Maybe the relevance of the books had as much to do with them?

Nothing stood out. Two women, one man. Varying degrees of popularity and success.

Maybe I just needed to dig in. No shortcuts, no summaries or reviews. I had to go book by book, chapter by chapter. I was a fairly speedy reader, but not like some people who read multiple books a week. Obviously, I was more motivated here, but it was still going to take time.

I pushed ahead, starting with *The Family Next Door*. I would just have to finish them one at a time.

My phone distracted me with its silence. The mom group didn't text every night, but close to it, and tonight's inactivity was unnerving. With no way to prove it, I worried a conversation was going on without me.

Geoff's breathing deepened with sleep. I gave in to temptation and went to the window one last time. The Sheller house was a charcoal cutout against a dark gray sky. The truck was gone.

I started tapping out a message on my phone, not caring whether the mom group was freezing me out or not.

Has anyone seen Eric Sheller or his sons?

Maybe they'd taken an Uber to the airport. Flown off somewhere to just get away.

I checked my phone. No response.

Because I haven't seen them for days, I wrote. *Just hoping they're all right.*

I hit SEND on the last one and climbed into bed. I went back to the book, and then it hit me: a person with a sick sense of humor had targeted me. *That* was the key here. Not necessarily what was in the books, but who had sent them and why.

I wondered again, Eric Sheller? Naomi could have been a victim of his madness. Someone caught up in a twisted game he liked to play. And now I was next. He'd dropped these books off to see how I would react. Maybe he was watching me as much as I was watching him. He'd seemed sane enough, but wasn't that how it went sometimes? Ted Bundy? Jeffrey Dahmer?

I didn't know.

But no one texted me back.

CHAPTER TWENTY-FIVE

On Friday morning, not long after I'd seen the girls off to school and Geoff off to work, Smith stopped by as promised. He asked me how I was, and I said I hadn't seen Eric or his sons in quite a while.

"They're in Tannersville," Smith said.

Which made sense, I guess. "Do they have family there?"

"Some family. Some friends."

I thought about the woman. Had Eric Sheller returned to the town to shack up with his mistress? If so, that would be a very bad move.

Smith studied me. "They're all right, I can tell you that much."

He had a few questions about Gary Latrelle. The Saturday engagement party. "It was the last place anyone saw Gary. What time would you say he arrived?"

"I'm not entirely sure. The soccer game ended at noon . . . Uh, most of us were there by one or so. I think Gary came along shortly after?"

"Do you recall when he left?"

"After me. That's my understanding. And I left at about a quarter to four."

"I heard that Cara Cormack wasn't happy he had to leave early."

"I don't know. I don't think we talked about that."

Smith raised his eyebrows.

"I mean, the group of women who text each other. The 'mom group.'"

"And no one in that group said Cara was unhappy?"

I don't know why I hesitated. Maybe just for a moment it felt like betrayal. But that didn't make sense. Smith was just getting information.

"Can you remember?" he pushed.

"No, but I can check."

It took me a few seconds to scroll back through my phone. I battled with the guilt until at last, I came to the beginning of those exchanges.

Terrible car accident.

Wendy.

He's barely holding on.

A little further down.

He had to leave for work. Cara was upset he didn't take the time off.

Theresa had written that. I told Smith, who countenanced it like he already knew. Which made sense — he was the one to bring it up.

"What else did you hear?"

"You'll have to be specific, I'm sorry. It was a busy day. And emotional."

"Anything about Gary's car?"

"I heard it may have had compromised brake lines."

Smith wasn't able to hide his surprise in time. "Who from?"

"Just people," I said, covering again for Martin and Wendy. We were back in the same territory as before. Smith and Cojuangco had wanted to know where I'd heard details about Naomi Sheller's death, like blunt force trauma. Martin clearly had a problem with keeping confidences. He wasn't an investigator, but still. He'd been involved with both cases.

"Wendy Baker said Martin told her 'faulty brakes.' That it could have been wear and tear."

"Was that all? No one said 'tampering'?"

"No."

Smith eyed me knowingly. Language aside, an officer familiar with the case had talked — if just to his wife — and it was a big detail to have floating around out there. If there was foul play, then a perpetrator who thought his MO was blown might run. But a perp who thought he'd gotten away with something was more likely to relax, slip up. Information sharing mattered.

"I'm sorry." I meant it on general principle.

"Is there anything else you want to tell me about?" Smith said after a moment.

I told him about the text I'd gotten from Courtney late last night. That a health care worker was living with a local family.

Smith looked at me with some confusion. "I don't follow."

"One of the books is about a housekeeper. A home health aide is similar in a lot of ways."

"Oh." He picked up the book.

The way he reacted, it struck me that Smith had used the books as a pretext to ask me more questions. About Gary Latrelle in particular.

But I tried to see it through a cop's eyes: Two very unrelated cases were taking time and resources. People had died. A housewife had some books that bore broad and probably coincidental similarities. So what?

Oh really, ma'am? You're gonna crack the case with a couple of paperback novels?

A profound thought in the middle of the night seemed less so in the sober light of day. Just like these books, and my investment in them. Smith needed physical evidence. Witnesses, timelines; not theories.

When he left a few minutes later, it was honestly a relief. As I watched him pull out of the driveway in his unmarked car, backing into the fast road passing our house, I realized I was going about this the wrong way. From his perspective, I was just another townsperson with a random tip.

I needed more. *He* needed more.

Something else my father used to say came back to me: if three people tell you that you have a tail, you better turn around and look.

Two of these books had thematic parallels to the real events in Buxton. It wasn't enough. I needed to connect the third.

CHAPTER TWENTY-SIX

The Hemlock house sat on a rise with a spectacular mountain vista to one side, Lake Champlain shimmering on the other. A two-story great room took in the views; the rest of the house was long and ranch-style, with a covered porch on the side facing the road and fewer windows.

I drove past slowly. A little red car sat in the circular driveway, maybe a Honda or Kia. A two-car garage in a separate building could've housed more vehicles, but I couldn't see in. If I'd been bolder, maybe I would've knocked on the front door with an excuse about car trouble and a dead phone. Or, since Courtney knew the family, I could say I was delivering a message for her.

But I didn't want to involve Courtney. She had her reasons for leaving — *escape* was maybe too strong a word — for her and her husband taking their two children and burning rubber out of Buxton. I knew she had a contentious relationship with some of the people she'd left behind. Other than that, simply spending your entire life in a fishbowl town could be challenging enough.

Courtney gave me the name of the home health aide, and I'd already looked her up. Janine Persad was a thirty-year-old Indo-Jamaican woman. I found her on LinkedIn and Facebook only; if she had an Instagram or TikTok account, I didn't know what it was. But Facebook showed her visiting family in Jamaica, celebrating her sister's birthday in the States. It looked like she'd emigrated to America for college, then stayed for work. A couple of pics of friends in nursing scrubs, a few scattered nightlife shots, images of cats. No apparent children. No listed relationship status, and I saw no signs of a significant other.

I put away the phone and sat idling a moment, then pulled back into the road. Someone blared their horn, and I hit the brakes. The vehicle swerved and I glimpsed an angry face. Chilled, I took a big, long look into the road and pulled out more slowly this time, my blinker on.

About a hundred yards further down the road, I pulled over, feeling indecisive. I needed to turn around, go back there, and talk to this person. Find out, above all, if she was okay. I just needed a cover story. I wouldn't involve Courtney. I'd say that I was a writer working on my first novel, and it was set in a house just like this one. Could I look around for a few minutes, take some notes? At worst, she could say no. Or consult her employer, and Hemlock would say no. But in that time, I could get a sense of things, a vibe. A little small talk, at least.

Come on, do it.

But I didn't move. I felt almost paralyzed, unsure why. For the past two weeks, life had been too full of surprises. I'd felt scared multiple times. When a woman was having a crisis in front of me, I'd wanted to help. But when her husband caught me watching him with another woman, I'd felt the first tendrils of fear. And then when his wife was found dead, I might've gone into a kind of low-grade shock.

Was I still in shock? Was I afraid? For months, I'd been thinking my husband might be having an affair and hadn't done much of anything about it. Maybe I just wasn't as tough as I liked to think.

Gripping the steering wheel — kneading it like flesh — I tried to force myself to decide. Go back and talk to Persad, or just wait and see what happened. Did I really believe she was in danger? Did I really believe she was going to *die*? Why? Because of some books?

I didn't know. I was just following a lead. But I wasn't police.

Do it anyway.

Done debating, I turned my blinker on and prepared to make a U-turn, go back to the Hemlock house with my writer story.

My phone buzzed.

I didn't recognize the number at first and was about to dismiss it as spam when I thought I might know who it was.

"Hello?"

"Elaine Barrister?"

"Yes?"

"This is Barbara Cantwell. I'm a friend of Courtney's?"

"Oh, yes. Hi. Courtney gave me your number."

"I know, and she wants me to apologize for her — she ended up calling me anyway." Cantwell sounded older, a sweetly husky voice. "She told me about a lot of what was going on there. Hoo boy, sounds like you got yourself quite a situation."

I thought of how I was sitting there on the side of the road, on a Friday afternoon, about to lie my way into a stranger's house.

"I think you could say that."

"I'm originally from Buxton. Well, I've lived in New York for most of my life. I used to babysit for Courtney when she was very little . . . Did she tell you I'm her godmother?"

"No, she didn't."

"Well, I'm actually in your area, and was wondering if you were free for a quick visit. Maybe we could meet somewhere and talk?"

"I could be, yes."

She may have sensed reluctance. "I was a private investigator for many years. I just want to help if I can. Even if it's just to listen."

I allowed myself to relax a little further. To feel a ray of hope. Maybe this was just what I needed.

"That would be great."

CHAPTER TWENTY-SEVEN

Cantwell picked the place: a small park in downtown Buxton. On a side street behind the local grocery store, it featured a defunct fountain and unkempt botanicals. We got scones and coffee from the grocery store bakery and sat in a paint-peeling gazebo. No one else around.

"I've never been here before," I said.

"I used to play here as a kid." Cantwell's age was hard to place. She was dressed for the heat, but in urban fashion: jeans and a tank top. Simple studded earrings and shoulder-length blonde hair verging on white. A sparrow tattooed on her shoulder. Fifty-five, in city years?

"We used to set up a jump right over there and ride our bikes, see if we could clear that little garden patch."

She had an easy, familiar way, like we'd already known each other a long time. I imagined her young, competing with the boys. Like Charlotte. When she took a bite of her scone, it left chocolate in the corner of her mouth. She licked it away with the tip of her tongue. "You live up over the valley? On the county route?"

"I do."

"I know your house. Used to be owned by the Bouchard family. They built it. Nice family."

"You probably know a lot of people from Buxton?"

Midway through another bite, she nodded yes. After swallowing, she said, "Sorry. I sort of skipped breakfast."

"Not at all."

"I was already here visiting when Courtney called."

"Where do you live?"

The quickest of suspicious glances was gone in an instant. Just a reflex, I supposed. "I'm in Brooklyn. Once Court laid everything out for me and I started looking into it . . . I get kind of hooked in by this sort of thing. Which is why I went into it, right? It's not all 'intrigue and mystery!' though, I can tell you that. You want to make a living in private investigations, you end up doing lots of insurance fraud and workman's comp claims. A lot of background checks. Most of the time, you're at the computer, or running the phones — it isn't Sam Spade. Well, let me get to the point." She chased a final bite of scone with some coffee and fixed me with her marble-blue eyes. "Your neighbors are the Shellers."

It was a statement, but she paused, and so I felt compelled to confirm. "Yes."

"They moved here from Tannersville. You knew that?"

"I did."

"Okay, so, I did some quick poking around down there, talked to a few friends. It's a bigger town than Buxton — three times the size — but by the national average, it's still just a wide place in the road. People know their neighbors. And the Shellers had lived there for years. He's from the region, but she was from Missouri. Unmarried name was Naomi Goddard. The story I heard was that he met her while traveling the country and basically brought her home. The people I spoke to described her as a little odd. She was quiet, driven, and extremely beautiful."

It squared with what I knew.

"What I heard was, they were having marital problems." Cantwell seemed to get lost in thought for a moment, looking around the park.

"Do you know why they left?"

She started ticking off the items on her finger. "I'm pretty sure they didn't move because of business or financial problems. She was a grant writer and worked mostly remote. Sheller has a solid rep as a lawyer. He does well. And their house in Tannersville has comparable value to the Marvin place they bought, so it's not like they were flipping it. The market is stronger now, but that means everything is up. You'll get more for your house if you sell it, but then have to sink more into the new home."

I was stuck on her calling the Sheller's home "the Marvin place," and she picked up on it.

"I remember Mrs. Marvin," Cantwell said. "She was a generation older than me, but she lived there when the Bouchards did. I babysat for them too."

She finished her coffee and seemed to check if there was more in the bottom of the cup.

"Anyway, marital trouble is the consensus. But people don't move because someone is cheating, right? They get divorced. Maybe they move separately. But to just hop one town over? It makes me think they ran into some bad social juju."

I felt a little flutter in my chest at that. I'd been trying to protect them from social blowback. Something they might've already been running from.

"And then, of course, there's the woman in Eric's truck. The one you saw. I'm going to try to get in touch with her. If that's okay with you."

I wasn't sure if this was the moment I needed to sign something. To pay a retainer, or make some formal agreement. But she made no indication of that, so I said yes, and she simply continued on.

"My guess — and I'm sure it's yours too — is the mystery woman is going to be Eric Sheller's mistress. And the family left to save the marriage. Maybe to escape the woman's husband. If he was making trouble for Sheller, or the kids were having difficulty at school, that could be the bad juju."

I let it settle with a deep breath. I felt disappointed in myself. I'd been so eager to protect them, I'd ignored the signs. The darker implications of Naomi's episode, the other woman, the argument.

"I was just at the Shellers' the end of last week," I told Cantwell.

She raised her eyebrows, and I relayed Charlotte disappearing over there. I told her how Eric had seemed genuinely heartbroken over his wife's death. But I also told her about seeing him come home late carrying a duffel bag. About the argument. About my feeling like Naomi was trapped in her home. Had I let an attraction to Eric subvert my better judgment? Had a woman been in trouble and I didn't do anything?

"I don't know." I put my head in my hands. I couldn't help it. I barely knew Barbara Cantwell, but I suddenly felt confessional. "I think I've just made one mistake after another. I don't know what I'm doing."

She said nothing until, a few seconds later, I straightened again and wiped my eyes.

"On the contrary. I think you've been kicking some ass."

It made me laugh.

"Seems to me like you're ahead of the game. Police have been to talk to you, you saw the other woman . . ."

"That was just circumstance."

Cantwell lowered her head and looked up at me, raising her eyebrows. "You've had your eye out since day one. Your radar is going, you're interpreting the information, and you're talking to me, which means you're smart." She winked. "Now tell me more about these books. One is about a fiancé? And he was in with some bad people?"

After we went over it, Cantwell said, "The Latrelles have a history in Tannersville too. About half broke bad. The other half are upstanding, do honest work. It's not a perfect binary; sometimes it's hard to tell who's who. Usually, you can. A couple of them have a shop down there, two brothers: Gary's uncles. They're all mechanics. Called 'Ideal Garage.' They're into vintage cars, go to the car shows, all of that. Henry Latrelle has got a plumbing and heating business. That's what Gary was doing. Works with his other uncle. One that didn't break bad."

"Gary seemed well off," I said, choosing my words. "He took Cara on a lot of trips, bought her jewelry. Not exactly conspicuous, but a little noteworthy, I guess." What had Renee said? *Getting into mischief.* Hadn't I seen a couple of men with axle grease under their nails, drinking beers off in the side yard? Were his uncles on the "good" side of the family or the "bad"?

But Cantwell wasn't finished. "A cousin of Gary's went to prison a few years back for fentanyl. And there's some family on that side that . . . I don't know what they did. Took the money and invested it, cleaned it, before the busts happened. And there's still a heroin and fentanyl problem in the region. It's bad. I'm not saying Gary was linked to that, that I have any proof he was. But those are the particulars."

It was a lot to think about. Though I felt better than I had on the side of the road, I still felt burdened.

"The bottom line is," Cantwell said, "this stuff with the Latrelles, that's pretty well-known. The cops know. It's not just what I've heard. And the fact that the police showed you the picture of this other woman . . . Well, they know about her too, and are running that down. This thing may very well get resolved on its own. I just don't know if they'll ever understand the significance of these books."

"Exactly," I said, feeling clearer on my position. On why I cared. This is what I'd been debating. "What if they miss something? Or someone else gets hurt?"

She nodded. "Right."

"I mean — what do *you* think?"

"I think there's a risk of doing more harm than good. But I'm sure you can weigh it all up." She reached out to me, but not for my hand, I realized — my empty coffee cup. Then she took them both, crumpled them, and tossed them in a trash can I hadn't even seen was there, hidden in the vegetation just beyond the gazebo. She stretched a little and looked around, nostalgia seeming to take her once more.

But her mind was still on the topic at hand. "Courtney said you went to school for criminal justice."

"I did."

"So, you know what victimology is."

"Relationships between victims."

"M.O. might be how a crime is committed," she said, turning back to me. "Some psychopath likes to put bugs in his victims' throats, like *Silence of the Lambs*. But victimology asks, 'What do they have in common?' If Naomi Sheller and Gary Latrelle are victims of the same . . . whatever this is — if they're part of a series — they don't really have anything in common. Naomi is from Missouri, transplanted to Tannersville, then to here. Gary Latrelle is more dyed-in-the-wool Tannersville, but he's different in every other way. Male, unmarried, probably voted for the opposite candidate than Sheller in the last election. And then this home health worker . . . Where did you say she was from? The Caribbean?"

I nodded.

Cantwell raised her shoulders and let them drop. "The books suggest someone wants you to see something in particular. And maybe this same someone wants to take credit."

"That's what I think."

She looked at me levelly. "I know you do." She gave me a slightly lopsided smile. "Forgive an older woman's bluntness, but somewhere inside you, you know exactly what you're capable of. I can see it," she said, pointing at my eyes. "Right there."

Then she lowered her hand and said, "You just gotta let it out."

CHAPTER TWENTY-EIGHT

The girls were quiet at dinner. Delia was tired, not sleeping well for several nights in a row. But Charlotte's behavior was unusual for her. It was Riley. The troubled student had planted the teacher's laser pointer in Charlotte's desk and told the teacher she'd stolen it. When Charlotte confronted Riley about the frame-up, Riley shoved her again.

"She said, 'Your ass is grass and I'm the lawnmower.'"

Geoff choked on his spaghetti, stifling a laugh. Ignoring him, I went to Charlotte and gave her a hug. Then I said, "Did you tell your teacher? Or a grown-up?"

"I told Miss Gramone, but she said since she didn't see it, she couldn't do anything about it."

I gripped her small shoulders. "Nobody has the right to put their hands on you like that," I said. "But if they do, you have the right to defend yourself. I'm not saying you go berserk on somebody, but if they push you, you can do a couple of things. Here." I gestured for her to get up from the table. Geoff put his fork down, watching. Delia perked up.

I got down on my knees. "Come at me like you're going to push me, okay?"

Grinning a little, since this had turned into fun, Charlotte stuck her arms out and advanced. Gently but firmly, I trapped her hands with my forearms, pushing down, which knocked her off balance. I caught her before she could crash into me. "Let me show you another."

We went through a couple more quick moves. Charlotte was laughing by the end, but determined, trying to shove me but unable. Then she wanted to try the tactics herself.

"Where did you learn those?" Geoff asked.

"College," I said. Which didn't quite cover it, but close enough. Years after Stacy Meyer, I decided to take some self-defense classes. A roommate was assaulted in front of me, and I tried to help. The aggressor was too big, too strong, and shrugged me off. Though more people arrived to help, I vowed to be neither a victim nor a bystander ever again. I'd changed my major from undeclared to criminal justice the next day.

"Well, it's the weekend," Geoff said as Charlotte returned to the table. "So at least you don't have to see Riley for a couple of days."

We did our best to cheer up both girls, and once they were in bed with teeth brushed and stories read, I texted the mom group, just to see if anyone else's kids were having issues with Riley.

An hour later, the only one to respond to me was Theresa, who indicated no problems. No one offered anything other than that. Which was weird, since Wendy had been so upset with Riley's behavior just two weeks ago when her daughter had been bullied too. Maybe Wendy was busy, but it didn't feel like it. If felt deliberate. Like they were ignoring me.

Geoff zonked out early again, so I propped up on my pillows to read. I'd downloaded each of the books on Kindle and was reading *The Housekeeper* closely when I thought I heard a car next door.

Going to the window, I saw headlights shaping out two small figures who jumped up onto the Shellers' front porch. Their voices carried across the joined yards. Boisterous, playful. A taller figure joined them, moving slower.

I heard a man's voice say, "Thank you," and the vehicle backed out of the driveway. As it turned into the road, the headlights swept Eric Sheller, walking up to his front door. The boys had already worked their way indoors. He went in and lights came on inside the house.

Home again. For now. As far as I knew, the property had been put up for sale again. But who was going to buy it after what happened? And where could Eric go in the middle of an investigation? He hadn't been arrested, but surely the police would have asked him to remain in the area.

I climbed back into bed with mixed feelings, hoping for answers soon. Barbara Cantwell had given me some confidence, but I didn't have the resources or insights of the state police. I wanted to know if I was living next door to a murderer.

* * *

Saturday

Charlotte's third soccer game of the season started hot and humid, rain clouds low and dark. Wendy, Renee, and I functioned as we had throughout the season so far. I had the water jugs and the two bags of soccer balls. I helped Charlie Shanley lace up his cleats and brought Lacy Peck to see her mother after landing on her back from an inadvertent bicycle kick.

The game was forty miles away, so on the way back we tried to entertain ourselves. Charlotte and I sang songs, told riddles, and played twenty-one questions. Halfway home, I let her use her tablet, and I turned on *The Housekeeper* audiobook. The skies opened up. The rain slammed down.

As I listened to the narrator tell the story of a live-in maid witnessing a crime, I thought about the real live-in health worker, Janine Persad. About what Barbara Cantwell had observed: Persad wasn't from Tannersville. She wasn't even originally from the country. The two people who'd died were already quite different, but Janine really departed from any possible pattern. Just as I was connecting Naomi and Gary, Janine seemed completely off base.

If something connected the three, it wasn't their backgrounds. Not their jobs or their hobbies, not school or extended family. The only common denominator: they each lived in the area. That was all.

Somewhere inside you, you know exactly what you're capable of, Cantwell had told me.

What was I capable of? What did I have? What, besides being from the area, connected the victims? What was their victimology? Someone they knew in common? The killer — if there was a killer?

The windshield wipers smacked back and forth, struggling to keep up. I slowed, visibility limited through the deluge.

I knew the books were ordered before Gary Latrelle had his so-called accident. Which meant whoever sent them *had* to be involved, right? This wasn't some casual observer making a point of how life imitates art. The killer was the book-sender, and he wanted to involve me, hoping to be witnessed.

Maybe hoping to be stopped?

I gasped and jerked the wheel as something dashed out in front of the car. An animal leaped across the road.

Charlotte looked up from her tablet. "What is it, Mommy?"

"Just a deer, honey."

"You sound upset."

"By the deer?"

Charlotte didn't answer. She didn't know. But she was intuiting my stress.

"Everything's okay. Mommy's just . . . working on a hard problem."

"Miss Gramone says when you're working on a hard problem and you can't get it, it's good to take a break."

It wasn't a bad idea.

Perhaps what I needed was to take a step back, get a fresh perspective. I could be coming at this thing entirely the wrong way.

I could use a long shower too. Maybe turn my phone off, set the matter aside. Everyone would be home tonight. I could spend a few hours enjoying normal life. The way things were before that morning in the grocery store.

It was a good idea, and it almost worked.

I found the text on Geoff's phone by accident.

CHAPTER TWENTY-NINE

That was so good. Xoxo

Geoff was in the shower. He'd gotten a call to the ER last night and returned home late, middle of the night. I was gathering laundry from around the house and stopped in the bathroom to get his clothes. His phone was in his discarded pants. Normally, I wouldn't even look at it, but the screen blinked on, and there was Mae's message.

That was so good. Xoxo

Had she been at the ER last night too? Maybe they'd saved a life? I could only imagine the intensity of it.

But the *xoxo*. *X*'s and *O*'s didn't follow tough-but-rewarding nights in the emergency room. *X*'s and *O*'s were reserved for family or close friends. Lovers, even.

Normally, I might've given him the benefit of the doubt. I might've put my suspicions aside and just waited. See if anything else happened. But for some reason, not this time.

"Hey, Geoff?"

The shower beat down on him. "Yeah?"

"What was 'so good'?"

"What?"

"What was 'so good'? Mae just texted you. I was picking up your stuff and just happened to see your phone. Mae said, 'That was so good.'"

He didn't answer but slid the door open. Blinked at me through the water coursing down his face. "Can I see?"

I didn't want to give him the phone. I wanted to see what he would say without knowing about the *X*'s and *O*'s. I asked again, "What was 'so good'?"

He put out his hand.

"You're wet," I said.

"Lainey."

I handed over the phone and he rotated it around to better read the screen. I watched his face carefully. Traces of frustration? Maybe with me. A little bit of shock? Guilt? This was unlike me; I wasn't the jealous type. Mae was being overly familiar, and that was all.

But Geoff was a married man. There were boundaries. She couldn't do or say whatever she wanted with him.

"She's just talking about a run." Geoff gripped the phone like he wasn't handing it back.

"You went for a run? In the middle of the night? After the ER?"

"No. Scroll up. Look at my texts before it."

I did. They'd had a run at lunch on Friday. Geoff had a Garmin watch that tracked everything, and he'd relayed the stats to her. As I read the details, he said, "It was a good run, 5K in under thirty minutes. Kept it under a ten-minute mile the whole time."

He stood there, naked, water hitting him from the side. Drops of it ricocheted out, getting me wet.

"And she's just replying now? Or last night? At 3 a.m.?"

"Yeah." He blinked away some more water. "I don't know why she did the, ah, *X*'s and *O*'s. It's weird."

"'It's weird'?"

He didn't answer.

"Fucking *weird?*" My voice went up.

Geoff closed the door.

"What else do you want me to say?" He put his head back under the water. "She's from London. It's a British thing."

"Not to married men."

"Why are you so worried about it? Do you think something is going on between us?" He said it like it was the most preposterous thing in the world. That he'd sooner be having an affair with the Statue of Liberty.

"I don't want you running together anymore. Or doing anything together besides work."

He didn't respond. I could see him soaping up through the opaque glass, although I was pretty sure he'd already done that. I set the phone down in the middle of the bathroom floor like detonated ordnance, picked up his clothes, and left the bathroom.

* * *

"I'm taking the girls to a movie," Geoff said later.

The nearest town with a theater was almost an hour away.

I sat in the dining area, now folding the clothes I'd laundered on the table. Delia and Charlotte played a board game in another room. "What movie? When?"

"There's that one that they're . . . you know, the one with the little alien who's like a gardener . . . I never get to do anything with them, and I figured you could have the night off."

"Geoff, I think if you want to do something with them, of course it's fine. But it seems like you're angry. Let's talk about it."

"Talk about what? Talk about *my* anger? I wasn't the one swearing and yelling a few minutes ago."

I squinted. "If didn't know better, I'd say that was textbook evasive maneuvering."

"Lainey, fuck . . ."

He started out of the kitchen, but I followed. "Your coworker just said your last run together was 'so good,' and sent you kisses and hugs."

For emphasis, I pronounced "so good" like I was Marilyn Monroe.

He turned. His voice was low but crackling. "It's just her way. I told you, she doesn't mean anything."

"You said it was 'weird.'"

"It's a weird custom. A weird habit to send that. She should know better."

"'She should know better'?"

"Because I'm married."

I stared across the space at him. Just a few feet but yet so far away. "She should know not to hit on you, you mean. Not to come on to you, make lusty statements about running together. About getting hot and sweaty together."

"You're being ridiculous."

I sighed, trying to let the tension dissipate. Geoff and I didn't clash often, but when we did, it was usually me who made peace.

I didn't want to let this one go.

He continued down the hallway to the bedroom and again I followed. I peeked in on the girls as I passed Delia's room. They seemed blissfully unaware of us, laughing over the game they were playing: Life. I tried not to see the irony.

"And what about you?" Geoff asked once we were in the bedroom, door closed.

"What about me? What do you mean, 'what about me'?"

"Come on — next door? The hunky lawyer you wanted to know everything about? Guy probably killed his wife, and you're still at the window, staring over there in a daze."

A twinge at that. And I found myself instinctively looking out the window. "I was worried about the boys." I turned my back to it. "Why, have you heard something? Or can you not tell me, like you couldn't tell me you'd met Naomi Sheller before?"

Geoff smiled at me, humorless, disappointed, and shook his head. He grabbed his wallet and keys off the dresser.

"I just need to get out for a bit, okay? And I want to spend some time with my daughters. You get all kinds of time with them."

That was true. I looked at my phone — it was going on three in the afternoon. Where had the day gone?

"You're not going to say anything about knowing Naomi Sheller?"

"No."

I bit my lip. "You're going to see a matinee?"

"Or we'll catch an early evening show. We'll be home by bedtime."

I didn't know whether to push back or just let him go. My momentary rock-solidness was gone. The comment about Eric threw me. Yes, I'd found him intriguing. But was that the same thing as Geoff and Mae? No.

I went for a hug then, thinking the fight was over, but Geoff stood rigid. He put one hand around me, the other holding his keys. The most perfunctory hug in the history of hugs. I didn't even bother trying for a kiss.

CHAPTER THIRTY

The older I got, the more I thought about my father. How people had respected him.

He wasn't showy. My father had been a precise man. The culinary industry was dynamic, and chefs often moved to gain experience or to advance. My father's career path had been strategic. He left every job on good terms and grew into each new position. It was disruptive for my mother and me, but we didn't begrudge him. We knew he had a plan, and he took good care of us financially and emotionally. He meant what he said and said what he meant.

His stroke was a shock; he'd otherwise been in good health. Seventy was young in modern times.

Geoff's father was a passionate, sometimes arrogant man who'd chased thrills and good times most of his life. Now in his eighties, he still drank and smoked. Geoff had opted for medicine and health, and, in many ways, was the better man. But he had those flashes of his father's narcissism.

Geoff was a good father. He could be a little absent, but that was both the nature of his career and his personality. I had to share him with most of Buxton and the neighboring communities. His typically low-key demeanor was his way of coping with the demands of his job. People came to him with problems. They poked out their tongues and said *Ahh*, pointed out the strange spot on their armpit, coughed, moaned, told him their troubled tales. Then they wanted him to fix it.

Being with Geoff made me feel safe. Not just from would-be burglars, but in some way that probably went back to my child-hood, to that girl from fourth grade afraid to traverse the woods home. It was still in me to take the long way around in order to avoid trouble, self-defense classes or not. Geoff took things head-on. Sometimes aggressively. Never violent with me, of course, but I knew he had a streak in him; I'd seen flashes of it before. A moment of road rage, an explosion over some dramatic current event, or just the stress of his job bearing down. There was a fighter in my husband that would defend what was his.

Marriage and a family were good things. But they could also be places to hide. They could be that long way around the trou-ble. Fighting with Geoff exposed all of this for me. It reminded me that I might eventually have to face something on my path, something I couldn't work my way around.

Did I really think he was sleeping with Mae? He never came home smelling like perfume. He continued to show attraction for me and initiate sex. And what kind of cheater would leave his phone lying around for his wife to find? Spend weeks or months covering his tracks, only to mess up so badly? To have told Mae she could text any time with saucy messages? He was too smart for that.

It didn't mean I wasn't bothered. I was. I wanted to find Mae Springer and give her a knock upside her head. Ask her just who she thought she was.

But that wasn't what my father would have done. My father would have been precise. He would have made his boundaries clear. If the ring on my husband's finger wasn't enough of a boundary for Mae, perhaps we needed to talk. I'd be cordial but persuasive. Only, I didn't have her number. I'd been so nonplussed by the message, I'd never checked for it.

I could've called the hospital, but that might've been going a little too far. And anyway, the more I paced around the house, the more I needed to get out.

Thunder rumbled over the mountains as I dashed to my car and got in. I pulled out onto the county route with hardly a thought about where I was going. But first I drove past the Sheller house. I could see a couple of lights on, squiggling amber blooms through the rainy windows of the car. And then it was behind me.

Buxton doesn't have much to while away the time. I'd been to neither of its two bars in seven years, and I didn't feel like eating. Not alone, anyway. There were a couple of gas stations, a hardware store, and the grocery store.

I drove west into the dark and gauzy rain. It wasn't quite sunset, but the weather hastened dusk. I turned right about two miles out of town, and as soon as I did, I knew where I was going.

Somewhere inside you, you know exactly what you're capable of.

Up the hill and onto the ridge, another half-mile and I was at the Hemlock house. I pulled over to the side of the road along a hedgerow, just able to see the house but mostly hidden from it. After a moment, I cracked the window so I could smoke a cigarette. It was a bad idea; I never smoked in the car — it would stink, especially in all the wet — but it was my little act of rebellion. If Geoff could go running with Mae and receive cutesy sexual innuendos, I could smoke on a stakeout.

A few puffs in, I slipped it through the gap in the window to tap the ash away and it got wet and extinguished itself. I rummaged around and found an empty can of diet coke behind the seat. I used it for the ash can. I thought about checking my phone, but I didn't want to look at social media. Or see the radio silence of my mom group.

I watched the Hemlock house instead as the heavy rain clattered on the roof of my car.

A vehicle approached from behind and I instinctively slouched in my seat. Grabbing the keys, still in the ignition, I prepared to drive away. But the vehicle slowed as it passed. I peered over the steering wheel as it pulled off the road ahead of me. The tail lights clicked off.

Had they seen me? Was that why they were stopping? The rain obscured my view, but it looked like they were just sitting there, on the other side of the Hemlock driveway. I waited for the car to take off again, but it didn't move.

My breath quickened, along with my heart rate.

Relax. They're pulled over, no different from you. Getting something from their back seat, maybe.

The driver's side door opened. Someone got out, slowly, not in a hurry. It wasn't clear that they saw me. Between the rain and the hedge overshadowing me, maybe they didn't. They didn't act like it, anyway, because the figure moved toward the Hemlock house, seemingly paying me no mind at all. Who was it?

The Hemlocks had children, according to Courtney, but one had died of breast cancer and the other lived halfway around the world. Perhaps a visitor, then — but why would they park on the street in the rain?

I waited for a motion light or porch light, but everything stayed dark. Just the bit of ambient light to see by.

The other vehicle at the house, the one in the circular driveway, had been here before. The small red one I'd presumed belonged to Janine Persad, the home health aide. Maybe the visitor was delivering something. But I didn't think DoorDash reached us in Buxton.

"Shit," I said, and turned the key. The automatic headlights bathed the scene. At this point, I didn't care if anyone saw me. I had a bad feeling. The Hemlock house had a turnaround driveway, and it was pouring rain. If this was family, a friend, or delivery, they would have parked in front of the house, not on the road. The person didn't want to be noticed.

I let off the brake and turned into the driveway. I could see everything in the headlights: the long porch with the red birch-trim railings, curtains drawn over the windows. A stately door with a large old-fashioned knocker.

Something flashed across my vision. A shadow streaking across the driveway. Where had the figure gone? Behind me?

I lifted my hand to beep the horn.

In the next instant, something hit the car. *Bang!*

I screamed. Blasted the horn and put the car in gear at the same time. I started out of the driveway, then stomped the brakes when I saw the figure running toward the road.

I exhaled. Was it a gunshot? I didn't think so. It had been a metal bang, a flat sound like they'd struck the car with something, maybe even the flat of their hand, before running past.

They reached the vehicle. An interior dome light illuminated a medium-to-large person getting behind the wheel in a hooded sweatshirt. The light blinked off as they closed the door and started the engine.

At the same time, the porch light snapped on and the front door opened a crack. A young woman leaned out, holding a baseball bat.

I was torn — stay and check that she was all right, or give pursuit?

The prowler roared off and I followed, decision made. I still had to get out of the driveway and onto the road. The turn radius wasn't quite tight enough and I clipped something, probably the edge of the porch. But I stepped on the gas and followed the red tail lights vanishing up ahead into the wild storm.

CHAPTER THIRTY-ONE

Wipers slapping back and forth, I plunged into the rain, chasing the red tail lights up ahead. We reached an intersection. The prowler turned right, away from town, and I followed, trying to close the gap. The road sidewinded and undulated, making it hard to gain ground.

Buxton Falls Road. I hardly ever came this way. This is where Gary Latrelle had his terrible accident.

Over the rises and into the dips. Tail lights winking out, then coming back into view. My speed climbing, then dropping. On the next straightaway, I was doing almost sixty miles an hour in the dark and rain and not getting any closer.

I came to my senses: this was insane! Even if I caught up to the person, what then? They'd just pull over? I wasn't a cop. And they wouldn't wait while I called the police either. Still, as I slowed, and the tail lights got farther ahead of me, it felt like a defeat. I'd been so close to something, and it was hard to let it go.

I continued at a more reasonable speed until I found a place to turn around. Pulling back onto the road, I saw headlights behind me and grew nervous.

They've turned around too.

They're following me.

The headlights closed in. Rather than speed up again, I kept a moderate pace. I could see the vehicle was different, the headlights mounted higher, yellow running lights atop the cab signaling a heavy-duty pickup truck. I eased off the road a bit, still doing forty, and the truck blasted past in a whoosh.

It took a few minutes for my heartbeat to slow. By then I was back near town and took the route to return to the Hemlock house.

As I neared, the trees flickered with red-and-blue cop lights. The county sheriff's car in the driveway became clearer the closer I got. I parked and got out. I hurried through the rain toward the house, and the front door opened.

Wendy's husband Martin held his hand up in a stop gesture. "Whoa, whoa, Mrs. Barrister. Take it easy."

Looking over his shoulder was the health care worker. Martin had his other hand resting on his sidearm.

I made a time-out gesture, shaking my head. "I'm sorry, so sorry. I understand, but there was someone else here. He took off going south on Falls Road. I actually followed him."

Martin slowly came down the steps. Still looking at me funny. I was getting soaked, but I didn't care. I was exhilarated. Someone had been here, clearly not with good intentions, and I'd chased them off.

"Did you get a license plate number?"

"I tried to, but it was too dark. And he was too far ahead of me." It also validated my theory that Persad and the Hemlock house were involved in this whole thing. Whatever it was.

"Make and model of the vehicle, maybe? A color?"

"It might've been dark blue or dark green. So many cars look alike now . . . It was an SUV, though. One of those crossover SUVs, I think."

He kept his hand out, like I might do something. At least his other hand had come off the sidearm. "Mrs. Barrister, let's—" The approach of a new vehicle cut him off.

I must've reacted, because Martin became agitated, saying, "Take it easy, Elaine. It's the state police. Ms. Persad dialed 911, who polled the call — put it out. I was closest, but others picked up on it and are arriving now."

The state trooper rolled into the driveway underneath the dumping rain.

"Why don't you go up on the porch for me, okay?" As I moved closer, Martin asked, "You're not carrying anything on you, are you? Any concealed weapons? Anything dangerous?"

"No. Of course not."

"I want you to get out of the rain, so it's either in my car or up on the porch, but I need to check you first."

"I don't have anything."

"I have to check."

And then he did, patting me down carefully while two state troopers got out of the troop car. One clicked on his flashlight and shined it on me. The other turned a light on the property and swept it around, studied my vehicle.

When Martin had finished with his body search, he led me over to the porch. Janine Persad kept her distance.

"I'm sorry for this," I told her as I climbed the stairs. "I just—"

"Mrs. Barrister," Martin called. "Please just move past the door. Stand right over there by the bench. Stay dry, okay?"

One of the troopers was really clocking my vehicle now. The first trooper had followed my movements onto the porch with his light. He and Martin conferred, speaking low under the crashing rain. I looked at Janine Persad some more, hoping to catch her gaze, to show her I was no threat.

The whole thing was ridiculous; I'd been trying to help. But I knew the police had their procedures, so I tried to be patient, soaked through as I was. I just hoped Geoff and the girls didn't get home before I did. At this rate, they might.

"Mrs. Barrister." Martin kept calling me that, like he hadn't seen me at countless soccer games, community picnics, and school events for the past several years. "Can you tell me what you were doing here tonight?"

"Well, it's kind of hard to . . . You know Investigator Smith?"

"Yes."

"It might be worth calling him. He could tell you about—"

"Because of the books?"

"Well, yes."

"I believe Investigator Smith advised you not to come here. To let us handle the investigation."

"I just . . . I was . . . I'm worried." I leaned around him to see Persad. "Hi, you don't know me, but I'm Elaine Barrister. I live here in town."

"Elaine?" Martin said, his tone taking on that condescension cops sometimes had. Usually when they were dealing with someone unruly. "Let's just leave Ms. Persad out of the conversation for a minute, and you just talk to me, okay?"

"I didn't mean to scare her. But I didn't approach the house. Not on foot. I was only ever in my car. I saw the other person exit their vehicle and approach the house on foot. I didn't know where they went. Then I—"

"Let's slow down, okay?"

I took a breath. My excitement was turning into agitation. Knowing how it looked, Martin's attitude, not being able to just speak to Persad. But the more I wriggled and fought, the tighter their grip would get.

I thought of Barbara Cantwell. Her sly smile. How would she handle this situation?

"Someone sent me three books. Psychological fiction novels. There are enough similarities between the first two books and things that have happened in Buxton to make me worry that the third book could be about Ms. Persad."

I could tell it wasn't quite landing with the police, who seemed to think little of the coincidences.

Persad was harder to read. Interested? Maybe.

"The story is about how a housekeeper exposes the secrets of a wealthy family." I left out the part about how the housekeeper, in a twist, was complicit.

Persad's expression cycled through several emotions. "I don't know anything about this book."

"I'm just worried that, since people had terrible things happen that are similar to the first two books, you could be in danger. I know it sounds crazy."

No one challenged that. Sensing I was done, Martin said, "Well, Mrs. Barrister, if you can just sit tight for a moment."

"Let me get you something dry," said the female trooper. She went to the troop car while the other trooper and Martin went into the house to presumably speak more with Persad.

The female trooper came back with a stiff wool blanket. "You don't have any injuries or anything like that?"

"No." I shrugged into the blanket. "Thank you."

"And you chased this other vehicle? How far?"

I told her what had happened. How I'd let the vehicle go on Falls Road. "I've never done anything like this before."

Her eyes showed compassion. "These events are a lot for a small town. I'm from a big city, and you don't bat an eye. But here, people are sensitive to it. And that's a good thing, why we need community. But you have to be careful. Chasing after someone in the dark and in the rain, not knowing if they're dangerous . . ."

"I know." I appreciated her concern, but I was growing more worried by the minute that the girls were getting home, that Geoff would be wondering where I was. I realized my phone was in the car and asked if I could retrieve it.

"It'd be best if you stayed right here, okay? Just for another couple of minutes until we get this all sorted out."

I tried to remain patient, and soon the other cops emerged. Janine Persad was not with them.

"Okay," Martin said. "You're free to go, Elaine."

"Oh, okay . . . What about—?"

"Ms. Persad is not going to press any charges, nor is Mr. Hemlock. He's aware of what happened; we spoke to him."

I started to respond, but Martin held up his hand again, a posture I was growing to resent. "Ms. Persad heard a prowler outside. It seemed like someone was trying to get in the back of the house, through a window."

"That's who I'm talking about! Someone was trying to break in."

Martin's cool veneer fell away. "Mrs. Barrister, the only one Ms. Persad saw is *you*. She heard someone trying to get in, got a baseball bat, and called 911. She then heard your door slam shut, looked outside, and saw you turning around in the driveway."

I realized the truth. "No, the person — they hit my car with something!"

"Is there any sign of that?"

The troopers, who had examined my car, shook their heads. One even reported, "There does seem to be minor damage to the front bumper, right side. Some streaks of paint."

"And," Martin said, "there's a chunk of the porch damaged right there. See that lattice work? See that broken piece? Same color as the paint on your car."

Mortified, I turned and saw the damage. It wasn't terrible, a patch job, but it was depressing.

"I came back," I said softly. "Why would I come back if I had anything to hide?"

"I don't know," Martin said. "But these are the facts as we have them."

"I didn't get out of the car. The person trying to get in the window was someone else. I scared them when I turned on the headlights. How does she think I turned on the headlights out here if I was at the back of the house?"

"Ma'am . . ."

"I drove off when they did. That's when I did that to the porch. And I'm sorry. I'll pay for it, of course."

"You can't give me a plate number, a make, or a model." Martin took a deep breath, like he'd been storing this up for last. "But Ms. Persad can attest that you've been here before, sitting out in the road. She's seen your vehicle."

Oh, crap.

Now I knew it was truly pointless to argue. Persad had seen me here the other day. Nothing I could say would help. I was a stalker.

"At this time, we're asking you to return home. We're asking you not to return to the Hemlocks' home. If you do, Folger Hemlock has indicated he'll file a restraining order."

I could feel the tears welling up but suppressed them.

"I hope nothing happens to her," I said.

"Mrs. Barrister? I hope that's not a threat. Should we take that as a threat?"

"Of course not."

A nerve twitched above Martin's left eye. "You say you're here because of *books*, Elaine?"

"All right," the female trooper said, trying to mitigate.

But Martin pressed on. "Smith said you could have given *yourself* those books. Ordered them up on the internet."

Quietly, through my teeth, I said, "I didn't."

He just looked at me, simmering with anger. I wondered if he knew I'd told Smith he'd been giving out information on the two cases.

"Go home," he told me. "And don't come back here, Elaine. Period."

CHAPTER THIRTY-TWO

Monday

People watched as I pulled up to the soccer field. Looking at me. Whispering to each other.

Charlotte jumped from the car and ran to her friends. I watched her for a moment, living vicariously through her free spirit. *Life only gets harder, kid.*

Theresa offered a wan smile. I wondered how much she knew. Only Kimber seemed guileless, chatting with me briefly as I brought the soccer balls out of the shed. Fynn was having his birthday party on the farm — his choice — and Charlotte was encouraged to wear her sloppiest boots. I had nearly forgotten the party, happening the coming Saturday, the twenty-sixth. September had nearly passed.

"Two things that boy cares about," Kimber said, both self-satisfied and genuinely humble. "Soccer and cows."

"The important things in life." It was an effort to sound upbeat. Kimber was easy to talk to, but a cloud hung over me. The night before, I'd managed to beat Geoff and the girls home. Before I could tell him what happened, he was apologizing. Admitting he'd reacted badly. He knew Mae's text was inappropriate; he just didn't know how to tell her. The emotion in his eyes had been unexpected. "I'm sorry, and you're right."

I'd wanted to check the calendar for the last time I'd heard those words.

"Okay," Kimber said. "Have a good practice."

Oh no — I'd spaced out on her. She'd been reminding me of Fynn's birthday party, and I'd drifted off. I continued dragging the ball bag onto the field, feeling worse.

"Sorry I'm running late," I said to Wendy as I unpacked the balls and rolled them onto the field.

She smiled, but her demeanor was tense. "Did you check your email today?"

"No, actually."

After Geoff's apology, I hadn't told him anything about what happened at the Hemlock house or with the police. I wanted to preserve the good vibe between us. I knew it was wrong, and that guilt carried over into today.

"Elaine," Wendy said. She sounded like someone about to deliver terrible news. "We need to have a talk."

She must've signaled Renee, who ventured closer.

Wendy then whistled at the kids. "Two laps! Get goin', hup-hup!" Some groaned and some giggled and some made charging sounds like soldiers into battle, but they all started running. I watched as they separated into the vanguard of faster boys and girls, the middle of the pack, the few slower kids trailing behind.

Feeling like one of those last kids, I didn't want to focus on Wendy or Renee. No lectures, please. But I'd been deluding myself that Martin hadn't told his wife what happened.

"Okay," I said preemptively. "I'm happy to talk to you about any concerns you have. But I promise I'm fine, and it's not going to affect my coaching or anything like that."

"It already has," Wendy said.

Her response took me aback. We hadn't had a practice or a game until now. How could the events of last night have affected anything here? I racked my brain.

"Because of what happened last week? That was an accident. That happens to all of us. Colliding with a player happened to *you* just the other w—"

Wendy patted the air. Even though we'd walked away from the field, I noticed some of the parents observing us. "It's not that," she said. "Well, not just that. We understand your situation is somewhat unique, because the Shellers were neighbors."

"Wendy, I don't—"

Renee cut me off. "Honey, the youth commission first discussed your situation well before your tangle with the player. Two weeks ago, then again last week. And today, after a lengthy phone call, we made a decision. Normally, we might let you finish out the season. You're a good coach, Lainey. But with everything going on, we think it's best you take a break."

My legs started shaking. My lips went numb. "I didn't do anything wrong."

Wendy got eye-to-eye. "You've been late to practice. You've been distracted. You've been talking about . . ."

"It's all in the letter," Renee said. "I'm sorry it's disappointing. Thank you for all of your help so far this season."

"I've been doing this for five years."

Wendy spoke through clenched teeth. "Lainey, you've been defending a man who murdered his wife. And you've been doing it in front of the kids."

"What?"

Renee put out a hand to stop Wendy, but she went on anyway, enumerating her points with her fingers. "You've compared Gary Latrelle dying to something you read in a book. You're going around saying we sent you books as part of a book club we never started."

Renee said something quiet to Wendy. Wendy's lips pinched before she returned to the field. She began rounding up the kids to get the practice officially started. When she blew the whistle, it pierced me like an arrow.

"Elaine," Renee said.

I watched the children gather around Wendy. Charlotte in her pink socks. She looked for me, saw me, waved.

Don't cry.

"This isn't about anything I've done," I said.

"Elaine . . ."

"I didn't say anything in front of the kids."

"Maybe you don't remember."

I looked at her. "We were all talking about what happened. Everyone. And you told me you worried about Gary Latrelle. You said you worried about the kind of life he led."

"This isn't personal. It's about the kids. We've all been affected by these tragedies. And everyone reacts in different ways. Maybe you've been so close to it you can't see how you're behaving . . ." She held up both hands and tightly pursed her lips. She would say no more about it. She started to walk away, but turned back. "Obviously, you can stay for the practice. But I can understand if you don't want to. And Charlotte . . . We love having Charlotte on the team. It's really up to you."

It was like someone ripped out my insides and left them there steaming on the grass for me to contemplate. Do I leave them for the animals? Put them in a plastic bag and bring them home?

I don't know how long I stood there. I felt like that little girl on the trail home from school. Only I was a grown woman now. With children. A husband who flirted with his coworker. People dying all around me. Friends I thought understood, who I felt safe with, turning into people I didn't know.

I was on the outside.

I'd always been on the outside.

Since I couldn't imagine talking to Kimber or any of the other parents, I circled the shed and took the long way to my car. I sat there for several more minutes, in shock and undecided. I thought about calling Courtney, but I'd bothered her enough.

So, I sat, and I thought, and I wondered if I was losing my mind.

* * *

I read the youth commission email on my phone back home in my driveway. It was worse than Renee and Wendy had intimated. I was done coaching soccer, not just this season, but forever. The wording was that I *should not apply for any youth commission coaching positions in the future*. They'd slammed a very hard, very loud door right in my face.

"I made dinner," Geoff said when I finally went inside.

I didn't have much of an appetite, but I tried to get through most of it. The girls chatted about school and friends. Geoff knew something was wrong but seemed unsure whether he should ask. He probably assumed it was about him. I shooed him out of the kitchen when it was time for the dishes.

Two weeks? Renee had said they'd been "discussing my situation" for almost that long.

It was two weeks since Naomi Sheller had been found dead. When we'd discussed it at practice, I'd asked if there'd been any manner-of-death ruling. Had that been wrong of me? Wendy had said, "I think she was attacked."

Alone in the kitchen, I opened the phone and went back to my email. It had come from the youth commission website, and there was a link. I followed it and clicked on the page for the board of directors. They last met on Wednesday, September 9. There were no recorded minutes, just an indication that it was their regular meeting for the month.

One of the board members was Nathan Hemlock.

I leaned against the counter and put my hand to my mouth. After a moment, I navigated to Facebook just to be sure. Yes, he was related to Folger Hemlock. His younger brother.

Of course. Renee said they'd been discussing me for weeks, but clearly what happened last night directly led to them letting me go. In a word, I'd been railroaded.

This was what happened in the world. This was life. People decided the truth about you, whether real or not. Yes, there were obvious misunderstandings, and I'd also made some bad choices. But it didn't mean I was wrong. *Someone* sent me those books — that was just an undeniable fact. Gary Latrelle's accident had been the result of perforated brake lines, leading the police to speculate foul play. And Naomi Sheller appeared to have been attacked.

If Eric Sheller did it, if he was involved in his wife's death, or even Gary's, why hadn't he been arrested? Because facts still mattered, evidence still mattered. Wendy had said, "You've been defending a man who murdered his wife." Well, Wendy, in this country, we're innocent until proven guilty. And I'd seen his face. I'd felt the emotion coming from him. If push came to shove, I'd say it out loud: I didn't think Eric Sheller was guilty.

"Honey!" Geoff called from the other room.

"Just a minute!" I called back. I wanted to finish up these dishes. I had a response email brewing in my head. I hadn't let Mae's floozy texting go, and I wasn't going to let this go either. I'd tried to do the right thing for Wendy and Martin. But I wasn't going to lie to Smith. And I didn't regret what I'd done at the Hemlock house. Now they were trying to close me out. I had to fight it, just like my dad would have.

"Mom!" It was Charlotte, excitement mixed with worry.

"Okay, okay!"

"Lainey!" Geoff again. Sounding alarmed.

What was going on? I followed the sound of their voices into my bedroom, where they were gathered at the window viewing the Sheller home. Blue-and-red lights flashed, and my heart sunk.

Oh no.

Once again, police crowded the Shellers' driveway. Spotlights turned the house bright white.

"Mom?" It was Delia who sounded nervous this time, and I held her.

We all watched as the front door of the Sheller house opened, and out came two state troopers, one on each side of Eric Sheller.

They had him in handcuffs.

PART IV:
THE MISSING WOMAN

CHAPTER THIRTY-THREE

Tuesday

I was wrong.

About how much, I didn't know. Maybe everything.

Geoff and I ate breakfast not talking, the air filled with our daughters' bickering. *You put too much cereal in your bowl! Well, you didn't get out of bed on time!* Geoff and I were back to a standstill, balanced in our guilt. He lied about a flirty coworker; I defended a man now arrested for murder. Which way did the scales tip?

"Mack and I are going to team up for four square today," Charlotte announced. "We have a strategy."

I was pushing her out the door. Geoff was already gone. My heart was heavy. "Honey, remember last night?"

"Yeah?"

"Mack might not be at school today." I wondered if someone would take the boys, keep their routine.

"Mack didn't do anything!"

"I know." As we drove to the school, I did my best to answer their questions. Delia wanted us to help. "Can they come live with us?"

"They'll probably go with their family."

She shook her head. "They won't. Jasper told me."

"What did he say?"

"He said his dad's family didn't like his mom. He said no one did. So, they moved."

I recalled the memorial, lots of people. "Honey, I don't think that can be true."

"It is," she insisted. Her face scrunched in pensive earnestness, visible in the rear-view mirror. "What if nobody will take them?"

"Well, then they'll go into state care. That means they get foster parents, and maybe someday, somebody adopts them." I kept thinking about the memorial; maybe I was wrong to recall "lots of people." Being wrong was a new habit of mine. I remembered a line going in, but how many had been in it? Five or six? Inside, I'd seen Wendy, Renee, Martin, and Smith. Several unfamiliar faces. Had it been packed to the rafters? Not quite.

"Why can't we be foster parents? We can adopt them."

I didn't have an answer. I'd felt an urge to mother Naomi's sons, but I probably wasn't the best candidate. I was asked to step down from coaching a second-grade soccer team. I was lurking outside of strangers' homes and risking restraining orders. My standing in the community was rapidly deteriorating, whatever standing there'd been to speak of in the first place.

"Mom . . ."

I was sitting in the road with my blinker going, the school drop-off area to my right. I finally made the move, and we began inching toward our spot. The vehicle ahead of us stopped at the safety officer on duty, the doors opened, kiddos bounced out. When it was our turn, we made our hasty goodbyes, the girls fighting to get in the last hug. Charlotte ran off ahead; Delia turned back. I waved and she waved, gave me a sheepish grin, and continued on.

There was nothing I wouldn't do for them. I was so lucky to have them, to be in the situation I was in. The Shellers had seemed like a similar family until they'd been shattered into a million pieces.

Leaving the school, I didn't want to go home. Didn't want to be there with the now-empty Sheller house beckoning me to look, to wonder how I could've been so mistaken thinking Eric was innocent. Killers didn't usually announce themselves, and true-crime tales were full of men who'd seemed harmless. But I'd studied criminal justice. I should be able to spot — or at least suspect — the quiet neighbor with the dark secret. The gentle soul who exploded with sinister rage when no one was watching.

I just couldn't get my head around it, though: the coincidences. The proximity of the crimes.

And what about the figure who'd hurried off in their car after I'd pulled into the Hemlock driveway? I'd definitely disrupted their plan. So, I was right about some things. I just didn't know what, or how many.

I drove out of town, taking Falls Road. I rolled the window down to hear the crash of the waterfall as I went past, to smell the tannins in the water, a coppery, woody smell. Two miles after that, a white cross marked the spot where Gary Latrelle had driven his Savoy off the road and into a massive evergreen tree. Adorned by ribbons, flowers, a picture.

I pulled over. The air was warm and breezy. A vehicle came cruising by, its tires clutching the sharp curve. I felt the wind of the vehicle, saw the driver's blurred face as she gawked at me. I imagined Latrelle coming around the hairpin turn, pushing the brake pedal to the floor. The screech of the tires as he tried to make the corner anyway. The rubber skidding instead, and the road letting go. Several thick trees bore the marks of the impact, and the loud boom echoed in my head as I envisioned the momentum carrying Gary Latrelle through the windshield, a slow-motion of spraying glass and flailing human being.

How long had he lain there until someone had come along, seen the accident, and called it in? How long until the dispatched ambulance wound its way to the scene? Ten minutes? Thirty? What had been going through his mind?

Had he expected this? Or had it come completely out of the blue?

After those few minutes spent on the roadside, I backtracked Latrelle's route until I reached the vicinity of Renee De George's home. I didn't dare pull into the long driveway. Instead, I stopped and observed from afar, remembering the kids running around that day, me desperate to keep my eye on Charlotte. Had I missed anything?

I'd seen the kiss between Cara and Gary. Sensed her love for him. The two uncles drinking in the background.

Cantwell had talked about the Latrelle family, Gary's uncles with their auto shop, Ideal Garage. I drove the rest of the way into Tannersville and slowed down a little as I approached it. There were two bays, one open with a car up on the lift. A man in a striped blue jumpsuit worked underneath.

A parking lot filled with vehicles served the business. Trucks, cars, SUVs, one old bus. Several of them were junkers. Some were in nice shape — I saw a sports car — and some looked like the vehicles of everyday customers who—

I almost slammed on the brakes, but luckily didn't, since someone was right behind me. I continued on until I found a place to turn around. Once I was going back the other way, I slowed again near the garage parking lot. And there it was: a dark-blue crossover SUV. Just like the one I'd seen outside the Hemlocks'.

What should I do? Stop and ask to see the vehicle registration? It was a common car for the region, one of those makes that looked like ten others. I could at least get the license plate. Only, as I pulled over to look, I saw there was none. The license plate was gone.

That's when I realized the same mechanic in striped coveralls was gawking at me, a hose to an air compressor in his hand. I pulled out into the road, checking back on him in the mirrors. He was filling the tires of the suspended vehicle. But he was watching me.

* * *

I sat with an ice cream at the Stewart's store. The same booth was free where I'd been with the girls that Saturday I'd seen Eric. The flavor this time was Cookies and Cream, packed with fat and sugar. Screw it. I deserved it.

My God. Gary's uncles? Using an unregistered vehicle? What did they want with Janine Persad? How did they connect to the Shellers? Did they?

Delia said no one in Eric's family had liked Naomi. At least, according to her son. I knew she hadn't been from here, but she'd been a transplant, like me. Cantwell said Missouri, and that her original name was Naomi Goddard.

I brought up Google and hit a couple of dead ends, but then I found the results of a 5K race in Parkville, Missouri. Someone named *Goddard, N.* had come in second for her age group, the 21–30 cohort. Sounded like her.

I ran a new search, modified to include the word "running."

Bingo. Naomi Goddard had been on a popular dating site where she'd kept her info public: *Twenty-six years old, loves running, grant writer.* In the picture, she wore a pair of horned-rim glasses, a tight blouse, and a short, ruffled skirt that showed off a pair of perfect legs.

I stopped mid-bite of the ice cream cone and slowly set it down.

Cleaning off my fingers with a napkin, I stared at her profile pic. I thought about the woman from Eric's truck, and I couldn't help but compare them. No contest. That woman had been pretty, but Naomi Sheller was a stone-cold knockout. And wasn't shy about flaunting it, either. Case in point, the "sexy librarian" look.

Not that looks were why people cheated, not all of the time. People cheated for all sorts of reasons, but I was pretty sure one of them was because they wanted to be desired. Still, Eric Sheller had been married to the most objectively attractive woman in five counties. So why had he been running around? Because nobody liked her?

I threw away the napkin and last bits of the cone, a small victory. I wasn't going to go back to Ideal Garage, so I headed home with no more answers than I'd started out with.

* * *

Maybe I'd gone as far as I was going to go. I'd been consumed with the Shellers for weeks, and what had I learned? Not much for sure.

Eric Sheller cheats on his wife. Potentially. She goes out for a run and disappears. He tells his sons he's going to look for her. Then he murders her — also potentially. Murders her, and rings the alarm on himself when he calls the police. Stranger things have happened.

But then it only got stranger.

Gary Latrelle has a fatal car accident. He's the fiancé of a young woman who's friendly with my mom group. His uncles own the garage where I spot a vehicle that resembles what I saw prowling the Hemlock house.

I'd been fired from coaching the soccer team, and on the youth commission board was Nathan Hemlock, younger brother of the man who owned the house where I'd seen the crossover SUV.

And, in the midst of it all, someone sent me books that mirrored these very events.

It was dizzying, but I had no idea what it added up to. I just couldn't see how it all went together.

"You've gone as far as you're going to go." As if speaking it aloud would have more effect. I'd felt this way before. But educational background notwithstanding, this wasn't my job. Real experts were working on this.

I was a housewife; that was the truth. And there was nothing wrong with that. The only thing wrong was pretending I was something or someone else. My amateur sleuthing had already cost me. The more I thought about it, the more I decided the youth commission board made the right call after all. Railroaded? I'd bashed into a little girl because my mind had been elsewhere. How many practices had I been like that? How many games? I cared about those kids — nobody could convince me otherwise there — but I'd been thinking more about the Shellers and the Latrelles than the kids at soccer. I'd been eager to get the gossip. Hell, I'd even chased someone in my car!

For the rest of the drive home, I listened to music. I took Falls Road because it was quicker. But as I passed the site of Gary Latrelle's fatal car wreck, I didn't look.

I switched to a podcast and listened to some politics for a while. Politics! Everyone was trying to get away from it. *Give me more. Let's hear about the wider world!*

Intense storms and record-breaking heat, the cost of everything going up-up-up, horrific wars that prompted protests, dysfunctional governments, technology that divided a nation while people suffered.

Okay . . . maybe not that.

I resolved to reconnect to what mattered. To the girls, my husband. To stop thinking about what I might want to do for a career. *This* was my career. Being a mother and a wife were the two best things in my life.

I pulled into my driveway feeling a burden had been lifted. Eric Sheller was caught. It was over. Gary Latrelle was gone, and

whatever or whoever had killed him — faulty mechanics or sabotage or just sheer bad luck — was none of my business. I needed
to keep my family together, to see if I could slowly work my way
back into the good graces of the mom group.

I walked up my front path, keeping my eyes on the door.

Don't even look over there.

I didn't. The Sheller house could have been burning and I
wouldn't have noticed.

In fact, something on my porch took my attention anyway. I
stopped walking when I realized what it was.

"No . . ." The word rode my breath.

Slowly, I proceeded. I started to breathe again, shallowly, as I
approached the thing like a bomb.

Another package.

CHAPTER THIRTY-FOUR

I was careful this time; I wasn't going to mess around. Not with everything that had happened.

"Elaine," Mae said. "He's with a patient. I'll have to have him call you back."

Cordial, but smug.

"No," I said. "I need you to interrupt him, please. Tell him his wife said it's an emergency."

She started to respond — her throat might've made a couple of clicks — but nothing else came out. I could hear her set the phone onto a hard surface.

You're overreacting.

Again.

No, I wasn't. The package came from the same address: Cozy Time Bookshop. The same plain brown box, same careful taping. It wasn't certified or priority, just basic media mail. Book rate. Probably had been traveling half a week. And the handwriting was identical. I didn't need an expert to confirm it.

"Lainey? Is everything okay?"

"There's another box."

Silence. "Another . . . box? Jesus, Laine, I was with a patien—"

"Geoff, shut up. Listen to me. People are dying." I let that sink in for just a second before hurrying on. "And someone was trying to break into the Hemlock house the other night. I'm scared, so I'm telling you."

"Someone what?"

"I was there. They saw me and ran. They *ran*, Geoff. I gave fucking *pursuit*. This is real, okay? This is real."

He was silent a moment. Then, "Elaine, I have a patient I'm with. I thought something had happened to the girls . . . Jesus."

"They're fine; they're still at school. Geoff, I'm telling you what's happening. I'm going to call the police. Emergency, bomb squad, troopers. They're going to come take this away and—"

"Doesn't the investigator already have a package? The other package? What has he said?"

"Nothing."

"Nothing? Lainey . . ." He was quiet. I wasn't sure which way it was going to go. It sounded like he was walking, closing himself in a room. "What if this whole thing . . . What if this is someone messing with us? Someone in this town, bored or hateful, maybe jealous. Sending you a book with a plot that's like the things that are happening?"

Hearing him like this gave me hope. He was interested and not dismissive, even a little excited. But he was wrong. "*Three* books," I reminded him.

"Well? So? Are there not millions of books?"

"And I don't think it's someone just commenting on these events. The books were in the mail before these events happened. The sender of the books is *involved*. I'm not crazy, Geoff."

"I know you're not crazy."

"And this isn't about me not working. That's your next idea."

"It isn't?"

"I'm just calling to tell you, as your wife. I want to be straight with you, to share what's going on. I'm seeing this through to the end."

I could hear him breathing. I think he sat down. "I blame myself," he said.

"Geoff, no."

"I blame this whole . . . I don't know. 'Trad wife' dream. It's stupid. You need to work. You need to be out there in the world investigating things. Being a stay-at-home mom — you need more. It's like your mom. And that's okay. Of course it is."

"Don't bring her into it," I said, but it was half-hearted, my mind wandering. I was thinking about Naomi Sheller again. Her dating site profile. Her short skirt and finger in her mouth and librarian glasses. Did that track with the forty-year-old trail-running grant writer I'd met? There's always more than meets the eye. At our age, you had a family, perhaps, you had a mortgage, and you had a past.

Geoff was still talking about equality and women working, when I interrupted. "Honey, thank you. But I have to go."

"Wait — *what?*"

"I love you."

I hung up before he could say any more. I felt a pang of regret — for interrupting him with a patient, but more so for using him to get an idea, even if it hadn't been my intention.

Naomi Sheller, and her sexy dating profile.

What if everything about the Shellers was backward from what people thought?

CHAPTER THIRTY-FIVE

Investigator Smith seemed to expect my call. He said he was actually in the area, and he would drop by in about an hour. He advised me not to open the package.

I sat staring at it for a long time, then went outside. For the first time in days, I felt clear. I lit a cigarette and called Wendy. She would be at work, but my bet was she'd be too curious not to pick up. I was right.

"Wendy, I'm sorry to bother you."

"Elaine, listen. There's nothing I can do right now. I'm not on the board. They control what happens with the youth commission."

"I'm not calling about that."

"Oh . . ."

"Remember the memorial? You said Naomi Sheller's family had wanted it fast."

"Elaine, I can't talk about this. And honestly, I'm a bit surprised that—"

"Wendy, please. If our friendship has meant anything to you, if my five years of coaching with you have meant anything, please. Just two minutes."

She sighed. "I don't know. That's what Martin said. That they should just go ahead and get it over with."

"Get it over with? Was any of her family there?"

"I don't know, Elaine. I have no idea. Probably not. Martin said they're all in the Midwest."

Missouri, to be exact. I thought about it. Naomi died on a Sunday; the memorial had been the following Wednesday. Certainly enough time to rally, to book a flight and a hotel. Just strange to want things to go quickly if you planned to travel. "Was it her parents?"

"Sister, I think. That's who the police notified for next of kin. Now, Elaine, I have to—"

"One last thing. The woman that Smith showed me the picture of. From Tannersville. Do you know who she was?"

"No. I don't have any idea. Whatever you're doing, you . . . I gotta go, Elaine. Goodbye."

"Thank you, Wendy."

But she'd already hung up.

* * *

Jaycie Goddard sounded like she smoked a pack of cigarettes a day. It almost put me off having another one, but not quite. I puffed from the anonymity of the backyard while I spoke to her.

"Naomi literally won a local beauty pageant when she was a kid," Jaycie said. "The boys were tripping over themselves from the time she was in fourth grade. She was fast, she was smart, she was strong, and she was beautiful." Naomi's sister cleared her throat. "Who did you say you were with?"

"I'm not with anybody; we were neighbors. Not for very long. They had just moved across from me. But . . . I first saw your sister at a grocery store in town. We didn't know each other yet, but she was having some kind of an episode."

"What does that mean, an episode?"

I described it, and asked, "Did she ever have any health issues?"

"Physical? No. Always healthy as a horse as far as I knew."

I waited. Voices sounded in the background, like daytime TV.

"But mental?" Jaycie paused. "I don't know if this qualifies, but Naomi was a nympho."

I almost repeated it in a question, just to be sure I'd heard her correctly. But she went on, so I didn't have to. "It's a double standard, everybody knows that. A man has relations with lots of women, he's a conquistador. A woman gets shamed for it. But Naomi liked sex, that's just the way it was. Liked it a lot. And one man was never enough. I think she cheated on every boyfriend she ever had. So . . . not the marrying kind, we all thought. But then this guy comes along and sweeps her off her feet. Eric. At first, we thought he was just another fling. But then she leaves with him. Like, five days after she meets him, just blows town with him. We kept waiting for her to come back with a good story, how much fun she had. But a year goes by. And then another. I find out she's settled down someplace out east. Settled down! They had a small wedding, I heard, didn't hardly invite anyone. Least, I didn't go. And our parents were gone by then, and it's just me and Naomi and Lenny. Neither of us went to the funeral, either."

I interjected there. "I heard that you asked for it to go along quickly?"

"Well, they called us. The police, looking for next of kin, making the death notification or whatever. They said her body was with the authorities. Something about the manner of death. They couldn't tell me more than that, just that it was an investigation. I haven't heard much from them since. Do you know anything?"

I told her what I could, keeping it to the facts.

"That's about what the police said. Then they asked us if we wanted to wait until the case was over, or if we wanted to do a memorial. I called Eric. Hadn't ever spoken with him, but the cop gave me his number. He just seemed in shock. Told me, whatever I wanted to do. I said, 'Well, she's your wife,' and he said, 'But you're her family.' I don't think he was in his right mind. So, I called the funeral home. Eric said he'd pay for everything. I called and said how about a memorial? Naomi wasn't religious or anything. Our parents were, but they're gone. So, I said go ahead. But it will be for her husband and her boys. We'll mourn her here. She's dead, so it doesn't matter to her. I felt bad for the boys, but to be honest, I've haven't seen them since they were babies. I don't think I even met the youngest one. Maybe Lenny did. But Naomi went off and got married and had two kids, and it just didn't have anything more to do with us, basically."

"Were you in touch at all?"

"Oh, you know. A text here and there. Vague plans to get together at Christmas, but nothing ever happened. We just kind of went on with our lives. People grow apart. Siblings can grow apart." Jaycie coughed, cleared her throat again, then resumed in her husky voice. "When I heard she was . . . that she'd died, it hurt. It hurt bad. But it also felt far away."

We were quiet a moment. "Again, I'm very sorry. Even if you weren't as close as you'd been in the past, it's still got to be a hard thing to experience."

"We were never close. Naomi is the youngest. Younger than me by nine years, Lenny by seven. She was kind of an 'oops' baby. Just did her own thing."

"And so, she was promiscuous, but that's it as far as anything that stands out? Was she ever hospitalized for anything? Did she ever tell you about any mental health treatment?"

"Ma'am . . . I'm sorry, I forgot your name."

"Lainey."

"Lainey, I'll just say this. Naomi . . . We had a rough childhood, but Naomi probably had it the worst. Lots of unsavory characters around. I don't know anything for sure. That's the thing. None of us ever had any definitive proof. But our parents left a lot of unattended. Unsupervised. Let's just say Naomi started doing adult things younger than she should have."

I didn't pry. I just thought, like I had before: *unprocessed trauma*. That the grocery store event had been psychological after all. A reaction to intense stress.

"I found a race online," I said. "Race results from almost twenty years ago. That's how I traced your sister to Parkville."

"She was always a runner. Naomi the track star. Made the parents proud. She was just thirteen when our father had his heart attack. He was young, fifty-six. Mom was diagnosed with breast cancer the year after. She went in and out of remission and then passed when Naomi was . . . fifteen? Sixteen? She spent a couple of years living with my aunt and uncle. That's why you found her in Parkville, even though she mostly grew up in Birmingham. They're both suburbs of Kansas City, but Parkville is much nicer. It's countryside."

"When was the last time you spoke with her? Can you remember?"

"My birthday. Three months ago. She said, 'Happy birthday, big sissy.' I remember that. Well, it was a text, not a conversation. Jeez . . . I can't remember talking. I don't know. I can tell you I haven't seen her since William Jewel."

My silence asked the question.

"A college. She got a scholarship, full ride. She went there for four years. I don't remember her major. English?"

"She was a grant writer, I believe. Worked for some pretty big nonprofits in the region."

"Huh," said Jaycie.

I sensed the conversation winding down. The last bits went over the same ground. I thanked her, said I was sorry again, and got off the phone with a biography in mind. Naomi Goddard, naturally athletic and incredibly beautiful. Potential that was largely untapped. Making her restless. She ran like she had to, like she couldn't stop.

I think she cheated on every boyfriend she ever had, Jaycie said.

And now I was betting that Eric Sheller was one of them.

CHAPTER THIRTY-SIX

It was going on noon when the unmarked car pulled into the driveway.

Smith snapped on a pair of plastic gloves and studied the box a minute before picking it up. The rain was gone, the weather balmy and still. We stayed outside — "for safety's sake," he said. "You never know about anthrax, stuff like that."

I couldn't tell if he was joking.

He sliced his penknife through the packing tape. The freed flaps lifted a little and he tried to peer in. Finally, he pushed them back and pulled out the contents of the box.

He held the first book toward me, cover out, so I could read the title.

The Girl in the Woods, by Georgia Raines. *A gripping psychological thriller*, according to the tagline.

I exhaled. Wearing gloves myself, I took the book from him and read the blurb on the back out loud. "'Jolee Beckman has seen things she can't explain. Coincidences. Signs. Like someone is playing a deadly game.'"

I looked up at Smith, who stared at the book, impassive.

"'When a young woman goes missing in the community,'" I resumed, "'the cops don't know where to start. But Jolee is tenacious, forging ahead. At the expense of her family, her job, even her sanity, she searches. What she discovers will change everything she understands about her idyllic community, the people closest to her, even the people she loves.'"

Smith seemed to study me.

"Do you see?" I asked.

I flipped pages now, fought back a groan. I didn't know if these books were meant to drive me crazy or they were a type of confession. The fact that Smith, giving me that flat cop look, didn't seem to quite grasp the significance made me feel even crazier.

I was also vaguely aware of traffic passing on the county route, drivers or passengers who might see me on the front stoop with a cop and another one of these damn books.

"Mr. Smith, I'd like to go inside please. I think the book is safe, don't you?"

"Hold on a minute." He went to the car and came back with an evidence bag, slipped it inside but didn't seal it. It had a clear back, so we could still see it as we went into the kitchen. I invited him to sit at the island with me.

"What's going on with the other books?" I asked.

"I've been reading them." Saying no more about it, he drew a breath. "On the phone, you said you had some new information about Naomi Sheller?"

"I spoke to her sister."

"Jaycie. I've spoken to her too."

"Did she tell you that Naomi was . . . She'd been a serial cheater when she was younger?"

He made a face like, *she might have*, and that it didn't matter much.

"Why do you think Eric did it?"

"It's an ongoing investigation. I can't answer that."

"And you can't say who the other woman was . . . Can you confirm he was having an affair with her?"

Smith only looked at me. A small, squiggly vein protruded beneath the skin under his eye.

Talking to Smith was like talking to a robot with limited functions. I tried a new tack. "You said you were going to come by. Can I ask why?"

He shifted his weight, as if preparing for something serious, and straightened his spine. "Folger Hemlock called his brother early this morning. He said Janine Persad wasn't there. Nathan Hemlock went to the house and confirmed her absence."

"What?" I got to my feet, like I needed to be ready for action.

He held up his hands in a *let's stay calm* gesture. "We don't know what it means yet. She could have taken off for the night. She could be sleeping off a hangover. It happens."

"Is she considered missing?"

"She's not officially missing. Nathan Hemlock tried her cell, and it went straight to voicemail. Folger Hemlock's vehicle — one of them, a Kia Sportage — is also gone. She sometimes goes out for groceries. She could have gone up to Plattsburgh. We're checking all area hospitals in case something happened to her."

"Red Kia Sportage?"

He narrowed his eyes. "Yes."

"I assumed it was hers. It was in the driveway both times I visited the house."

"Ms. Persad doesn't own a vehicle. Wait — there was another time?"

"I just drove past. But there's been nothing?" I asked.

"At the moment, no. We're still checking."

"Do you see what's going on?"

"What's going on is, I'm looking into it. Part of me looking into it is sitting here and talking to you."

I had an idea what was coming next.

Smith said, "I know police spoke with you at the Hemlock house. That you'd been there the other night. Nathan Hemlock mentioned your name. He—"

"He's on the youth commission board," I said, probably with an edge. "So, he mentioned my name and you decided to swing by? See if I had anything to do with Janine Persad's disappearance?" Feeling tired all of the sudden, I eased back onto the stool.

"Listen," Smith said. "Go easy."

Something in his voice made me look up.

"I do think something very . . . unusual is going on here. You're not off base. I don't think that. But there's a way I have to do things. Now, if I ask you this, it doesn't mean I don't believe you, or haven't taken your concerns into consideration. But I have to ask you, as a matter of course. Do you know anything about Janine Persad, or where she might be?"

Mixed emotions competed for attention in my brain and body. I was still upset to be asked, but Smith was right. I understood procedure and the need for discretion. I even believed him that he was taking everything I'd said into account.

"I don't know where she is, and I have nothing to do with her being missing. But I'm worried for her. Very much." I picked up the evidence bag. "That's four books now."

He studied me in that way again, like he hadn't fully decided something. "Mrs. Barrister, the fact that you're holding a book about a woman's disappearance . . ."

"Someone is sending me these."

It finally seemed to get through. His eyes softened now.

"Okay," he said. "Well, we need to find out who."

No shit.

CHAPTER THIRTY-SEVEN

Thursday

As Smith grew to appreciate the importance of the books, I got more involved. As a witness, naturally, but, for good or bad, privy to things the general public was not.

The search and rescue effort launched out of the larger town of Tannersville. It was standard police, fire, rescue, and volunteers. Within a couple of hours, the car was located: a 2007 Kia Sportage, red, with New York plates registered to Folger J. Hemlock. It was discovered just before 5 p.m. at the Stock County transfer station — aka the dump.

The newspapers had all of that. What they didn't have was that the responding forensic technicians identified blood in the front seat of the car. And on the steering wheel.

Pictures in the paper were taken from outside the cordoned-off area. The red car through a chain-link fence. But the dump had been closed all day, no one saw anything, and the one camera was a dummy. Dump thieves weren't exactly a problem. *You want junk metal? Plastic laundry jugs? Have at them. We don't even lock the gate.*

Police couldn't know whether Persad had driven herself there and abandoned the vehicle, if something had happened to her once she arrived, or if the blood had come from an earlier incident and the car was stashed. It all needed to be properly analyzed. In the meantime, Persad was on the nightly news. I watched searchers fan out from the dump into the surrounding woods — south into Tannersville, north into Buxton.

East was the lake, and scuba divers were going in. West was miles of rugged terrain rising into the mountains. The search got more intense there, with rough-terrain specialists and air support.

But Persad stayed missing.

* * *

Midway through the second day, the news media found a new angle.

Initial stories had framed Janine Persad as an immigrant with a heart of gold. Having emigrated from the Caribbean Islands and gone to school for nursing, she'd found her way into the live-in health worker field, a round-the-clock job that saw a caregiver doing everything from feeding and bathing their patients, to making meals, doing light housework, administering meds, and sometimes being the sole companion. The pay was only so-so for the type of commitment it entailed; live-in caregiving was broadly considered a selfless position. Only the most empathic of people could handle it.

But as searchers hacked further into the woods, and police door-to-door interviews spread into the outlying towns, journalists dug deeper too.

Allegations surfaced that Persad had mistreated a previous client. A wealthy family in the Pacific Northwest claimed the aide cajoled their sick patriarch into writing her into the will. The criminal complaint remained unproven, but it marred her record anyway.

Yet another family, this one in Wisconsin, claimed a burglary of the home seemed coordinated. Persad had worked with local thugs, the accusation went, to steal from the family and to give her a cut of the take.

This was also unproven, the case still open.

"I never heard one word about it," Courtney said, when I finally drummed up the nerve to call her. "And she's been there for almost two months. I never heard any complaints from Nathan or anyone else in the family."

"That might be part of it," I said. "They dropped the allegations in Oregon. And the investigation in Wisconsin is ongoing, but she was never formally charged. If Nathan did a background check . . ."

"Honestly, he wouldn't have. He's not going to waste the time and money. The referral service he used is supposed to vet all their subcontractors. And they're good about it, as far as I've ever heard. Tell me about the most recent book."

I'd only read the first third of it, with so much happening, but I filled her in. It set up a conflict between a woman — the protagonist, Jolee Beckman — and her small town. In the story, another woman is missing, but it's been years, and the town has long considered her dead. Beckman thinks she's still alive, being held captive. Finding her would reveal a dark and terrible mystery at the heart of the town involving some of its wealthiest, most powerful families. But Beckman persists, even though it costs her dearly.

"It's the same as the others," I said. "Strong thematic similarities. Different details. In terms of victimology, the thing that links our real-life victims is that they're each in their own way kind of like characters in a book. A mysterious housewife. An untrustworthy fiancé. A nosy housekeeper. Someone abducted this woman, Court, and I think it's the same person who killed Naomi Sheller and Gary Latrelle."

"I mean, holy shit," she said. "And the police are all over this, right?"

"As far as I know." I told her about the meeting with Smith. The more we talked, the easier I felt. As if, somehow, this was all just another conversation with a friend. About something happening somewhere else, to someone else, which it usually was.

I asked Courtney about Yellowstone.

"Amazing. There's no crowds now, nothing. Just the bison roaming in these massive herds. Not a lot of bugs, golden eagles. The aspens are turning yellow. Wolves are the only thing," Courtney said, dampening my fantasy of the perfect place. "They come into the valley to eat."

"Do they bother you?"

"We make sure the boys are in at dusk. You can't let your guard down around Mother Nature. She'll remind you who's boss."

It was still warm here, but nights were dipping down into the forties. October was close. I thought of Janine Persad enduring those nights alone in the Adirondack wilderness.

But in my gut, I knew she wasn't there. And I didn't think she was sipping piña coladas somewhere lush and breezy after Folger Hemlock unwittingly wired her a million dollars either.

"You think she's dead?"

Courtney's question brought me back. I'd been quiet, and she'd intuited what I was thinking.

"I don't know," I said. "Maybe. Can you tell me more about the Hemlocks?"

"Well, they're old money. Rich for decades, maybe centuries."

"Any scandals or anything like that?"

"Not that I was ever aware of. They're actually big into philanthropy, community. But, you know, their kind of community, I guess. Giving money to artist communes and private schools, things like that."

I tried unsuccessfully to stifle a yawn. It was getting late. Courtney was three hours behind me. She heard it and told me to get to bed. "Thanks, Court," I said. "For everything."

"Be good."

I tried resting, but my mind wasn't ready yet. And each time I thought about Nathan Hemlock recommending my dismissal from soccer, I got angry. So, I channeled it into critical thinking.

It seemed two books pertained to Janine Persad as a victim: *The Housekeeper* and *The Girl in the Woods*. In the first, a live-in housekeeper witnessed a crime — or so the reader was led to believe. I'd skipped to the end to know she was complicit in the very crimes she was reporting. If what was being reported about Persad was true, it tracked, and Hemlock was a potential victim, not a perpetrator.

But the second was a missing-person story. Persad was missing, but the analogy seemingly ended there. In the book, it was the daughter of a wealthy businessman living in a resort community that mixed powerful families and generations of secrets. Maybe that referenced the Hemlocks?

I'd see if Cantwell could get some more background on them. I hadn't heard from her in a few days, and I was curious what she might have turned up. I sent her a quick email through my phone. And then tried to, at last, get some sleep.

CHAPTER THIRTY-EIGHT

Friday

"The books came back from fingerprint analysis," Smith said on the phone.

"Mom?" Charlotte said. I was pouring the milk into her bowl of cereal and hadn't stopped. It was almost over the edge. Charlotte grinned, thinking it was the greatest thing.

"Sorry," I whispered, and gave her and her sister some paper towels.

"We didn't expect much, given these were purchased by an anonymous third party," Smith said. "Prints all over the books, dozens of types. We're running them, but probably nothing helpful."

It made sense. The books were well-used.

"No two are alike. Partials or otherwise. They could be anybody's. Previous owners, other booksellers, people who might've browsed them in the bookstore."

Charlotte bent to the bowl and slurped up the milk no-hands style. I snapped my fingers a couple of times and she stopped.

"What's that?" Smith didn't know who I was with.

"Just getting my girls off to school."

"Ah. I remember when ours were that age."

I hadn't pictured Smith with a family. Or old enough to have kids already out of school. He had sort of an ageless face and had just struck me as a bachelor. Had he even been wearing a wedding band?

"And the seller still can't give us any information?"

"It's going to require a court order. The book buyer could just as easily have made up an Amazon account; they can do it all anonymously. So, we'd have to break through that. A credit card is a little harder to fake, but obviously not impossible. To get into it all means more resources, some deep cyber forensics."

I waited.

"And right now, my supervisors aren't quite feeling it."

Also to be expected, I figured. Some books are broadly similar to recent crimes? Someone pulling a prank? No judge was about to sidestep the Fourth Amendment for that.

"Nothing proves that the books are any more than someone finding a thematically similar story after the fact," he said.

Charlotte blew bubbles in the milk.

"But what about the people?" I asked.

"Yes, there are some people in common. But no one directly involved. Honestly, the common denominator is you."

I knew it was true. And that was probably part of why Smith was engaging with me. Seeing what I would do. Seeing what else might turn up on my doorstep.

"You were Naomi Sheller's neighbor. Gary Latrelle was marrying someone in your friend group. And Janine Persad is working for a family your friend knew — Courtney Whitmer."

He'd been checking up on me too. Getting the full picture.

"Not only that, Persad worked for your former neighbor."

"What?"

"In going through her employment history, yes, she worked as a live-in aide for Regina Marvin for the final month of her life. Not even quite a month — three and a half weeks."

Which perhaps explained why I didn't remember. Also, Persad had no car of her own. If she'd been coming and going, it may have been in Mrs. Marvin's vehicle.

"Mrs. Barrister?"

"I'm just . . . sorry, that shocked me a little. Does that not seem significant to you?"

"Maybe. Only, again . . . It simply points back to you."

I didn't know what else to say.

We got off the phone a minute later and I focused on the girls, getting them out the door. On the way to school, Delia asked me to explain what I'd been talking about. Her night terrors were ongoing, so I was reluctant. But better to tell her the truth than have her come up with something on her own. "A woman is missing. But they're going to find her."

"Will you find her?" Charlotte this time, in the back seat.

I found her round little face in the mirror. "No, honey. I won't find her. The police will. The search and rescue operation."

"But you're searching," Charlotte said, scrunching up her face. "You're helping them. Aren't you?"

* * *

I lit a cigarette. The girls were in bed. I was getting bolder; before, I'd only smoke when no one was home. Geoff was due home from work at any minute. I didn't care if he found me. No more secrets.

I opened the texting app on my phone. I'd gotten used to the radio silence from the mom group. I had no doubt they were all still talking, just not with me. It hurt a little less each day. But I had a text. From an hour ago.

Hey, Renee had written. *You there?*

I drew a breath, feeling a little shaken by what came next.

I know you've got a lot going on. I know everything that's been happening has been especially tough for you. And I'm sorry about the board.

It was good to read that, I can't deny it. I'm human. I'd been telling myself it didn't matter, being asked to step away from the team, the ensuing silent treatment. (Who coordinated that, anyway? Or had they all just independently decided to cut me out of the loop simultaneously?) The fact was, I wanted things to be better.

Renee asked if we could meet. She wanted to talk, thought there was a way we could put all of this behind us. I agreed and thanked her, and fifteen minutes later she wrote back. We set the meeting for the next morning.

My phone buzzed again, this one from Cantwell.

Hi. I have something for you. The other woman.

I mashed out the cigarette, staring at Cantwell's next message:

I think I know who she is. Call you tomorrow.

224

CHAPTER THIRTY-NINE

I pulled up to the soccer field. The goals with their sagging nets. The scraggly field, all dirt patches and crabgrass. The small set of rickety metal bleachers. It all looked so good to me. I inhaled and my breath trembled.

Scraping, banging noises emanated from the hut. I went in as Renee's rump pushed the door to the back closet open. She shoved the box she was dragging off to the side. "Oh, there you are," she said to me. She wore carpenter's overalls and had her graying hair done up in a loose bun, strands pasted to her dewy forehead.

I looked at the box of equipment. "Spring cleaning in the fall?"

"So much stuff in here," she said. "Trying to sort it all. I mean, some of these cleats have literal mold growing in them."

I waited a moment, hopeful but anxious. I was glad Renee was talking to me, but I felt increasingly uncomfortable being here. I could hear the laughter of the kids in my memory. I knew every inch of this hut, but it was no longer my territory. I'd been evicted.

"Sorry," Renee said, perhaps picking up on this. "Hot in here."

"It's fine," I lied.

She stepped over some boxes and walked to the door, passing me, smelling faintly of sweat and some powdery scent, her key ring jangling. "Let's go outside, get some air."

I followed her to her truck, a rusty old beast on the edge of the long grass. She took her phone out and looked at it for a moment, then put it away. Then she turned and, sticking her hands in her pockets in a way that reminded me of a farmer, leaned against the vehicle.

"So, I don't want to presume anything. I mean, I don't want to presume what you want. I was hoping you could tell me."

It wasn't how I'd seen this going; my response was unfiltered. "I want to keep coaching."

Renee nodded, smiling a little. "Just wanted to be sure. Well, I want you to keep coaching. I think they made a rash decision."

It was a tremendous revelation. The weight lifted off my shoulders like a jumbo jet taking off. I literally felt *lighter*. But then I tensed again. Nothing was ever this easy. Some kind of catch was coming.

"My kids are grown," Renee said. "I had a boy and girl, both off in the world."

I knew from the mom group Renee had kids. But not much more about it than that.

"There's something about having a family. You realize at some point you can't hang on. You can't stop time. And you never know what's going to happen either. So, you just have to appreciate every moment, I guess." She pulled a Zippo lighter from her overalls and started flicking the lid back and forth.

She saw me looking at it and put it away. "Yes, the point is — I don't think the board properly took your experience into account. And honestly, some of what happened wasn't your fault at all." She raised her eyebrows at me, as if inviting me to take a guess at what she was driving at. I didn't feel comfortable doing that. Because I had an idea.

"Martin," Renee said. "And Wendy."

Still quiet, I remembered Martin coming across the yard that night, asking me and Geoff if we'd seen Naomi Sheller. I recalled Wendy texting updates about Naomi's disappearance. Texting about Gary Latrelle, things that only police should know.

"If Martin hadn't been saying things he shouldn't have been saying, frankly, it wouldn't have been preoccupying you. Is that fair to say?"

"I can't . . ." I started.

Renee shook her head and dismissed it with a wave. "You're a good person. And we know that. The board knows that. But what I'm saying is, some of the grounds they cited — you being too distracted by all of this — it's arguable you wouldn't have been if Martin had done his job correctly."

"They basically banned me for life," I reminded her.

"That's not . . . no. Listen, here's what's up, okay? Wendy knows a lot of people on the board, and I think she was covering for Martin."

"What about Nathan Hemlock?"

Renee had been about to say something else, but my question cut her off. She narrowed her eyes a little. "What about him?"

"No, nothing."

"The Hemlocks are another story," Renee finally said. "What I'm talking about here is that you were given information you shouldn't have been given. The board can't fault you for having been distracted, or preoccupied."

I was about to protest, to tell Renee it wasn't worth my reinstatement if it meant throwing Wendy or Martin under the bus. But she held up her finger to stop me from speaking. "All they're going to want is a promise that you're letting all of this business go."

Sound of record stopping.

"What does that mean exactly?"

It wasn't a record stopping. It was my phone jittering in my front pocket. I ignored it, focused on Renee.

"What it means is, I think that you should let the whole thing go as best as you can. Eric Sheller has been arrested. Gary is gone, and no one is pressing any charges about tampering with brake lines. I'm saying if I go to bat for you, remind the board of your circumstances, that you were neighbors, that you were given access to information you shouldn't have had, they'll get what I'm saying. And Wendy knows too. She and I have talked."

Wendy knew? I was losing the thread a little, the phone still vibrating against my thigh. "I'm sorry, let me just see if this is the school or . . ."

"Sure." Renee looked off into the gloomy day, playing with the lighter again.

I recognized Cantwell's number. *Oh, for the love of* . . . I'd have to call her back.

Renee looked over. "Do you need to take it?"

I slipped the phone back into my pocket. "No."

Renee stared at the hut. "Okay. Want to give me a hand, then? I know it's hot in there, but it'll go quicker with two."

"Sure."

* * *

"Ow!" A crash from the storage closet. I sat cleaning cleats with an old toothbrush while Renee pulled more stuff out.

One of the shelves had broken free and landed on top of her; she was holding it up above her head.

I rushed in to help support the weight, and Renee was able to maneuver herself out from under it. We both lowered it down to the ground together, more cleats and old shin guards, goal nets, and orange cones falling off and pelting us. We laughed then, and I didn't care anymore about the sweat.

It was hard to stop thinking about the unanswered Cantwell call, though.

We cleaned it all up and continued to use the main area to sort everything. Renee decided what was too old and worn out and we threw those items away. The rest were salvaged with more scrubbing and cleaning. There was only the toothbrush, a Windex bottle, and some brown paper towels from the bathroom, but it worked.

"Gonna redo this whole thing," Renee said about the hut. "Maybe tear it down, start from scratch. There's grant money."

I smiled at the thought, though the word 'grant' prompted an image of Naomi Sheller and her dating profile, smiling coyly. In the next instant, she was bludgeoned by her husband along the running trail, dragged off into the woods.

"I guess I was wrong about him," I said out of nowhere.

But Renee seemed to know exactly who I meant. "Sheller? Well, the world has always had dark corners."

I pictured a version of his face in a lunatic rage, overcome by hurt and shame. Maybe Renee was right.

"But you shouldn't be too hard on yourself," Renee said, swiping away some sweaty hair as she looked at me. "We live and learn."

* * *

As soon as the soccer field was in my rear-view mirror, I called Cantwell to find out what she knew.

"At this point, it looks more to me like Naomi was cheating on Eric," she said.

"I think so too."

"Well, there's more. Someone wrote 'cuck' on his door."

"*What?*"

"They etched the word in the door of Eric Sheller's truck. C-U-C-K. For 'cuckold.' That's why it's two-tone. He replaced the door. And there were other threats. People coming after him online — he lost work because of it, a whole mess. Basically, in a town like Tannersville, you get branded as someone whose wife is running around and you're not doing anything to stop it? It's tough to slough that off. So, they moved."

I remembered the look of pure astonishment on Naomi's face as she reached for the grape juice. A woman whose husband had discovered her affair, but instead of leaving her, moved her to a new community.

The tangled webs we weave.

"But he didn't move far," Cantwell said, "so he could keep the clients he still had. And he stayed married to her, wanted to keep the family together. Did he forgive her? That part, I guess only he and she ever knew."

"Why would she stay?" I asked. "She clearly wasn't happy in the marriage . . ."

But I knew, and Cantwell articulated it, "She would lose everything. He's a lawyer, makes good money. She cheats on him, that's infidelity. Courts get a reputation for siding with the mother, but it's gotten more even, looking out for the best interest of the kids. And he would seem the stable parent. She'd get no alimony, maybe limited custody."

I remembered Naomi's detachment. Her resignation. Trapped, yes. Not by an abusive husband, necessarily. Trapped by the circumstances.

"Okay, but who is the other woman?"

"Naomi Sheller cheated on Eric with a man named Roger Nesbeth. The woman in the truck was his wife, Alice Nesbeth."

"So, revenge sex?" I asked Cantwell.

"No. Alice Nesbeth doesn't drive, so Eric was taking her to see a divorce lawyer. Apparently, she didn't have a job either — I checked. I can't speak to Eric's motivation; I can only guess. Maybe he felt sorry for her? But it would be a conflict of interest for Sheller to represent her himself, so he recommended a divorce lawyer he knew personally. They ski together, their kids were play-mates, that sort of thing. And then he picked her up and took her to the initial appointment."

"Maybe he just wanted to be seen as magnanimous because he planned to kill his wife." I surprised myself a little with the coldness of it.

"That's possible."

"The police know about Alice Nesbeth," I said, recalling Smith and Cojuangco showing me the photo. "Do they know all of these details?"

"They know about the affair. I'm sure they do."

"So, they could think that too. That he was just helping her for show. That he felt pressured from all the social recrimination, so he hatched a plan. Move twenty-five miles away and kill her while running in the woods."

"Also possible. But if he did it, it just seems hard to reconcile those premeditated elements — get her away from town, from any support network she might have — with the seeming spontaneity of the murder. The evidence — her injuries, the crime scene — makes her murder look more like a crime of passion."

I thought it through even further. Naomi Sheller is having an affair; Eric finds out. After some time — weeks? months? — Eric decides they're going to move. Maybe he makes it an ultimatum. He can't face the town anymore; people talking behind his back, scratching cruel epithets into his truck.

The old Marvin place is for sale, so he snatches it up. Moves in as soon as it goes to closing. His wife is still with him, there in the flesh, but something inside her has broken. She has a fugue in the grocery store, first day in the new town where her husband has taken her and her sons because of her sleeping around.

Eric goes back to Tannersville to help Alice Nesbeth initiate her divorce. And then, that same day, he returns home, follows his trail-running wife into the woods, and clubs her to death?

I wished I could talk to Nesbeth. Get a better sense of Eric, his state of mind that day. Had the cops spoken to her for the same reasons? Cantwell said she didn't know. But they must have. And they arrested him anyway. Maybe that was that. Maybe talking to her had been the thing that gave them the final push to charge him.

"Okay," Cantwell said. "Now let's talk about these other cases. Janine Persad — all over the news, huh? My God, Elaine Barrister, what have you gotten yourself into?"

She clearly meant it as a joke, but Cantwell's comment froze me up for a second.

"And she's got a bit of a background too," Cantwell continued. "I probably don't know any more than the media, there. What do you think? Part of all of this?"

I said I wasn't sure.

"Maybe Persad made herself disappear," Cantwell said. "Like the complicit housekeeper. We could end up hearing how she swindled Folger Hemlock. And who was the person you chased away that night? That could have been an accomplice of hers."

I'd had a lot of these thoughts too.

"Finally, I called in a favor and spoke to someone from law enforcement about Gary Latrelle. Don't ask who, because I can't say. But that car's been gone over inch by inch. The brake lines were cut. Latrelle was definitively murdered."

It felt solid. It felt right. "But why? Did he owe money?"

"You don't kill someone who owes you money, then they'll never pay. I did find a trial in Albany that's coming up involving someone with ties to the family. But I spoke to one of the lawyers involved and Gary Latrelle had nothing to do with it. He wasn't going to testify, nothing like that."

Renee had said no one was pressing charges over Gary's death. I told Cantwell about my meeting with Renee and the whole thing with Martin and Wendy. I explained that the mom group had sort of cut me out for a while.

"And I thought Brooklyn was bad! These small-town social circles are brutal. Let me look into it, okay? I'll check everything out there with Martin and Wendy, see what turns up."

"I don't know," I said. I explained that a condition of my return to coaching soccer — and to the community's good graces — was to let all of this book business go.

"Huh," Cantwell said. "Well, I don't suppose you want Alice Nesbeth's number and address, then."

CHAPTER FORTY

The gravel driveway was steep, winding through maple trees. At the top of the rise, the hill rounded off to the right and the view opened up. A sweeping deck buttressed large, south-facing windows. Adirondack chairs surrounded an outdoor fire pit, and a massive stainless steel barbeque grill sat to the side, looking unused for the season. The Nesbeths appeared to be among the few well-to-do in the otherwise working-class community of Tannersville.

I turned off the engine. Dogs barked somewhere inside the home.

A woman opened the door and peered out cautiously, her finger hooked into the collar of a black lab, her hip blocking a golden lab. She was no match for them; I could see her polished fingernails from here. The golden broke free, pushed past her, and ran to my car, where it pawed the windshield.

I gently opened the door and had to push a little against the exuberant pooch. "Down!" Nesbeth shouted. "Blondie, down! No!" She still had the straining black lab by its collar.

"It's all right," I called. "Hi," I said to Blondie. The dog got up on its hind legs, trying to lick my face.

"Sorry. They're just puppies. Two-and-a-half years."

As I worked to keep Blondie happy but calm, Alice Nesbeth said, "Roger's not here."

I made my way over. Blondie finished greeting me and bounded off to further investigate my car. At the same time, Alice finally lost hold of the black lab, who came running. "Gypsy! No!"

I prepared to be knocked on my butt, but Gypsy ran past me, more interested in what the other dog was doing.

"Are they siblings?"

"They are, brothers. Blondie with the two *e* genes, Gypsy with the *b* and the *e*."

Alice Nesbeth knew her dog pigmentation.

"Boys!" she called. "That's enough!"

They paid her little attention, but finished with my car and moved off on their own, now hooked on other interesting scents, noses down and tails up.

"I'm Elaine Barrister," I said, offering my hand.

She came down the two doorsteps, scowling. "Are you related to Dr. Barrister?"

"I'm his wife."

"Oh," she said, shaking my hand. I could see her trying to work out why I was there.

"We're neighbors with the Shellers."

Her face drew in, eyes seeming to shrink as she searched my gaze for intent. I had the feeling I had maybe one chance to say the right thing, or she'd ask me to leave.

"Forgive me for being blunt. But I'd like to ask if you think Eric Sheller killed his wife. Because I have my doubts."

She stayed locked on me a moment, but I could see her guard coming down. Then she pushed open the door. "Come in," she said.

* * *

"Of course he didn't do it," Alice said. She'd made coffee and we sat at a wood block table in an immense room, light streaming in. It was overcast outside, yet the place was luminous. Pictures on the wall were of old-fashioned guides, men in high trousers with fishing rods and ancient boats. A contour map of the region must've been six feet high.

Other framed pictures included pugilists. The old-timey, white-guy kind, where the boxer's name was Joey Morano or Smitty and looked fifty even though he was thirty.

"Eric is not that kind of person," Alice went on. "I know everybody says that, but it's true. He's a good man. He was helping me."

She breathed, seemed to settle.

"I think being frank is the best policy here," I said, "so I'm going to keep up with that. Okay? I saw you and Eric together, two weeks ago. Here in Tannersville, at the Stewart's."

A light came into her eyes as she searched the memory, came up with the details. "Yes. He was taking me to see my attorney. Which worked out. We've already had the provisional hearing."

"Because your husband . . ."

"Had an affair with Eric's wife. Yes."

That difficult part past, I breathed a little easier. "And that day . . . How did Eric seem?"

"That's the day Naomi died?"

"Yes."

She shook her head, still looking at me. "Eric had nothing to do with it. You don't know me, but there is no way the man who took me to see a lawyer that day killed his wife later that night."

"Can I ask why you're so sure?"

She leaned back and opened her arms. "You see this place? Empty. Just me. Roger is gone. Hasn't been here for two months. When we met, I didn't have a driver's license. In the city, you don't miss it. But when we moved here, I thought I'd need one. Roger didn't want me to. He said no. No wife of his would need to drive. I thought it was maybe chivalrous — a little overboard, old-fashioned, but sweet. It wasn't. He was a misogynist pig. Eric

Sheller is everything Roger is not. Eric Sheller was the kind of guy who would take the wife of his own wife's lover to see her attorney. That's why he didn't do it. I don't have a driver's license, and Roger took both cars, the son of a bitch. Left me with two dogs to feed, no way to get anywhere. But that all came up in the discovery. I'm going to get a car. I'm going to get this whole house."

Fair enough. "Can I ask — what do you think happened to her?"

Alice squinted like she might be catching me in something. I realized it was a bit of a cop question.

"I have no idea. Maybe she fell, hit her head, was disoriented. Maybe someone else who didn't like her did that to her. Could be anything."

"Can you think of who that might be?"

She gave me that same look, this time over the rim of her mug as she was about to take a sip. "You mean besides me?"

I felt a chill then, realizing that I was in this person's home, and no one knew I was here. Well, Cantwell. But for all I knew, Alice Nesbeth could've had her own revenge affair, and he was just in the other room, eavesdropping on us, biding his time. Waiting to hear what I might say.

"Besides you," I said, trying to keep it light.

Her gaze held. "Well, Roger wasn't the only one."

"Wasn't the . . . ?" But I didn't need to finish. Even more light seemed to flood the space. Roger wasn't the only one Naomi had had an affair with. "Do you know that for sure?"

"Sure, I know it. The same way you know who I am, the same way you know about Naomi and Roger. It's a small town. People see things. Wives talk to wives; husbands brag to husbands. They can hardly help it. Who caught the bigger fish?"

Again, I noticed the animal trophies and the pugilist art. No family photos or pretty things. From the bearskin rug to the wall of antlers, the vibe: generations of men who had conquered Mother Nature.

It might have been tactless to ask how many other men Naomi Sheller was rumored to have slept with, but I did it anyway.

"At least two, besides Roger. Maybe more."

"Do you know their names?"

Now Alice Nesbeth seemed amused. "Are you going to track them down and interrogate them like you're interrogating me?"

"I'm sorry. I didn't mean to make you feel that way."

She smiled. "You're fine. I'm not a hundred percent sure of the other men. But one of them might be Brady Latrelle."

It felt like a pop to the back of my head. "Brady Latrelle?"

"Might be."

"Is he related to Gary Latrelle?"

"His uncle. Though not much older. Brady is barely forty. He works down at the Ideal Garage? Here, let me get you some more coffee."

Before I could answer, she took my mug and walked into the adjoining open kitchen. Her movement displaced a constellation of dust motes floating in a shaft of light. I watched, trying to connect dots in my mind like those motes of dust. *Brady Latrelle, uncle of Gary. Sleeps with Naomi Sheller. Doesn't like something she does, or says, or knows about him. He attacks and kills her. Then for some reason he goes after his own nephew.*

Maybe because Gary knew something?

It was heavy speculation, but it linked the two deaths at last.

Alice came back with the coffee.

"How did you find out about your husband?" I asked. "Did you suspect something? I know this is so personal, and I'm sorry."

She sat across from me, frowning. "He told me."

It took me a second. The man who had all of this to lose — his marriage, this house — just confessed to his wife? But then I realized she meant Eric.

Warmed up to me at last, Alice Nesbeth was now rolling on her story. She'd met Roger in New York City. It'd been at a real estate conference, and he was at the hotel bar afterward. He'd sold a medical start-up and was now into electric charging ports. "He had eyes so intense they almost made you look away," Alice said. "He was smooth, he was handsome. I should have known better."

Alice was a New Jersey girl, she said. She'd never learned to drive, instead going from the bus to school to the train into the city for two years of college and eventually a job, working for a large realty company.

"I was a girly girl," she said, her red fingernails ticking against the ceramic coffee mug. "And he was a manly man."

Roger had always liked the Adirondacks, the history of it, the guides and explorers. He was particularly fond of nearby Lake Placid, which had twice hosted the Winter Olympics. Eventually, they'd bought a house. Roger's children were already teenagers when he and Alice met; by the time they moved into the place in Tannersville, the kids had mostly flown the nest. But they came to visit, and it had, for a time, felt like a family. Roger worked from home but also traveled. "He didn't want me to have a job. Said a woman's place was in the home, taking care of her man."

That pricked some nerve in me, but I paid attention to what she said next.

"We traveled together less and less. And he was home more. We befriended lots of local people, mostly like us, kids gone or none at all." She took a beat, looked down, drew a slow breath. "But then there were the Shellers. Roger had been dabbling in not-for-profits, and he found a local grant writer. They got together a few times for business. And then they started fucking."

The shift in tone was abrupt, and I realized Alice still carried lots of anger. Understandably. I also realized the reason she'd looked dolled-up to me the day I saw her in Eric's two-tone truck, like she'd been going on a date, was because that was how she always looked.

The rest of the story was sadder still, with Alice eventually confronting Roger about it. He denied it at first. But by then Alice had privately met with Eric, who'd confided he suspected something too.

"Eric seemed so disappointed. And apologetic. I remember being struck by that. Like it was his fault. But he said he was worried about me because not only was she fucking Roger, she'd been fucking Brady Latrelle too. And Eric thought Brady was jealous. That he might even do something. So, Eric wanted to help me. Whatever I needed, he said. I said, 'I need a good lawyer,' and he said, 'Done.' I said, 'I don't have a car or a license', and he said, 'No problem.' Which is why I can look at you and say, without a doubt in my mind, Eric wouldn't have killed Naomi. No way. If anyone had a motive, it was Brady. He didn't like it when she started fucking my husband, and he liked it less when she moved away."

"And you've told all of that to the police?"

"Who — Smith? He's a bit of a wingnut, if you ask me. Nice enough, but not sure he could find his own butt with two hands and a flashlight. Oh yeah, I told him. He sat right there, and I told him before he arrested Eric, 'It's not him.'"

"But did you mention Brady Latrelle to him? That he might have a possible motive?"

"I did. But it was just Smith. The other one who'd come with him, the pretty Filipino woman, Cojuangco or something, she wasn't with him the last time he came. And then I found out that those guys all went to school together. Latrelle and Smith."

Alice said so much, so fast, I'd gotten a little lost. "Wait, I'm sorry — who?"

"He's from here, you know. Investigator Beaufort Smith is from Tannersville. He and Brady Latrelle grew up together."

CHAPTER FORTY-ONE

Red flares on the shoulder slowed me down. Around the bend, the flashing lights of police vehicles shone in the road.

Roadblock.

I slowed to a stop and a couple of state troopers checked my ID. One looked in my back seat. Nothing there but a booster seat, crumbs, and a crumpled juice box. Another trooper circled the car, bent, and looked beneath.

"Can I ask what this is for?" I had an idea, but I didn't want to assume.

The trooper at the window handed me back my ID. "We're looking for a missing person."

"Janine Persad."

"Yes, ma'am. Anything you'd like to report?"

The way he asked it, I almost blurted out everything. The books, Alice Nesbeth, Naomi sleeping around. But I was miles away from connecting all that to Janine Persad. I could only cause confusion here. "No, sir. I just hope she's found and she's okay."

They waved me through.

But I drove the rest of the way home thinking about Brady Latrelle and Investigator Bo Smith growing up together. Jumping into swimming holes and knocking back beers and having each other's backs when the chips were down.

Hey, Bo? I imagined Brady trembling, eyes wide and haunted. Blood staining his fingers. *I did something bad, man.*

I imagined he'd found out that Naomi Sheller had moved on from her affair with him to another man. A guy with much more money, multiple houses: Roger Nesbeth. Naomi wouldn't take Brady back, so he'd been stalking her. Obsessed. Couldn't live without her. She was just too beautiful.

She knows it too. He texts her all the time. Calls and leaves messages.

Naomi doesn't know what to do. One morning in the grocery store, a panic attack seizes her. In the grip of fear, she literally can't move. She feels death breathing down her neck.

Days later, she goes trail-running, and Brady follows her into the woods. He waits until she's on her way back out, where he confronts her. When she doesn't like what he has to say about spending the rest of their lives together, she tries to run past him. But he hits her in the head with a rock.

Down she goes, and she doesn't get up.

I imagined Brady dragging her off into the woods. Tossing some leaves and sticks on her. What more can he do? These are public trails. It's dusk, but there's still a chance of running into someone. He's got no time to bury her or take her with him, maybe chop her up.

So, he runs.

Police investigate, of course, but one of them is Brady's old high school buddy, Bo Smith. Bo knows his beat, knows Brady and Naomi had something going, and so rolls up on Brady to question him. And that's when Brady breaks down, confesses. *You gotta help me, man.*

What's left? Eric Sheller already looks guilty. He's a cuckold and everyone knows it; someone even wrote it on his truck. He leaves town to get away from prying eyes, so he can kill his wife the first opportunity he gets.

Smith, anyway, figures there's a better-than-average chance a judge or jury will come to just such a conclusion.

But there's a loose end. Not Alice Nesbeth, because who cares what she thinks about Eric Sheller? She's no character witness. And if anything, her story about Roger sleeping with Naomi only speaks to the woman's promiscuity and, indirectly, Eric Sheller's ensuing madness.

The loose end is Gary Latrelle. Gary knows the truth. Maybe he saw something, maybe he overheard his uncle saying something. Gary could have been in the background when Brady confessed to Smith. And now he knows, and he's a threat. Doesn't like his uncle, maybe plans to blackmail him.

But then one day, Gary goes flying off the road at sixty miles an hour straight into a tree.

Lights out for Gary too.

That just left Janine Persad. She was tied in somehow, working for the Hemlocks. Working for the woman who lived in the house before the Shellers moved in. What if the rich, criminal side of the Latrelle family had employed her too? Peeping through the proverbial keyhole, Persad could have witnessed an incriminating moment. Brady stripping off his dirty, bloody clothes to burn in the backyard . . .

I pulled into my driveway, surprised but grateful to see Geoff's car already there. An hour remained until the girls got out of school, so what was he doing home?

As I approached the front door, it opened. Geoff was there with a worried look on his face. "Where were you?" he asked. "You didn't answer."

"I must've been out of range." I surprised both of us by falling into his arms. I told him everything I could think of. About Naomi's sister in Missouri, about Alice Nesbeth. About Brady Latrelle and Bo Smith. "We're caught in something, we're right in the middle of it," I said, breathing into Geoff's neck. "And Janine Persad is still out there. And I'm really, really worried she isn't going to be okay."

He held me, and then he said, "What do you think links her? Besides the books."

I started to tell him, but partway through, I stopped. I realized what was in his hand. What he'd been holding this entire time. My Kindle.

"What are you doing with that?" I stepped back a little, drying my eyes. I looked from him to the tablet. We were still half in the doorway, so Geoff pulled us inside and shut the door.

"I decided to come home for lunch today. Wanted to see you, spend some time. When I couldn't get a hold of you, I picked this up and started reading."

Getting into the tablet was no mystery — the passcode was 1111. I let the girls use it. But I didn't like the look in Geoff's eyes. I didn't understand it; he looked chagrined. Like he'd done something he shouldn't have.

"We need to talk," he said.

CHAPTER FORTY-TWO

When Geoff and I entered the house, he closed the door. Now he stood between me and it.

"What's the matter?" I asked.

His eyes were sad, droopy, darker than usual. "I liked it. I let it happen."

I took another step backward. It was automatic; after everything with Alice Nesbeth, I was on alert, adrenaline running high. "What are you talking about?"

"I liked Mae flirting with me. I actively encouraged it."

I didn't know what to say. I'd suspected that there might be more than the "she's just British" excuse Geoff had used for Mae's overly familiar text, but I'd taken him at face value. And I'd honestly been preoccupied. Now I just felt numb.

"I'm sorry," Geoff said. "I just . . . I don't know. It's an ego thing, I guess. You start to feel, you know . . . the grind. Start to reminisce about your old self. It's a fantasy, that's all. It's just . . . It's the way they look at you. Like you're not, you know . . . the same old guy."

He stopped talking when he saw the look in my eyes. Maybe because I was flashing on a recent memory — thinking he was getting old. But the second I became aware of it, something else swept over me. An overwhelming urge to know what he was doing with my tablet.

"So, you've been sitting here reading?"

He looked at the tablet in his hand like he'd forgotten about it. "Well, yeah, I picked this up and it opened to the book you're on. *The Girl in the Woods*? I didn't lose your place — I think it remembers that. But I wrote it down anyway."

As he talked, I noticed the dark stains on his finger.

"You've been working on the car too."

"Yeah. Just tinkering. For a minute. But I didn't want to be out there and not hear you come in."

He seemed weird to me. Nervous. Like one of the girls caught in a lie. But I didn't understand why. Maybe just the confession? That he liked the way "they" looked at him. These men — Roger Nesbeth, Brady Latrelle — needing women to validate them, sex to validate them.

"You never told me about Naomi being a patient," I said. "Even after she died."

"Lainey, we talked about this."

"No, we didn't. I mentioned it, but then I let it go."

"Because you know how that goes."

"It's not like you were her psychiatrist, okay? You saw her kids for a checkup. Why didn't you tell me?"

"I don't know. Just that. Standards and practices. Muscle memory."

"Bull."

"It's not bull."

"Alice Nesbeth knew you too."

"Who?"

"The woman I just spoke to. Her husband cheated on her with Naomi." I let that sink in for a moment. "Eric was helping her."

"Oh."

"You know a lot of people, Geoff. You saw Folger Hemlock the other day. You told me *that*."

I gave him a chance for an excuse, but he didn't take it.

"You know Folger Hemlock, Alice and Roger Nesbeth, Naomi . . . Did she come on to you a little? Like Mae? And that's why you haven't said anything?"

Again, he only watched me. His face was now harder to read.

"I'm not the common denominator," I said, realizing it at the same time the words came out. "You are. You even work on old cars. Like Gary Latrelle. Do you know how to cut brakes?"

"Are you kidding?"

It was my turn to go mute.

He lifted the Kindle. "Listen, how much of this did you read?"

I didn't answer. I was too busy suddenly picturing my husband making small cuts to the brake lines of a 1963 Plymouth Savoy. When would he have had the chance? Maybe Gary had had a doctor's appointment one day?

Geoff took a step forward, and I took another step back.

Through the kitchen, into the back study, out the side door. If I had to run, that was my route. But would he just go out the front door and beat me to the car?

My butt bumped up against something, and I realized I'd let him push me all the way back into the kitchen and was stopped by the kitchen island.

"I'm asking you how much you read of this," he said, "because I read quite a bit of it. Skipped around, but I got the gist of it."

I thought of Cantwell, then, saying, *You know exactly what you're capable of.* The book too. The blurb on the back of *The Girl in the Woods*, the part that read, *What she discovers will change everything she understands . . . even the people she loves.*

"Geoff, just—"

"Here's what I think. Each of the books you got are analogs for someone we know. The first book, Naomi. The second book, Gary. The housekeeper one is about the missing woman."

"So is the fourth book," I said.

But he was shaking his head. "No, it isn't." His eyes locked on me, shining. "The fourth one is about you."

I swallowed. I stared at my husband through a prism of tears. One minute I was fine; the next I was crying. There were many of him, standing there with my tablet, talking about books I suddenly wondered if he might have sent me himself.

He tapped the tablet with a fingernail. "Jolee Beckman. She sees things she can't explain. She's tenacious. It's her against the town. That's all kind of come true for you, hasn't it? So, if something has happened to everyone else — they're either dead or missing — what if you're next?"

My insides went cold, my mind seizing on one thing only: we'd come so far into the kitchen, he wasn't quite blocking the door in the same way. I could get past him on the left; there was room. And out the front door and into my vehicle.

Maybe he didn't mean it the way I was taking it. Maybe all of this had finally overwhelmed me to the point of a nervous breakdown, and I was having my own "grocery store" moment. But it felt like a light turning on, one of those big slow sodium lights in a parking lot that glows brighter until it illuminates everything. I saw my husband, previously married. He'd had a whole other life before me. One I barely knew much about, one he rarely spoke of. I saw him running with Mae, her grinning at him through a sheen of sweat as they stretched together afterward, him grinning back, liking it. And Naomi stepping into his office, drop-dead gorgeous, a runner too.

Maybe he was afraid I'd suspect him, so he started sending me these books to throw me off, get me going down all these blind alleys.

"Geoff, I need some air."

I turned and stiffly walked past him. He made no move to stop me, and I avoided eye contact. I just kept going until I was out the door. I knew the keys were still in the car, but I wasn't sure if I even had my phone or wallet or what I'd done with them. I wasn't going back.

Geoff stood on the front porch. He gripped the tablet. His expression was blank as he watched me leave. But then he stepped down off the stoop and started walking toward me.

I wasn't stopping. I wasn't listening. I just needed to get away right now, clear my head. Too many things were off about my husband, too many coincidences. Back behind the wheel, I stabbed the ignition and twisted the key and the engine roared to life. I switched into reverse and hit the gas and started down the driveway. Geoff picked up speed, trotting now, saying something.

Nope, I thought, *sorry*.

I used my side mirrors as I reversed but also watched him. Now he was flailing his arms. I didn't know what he was doing. I went out into the road and heard a startling sound — a blaring horn — for just a split second before the back of my car was clipped by a motorist passing by.

The impact spun the car around in a circle, my head smacking against the driver's side window first, then my entire body lurching toward the passenger seat. With no seat belt on, I was like a rag doll in a clothes dryer. And when I connected with something solid a second time, the world went black.

PART V:
THE HERO

CHAPTER FORTY-THREE

A faceless killer stalked my dreams. I was in perpetual motion, my gown flapping in the wind. Running one place to the next, always in a hurry.

People surrounded me. The killer lurked among them, anonymous. Voices whispered in foreign tongues. Somehow, I understood what was being said, bits and pieces of conversations. About a woman's wrist, her head, her spine. Then it was dark. And something in the darkness moved. Down a long hallway, a shadow in the gloom.

Time went backward. I watched a woman thrown around in her car suddenly sitting still, glass having congealed into intact windows around her. She drove toward a house that looked familiar.

It was my house.

And then it shook, like the earth was quaking, and the whole thing abruptly slid from view — a slide changed in a projector. And Geoff's face was there instead, and I felt him holding my hand.

"Honey?" He turned to someone I couldn't see. "She's waking up," he said, and there were tears in his eyes.

* * *

I recovered. The girls were there. Charlotte fed me Jell-O. I cried. I'd had a bad concussion and lost some time — almost two days — but I was going home with a few minor bumps and bruises. I knew I was lucky. More than lucky. Even Delia seemed relieved. Vindicated — her worst fears realized — but relieved. It was over. She'd been worried something terrible was going to happen, and now it had. "And you're okay," she said on the car ride home.

Geoff glanced over at me as if to ask, *Are you?* And I put my hand on his, which rested on the shifter. He smiled, but the expression couldn't rout the sadness and worry from his eyes.

* * *

I tucked Delia and Charlotte into bed, lingering long with each one, answering all questions. "Yes, Mommy was injured. Yes, I'm going to make a full recovery." I let Delia study the Ace bandage around my wrist, the three small lacerations on the left side of my face, explained that I hadn't been looking both ways when I pulled out into the road. "What about the other driver?"

"He's okay. He was from out of town, a businessman just passing through. He's going to pay for everything."

"But didn't you say you weren't looking?"

"I wasn't, but he was speeding. He swerved to go around me but if he'd been going slower, he could have made it. Instead, he clipped the back bumper. His airbag deployed—"

"So did yours—"

"Yes, so did mine. His airbag deployed and bent his thumb, but the momentum caused me to hit my head against the window just as the airbag was slowing me down. That's why I have the small cuts here and the mild concussion."

She kept asking more questions, but I steered the conversation back to her, to her life, to school. She didn't want to talk about herself, but she did anyway, humoring me. Eventually I gave her a peck on the forehead and, after more assurances that everything was all right, blew her a kiss from her doorway. She never asked about checking for spiders.

Geoff helped me change into my bedclothes. My wrist was sore — I'd suffered a sprain from the airbag. The pain meds were doing a good job keeping a headache at bay. After I was dressed in some cozy pants and a favorite T-shirt, I went to the window. Geoff joined me looking out at the Sheller house. The place was pitch black, no one home. Even the cars were gone.

"It's so eerie," I said. "Like it never even happened."

But it had. Naomi was dead. So was Gary Latrelle.

Geoff's touch felt tentative; he wasn't sure how I'd react. But I turned to face him. "I don't think you killed anybody."

His shoulders visibly dropped, his hand on my shoulder settling in his relief. "Oh good."

"I don't know what I was thinking. Well, I do. I didn't know why you were home. Why you had the tablet. Then you told me about Mae, and I had a headful of this information about affairs and Naomi Sheller . . ."

"You don't have to explain. I get it. I haven't been myself. I've been keeping this in. I'm sorry."

"I think I was just on edge."

He moved even closer. "Lainey, I'm sorry."

I looked up into his eyes. He could have felt sorry for himself; he could have made an issue that I'd ever entertained the idea that the father of my children and my lover for over a decade could have been a murderer. Instead, he felt sorry for *me*, he said, for everything that was happening.

We got into bed, and he snuggled in close behind me. It felt like the old days. Geoff and I had spooned a lot, especially through my pregnancies. "And I think it's important for us to realize," he said, "someone has been putting us through some of this. Whoever sent those books. And Lainey, do you remember what I was saying?"

I'd been thinking about it, off and on.

The fourth one is about you.

"I remember."

"I read the whole thing while you were recovering."

We talked about it, the plot of *The Girl in the Woods* and the ending, and Geoff stayed adamant it was meant to parallel me and my experience while the three other books had mirrored Naomi, Gary, and Janine.

"It worries me," he said. "It's like you've been targeted."

I knew he was right. I'd misinterpreted his fear as aggression. I'd thought — for a few frazzled moments — my own husband could somehow be behind all of this. That wasn't healthy. None of this was healthy. I regretted the day I saw Naomi Sheller in the grocery store. Somehow, everything extended from there. A cascade of cause and effect.

Geoff held me. "I don't want anything else to happen to you, Lainey. I think you have to just lie low. Rest, recover, let the police handle everything. Okay?"

I nuzzled into him and yawned.

"Get some sleep," he said.

* * *

The next morning, I waved from the porch as Geoff took the girls to school and headed into work. I'd had to convince him that I was okay, that he didn't need to stay home. Plus, I reminded him, Columbus Day weekend was coming up and the girls would be home for an extra two days. I was looking forward to it. Even the soccer games. Two of them were scheduled, one home game and one away.

Once they were gone and I was back inside, I sat at the dining room table, still in my bathrobe, languishing with a cup of coffee.

I stared into space for a moment, thinking about what I'd make for dinner that night. Thinking I might attack Charlotte's room — it was a mess in there, barely any visible carpeting beneath the clothes and toys. In fact, there were a dozen little things around the house that needed tending. The shower had been backing up; I should unclog the drain . . .

Who was I kidding?

The heat had finally broken, and the day was comparatively cool, hovering around seventy. So, when I went into my room, I dressed in blue jeans, a black V-neck, and hiking sneakers. I needed to cinch my belt tighter; I'd lost five pounds over the past couple of weeks. Harrowing investigations and automobile collisions were apparently good for my waistline.

I made two phone calls, grabbed my keys, and headed out.

* * *

I drove toward Tannersville in a rental car, because my own vehicle was being repaired. It wasn't lost on me, at all, that a momentary derangement — thinking my husband could be a dangerous killer — was a result of my extrajudicial investigating. And it had almost resulted in my death or permanent disability. I hadn't lied to Delia about the accident, but I'd omitted how lucky I'd gotten. According to one of the troopers I'd spoken to, an accident like mine usually resulted in critical injury, if not at least one fatality.

But it didn't mean I had to stop. It just meant I needed to slow down, stay centered, not jump to any conclusions. Stopping was impossible. I was too close to an answer.

Taken as a series, Naomi Sheller was Victim One. Victim One had slept with Brady Latrelle, the uncle of Gary Latrelle, who was Victim Two. Those were connecting better all the time. But there was some missing link that would then connect those victims to Janine Persad. Like the main character in *The Girl in the Woods*, I believed she was still alive. And not hiding in Mexico or Italy either. The search for her was winding down, with people believing she was likely dead.

Maybe she was. But if she wasn't, if she was still alive somewhere and in trouble, maybe I could help her. If I could figure out how she connected, I could possibly save her life.

CHAPTER FORTY-FOUR

I turned down the long driveway toward Renee's massive brick house. Bales of rolled hay dotted the stubbled field off to my right. To my left, the barn, the several outbuildings. A massive lawn between the house and the lake. One woman by herself couldn't take care of this. The groundskeeping, the cleaning, the maintenance. Obviously, she had help.

The barn was in better shape than some I'd seen in the region, falling over or already fallen. The world had moved on from subsistence farms. Now you either had to be a commercial grower with a big monocrop, or a market gardener specializing in tomatoes or Jerusalem artichokes — whatever the hipsters wanted. My own garden had been neglected these past couple of weeks. I'd barely been able to keep up with the harvest, and my tomatoes were dying on the vine.

I got out of the rental car in front of the house, no one else around. I'd arranged this meeting just an hour before, and I was early by about fifteen minutes. Renee was at the hardware store in Tannersville when I called, and needed time to get back.

First, I walked toward the water. A million chips of light glittered across the surface. The lawn sloped gradually toward it until it met a steep escarpment. A long set of stairs that looked too rickety for my taste descended to a small beachy area below. I could just see it if I got near the lip and craned my neck out to look down. Close enough. Heights were not my thing.

I walked back toward the brick house. Old house, modern kitchen and appliances. We'd spent time in the kitchen, but mostly we'd been out on the big, wraparound porch.

Gary Latrelle had arrived with his two uncles, one of them Brady. I'd thought it was a little odd at the time, but figured family came in all shapes and sizes. Now I wondered, had they been keeping a watchful eye? Had Brady, at least, been keeping an eye on the car, waiting to see when the cut brake lines finally gave out?

I heard a vehicle approach and turned, but it was passing by on the road, some distance away. I checked my phone: still ten minutes to ten.

My phone wiggled with a voicemail. Service was spotty here, so it hadn't even rung. But I was able to listen to the message from Cantwell.

"Elaine, it's Barbara. Listen, I got that background on Martin and Wendy Baker. Turns out, yeah, he's got a reputation in the department for loose lips. He's been accused of blowing a case before because of information leaks. He has a problem with boundaries, is what I was told."

Listening, I drifted toward the small tenant house with the blacked-out windows. Cantwell was saying pretty much what Renee had said. Because Martin told stories out of school, I'd been privy to information I shouldn't have been. But whether the board took mercy and rescinded their decision seemed to depend on Renee. Me, really. Whether I stopped all this armchair investigating.

But here I was, waiting to meet with the very woman I wasn't supposed to be asking about this stuff.

Curiosity overpowering etiquette, I tried the front door of the tenant house and found it locked. Too bad. I remembered thinking Gary and Cara had been in here. They disappeared for a little while, and the mom group had exchanged knowing glances. *Two kids in love . . . whaddya gonna do?*

"Now, Elaine — I hope your voicemail doesn't cut me off — I also took the liberty of looking into the mom group. Just getting some background. You said they'd 'cut you out,' and that made me curious."

I checked beneath the two steps rising to the front door and along the windowsill, feeling along with my fingers for a key. Nothing. And then I saw the two rocks at the corner of the building, stacked in a purposeful way. Between them, a silver key.

"Wendy, Kimber, Theresa, and Renee. Wendy, we talked about. Kimber and Theresa didn't turn up much. But Renee was interesting. She lived in Manhattan, where she taught at a university. She was fired from that school, actually. For getting abusive with a student."

That stopped me for a second, but I pressed forward and tried the key anyway, half expecting it to not work. It slotted in smoothly. I gave a twist and met only minimal resistance.

"Not only that," Cantwell said on the message playing in my ear, "her husband is dead."

The door squeaked when I pushed it in. I found a light switch on the wall and flicked it.

"Apparently, the cause of his death was suspicious. He fell down the stairs of their Hell's Kitchen walk-up."

My breath caught.

"And her children don't speak to her. I know because I emailed the daughter, and she said both she and her brother are estranged from Renee. Says she's mentally unwell. Oh, and she's a hoarder."

The room was filled with books. Bookshelves packed to the hilt. Books upright and sideways. Towers of books. Books on furniture, in piles on the floor, overspilling boxes. Besides a couple of narrow walking corridors, an old couch was the only available space.

I didn't know what to do. I couldn't think. I tried to process what I was seeing, what it meant. But it was like my brain was stuck on pause.

"So, that's what I got. Give me a call, okay? And Elaine — might be good to steer clear of this person, yeah? All right. Ciao for now."

I slowly lowered the phone from my ear and, hardly aware I was doing it, took the top book off the closest stack. *Cop Hater* by Ed McBain. Beneath it, *Fear Thy Neighbor* by Fern Michaels. The more I looked, the more they seemed to all be genre fiction. Police stories and psychological thrillers and murder mysteries. Paperbacks, mostly. Hardbacks here and there. I spotted thrift store stickers and library stamps. The musty smell of pages permeated the air.

This time when I heard a vehicle, I stopped and strained to listen. Tires popped beneath gravel, getting louder.

Someone was here.

CHAPTER FORTY-FIVE

I went outside and saw Renee's rusty old pickup truck trundling down the long driveway. She pulled up alongside my vehicle and got out. She leaned in the cab of the truck, out of view. I thought of running, but I'd done that before, nearly gotten myself killed.

I stepped down the couple of wooden steps to the grass, rationalizing what I'd just seen. *It's just a stash of books. You don't know what it means yet.*

But of course, together with Cantwell's background report, it was compelling.

Renee finally closed the truck door, cup of coffee in hand. She took a drink. Seeing me, she smiled. Though seeing where I was located, I wonder if her smile didn't flicker a little. She closed the distance with a bemused look on her face. "Hi! How ya doing?"

"Good. How are you?"

"Well, you don't look too bad at all. When we talked this morning, I didn't know if you were downplaying your injuries. But let me look at you."

I moved a little closer. I turned my face to show her the scratches. Held up my hand to show her my wrapped wrist.

"Wow, Lainey. Just, wow. You've got someone looking out for you." She wore paint-stained overalls, her hair threatening to come loose from a hasty bun. Only when she reached me — I'd walked a couple of yards from the cottage, leaving the door open — did she look there.

"You got it open, huh?"

I hadn't bothered to close the door behind me because I knew she'd seen me.

"Yeah, I found the key. I'm sorry."

"What are you sorry for?"

"Well, it's locked for a reason."

She sipped her coffee. Her response seemed to take a beat longer than it should have. "It's just to protect my stash. They're not expensive. It's nothing mint or anything like that, but they're mine. Garage sales and thrift stores, lots of stuff ordered online. Did you see?"

"I saw," I said, my voice catching. I cleared my throat and continued, "That's . . . an amazing collection. Is that a thousand books? I'm pretty bad at estimating."

"You're not far off. One thousand, two hundred, and fifty-two, at my last count."

"Did you read them all?"

"Pretty much. Might be a couple I didn't get to. I don't even know when it started. One day, I just realized I had all these books. Been collecting them my whole life, I guess. I don't even like most of them. They're crap. But they . . . hook you in."

She stopped talking, and I tried to think of something to say. But my thoughts were swirling, my heart beating too fast. I finally managed, "With the book club idea, you always seemed to want us to consider more challenging stuff."

"I like to read what's good," she said, moving past me toward the cabin. "The problem is there's nothing new under the sun. Or there is, but you have to really search. It's buried under layers and layers of trash. Like in here. Some gems in here, but mostly trash." On the top step, she looked around the piles and stacks, seeming to soften. "I grew up liking science fiction. But lately, everything is about women running around, ignoring the authorities, 'questioning their reality.'" She made air quotes with her free hand. "A lot of these go way back. Blow on them and they'll fall apart."

"It's impressive."

I continued to find it hard to talk, but I knew I had to. This was more than a hobby. This was hoarding that fixated on a specific thing. And in the context of the past few weeks, the unexpected deaths, the missing person, the books arriving at my doorstep? It was incredibly worrying. But I couldn't lose it. Not now.

She came back down the two steps, closing the cottage door behind her.

"I talked to Alice Nesbeth," I said quickly, trying to keep my voice steady. "She told me about Naomi Sheller being with her husband Roger."

"Lainey . . . I thought you wanted to talk about getting back on the coaching team."

"I did. I do."

"Well, I mean . . . I thought it was clear . . ."

"Alice said Eric Sheller was worried. Naomi had slept with Roger Nesbeth, but it was after Brady Latrelle. And that Brady was angry. He felt cheated on. He might've written something on Eric's truck."

Renee's eyes reflected the bright day. That bemused smile played on her lips. "You couldn't let it go, huh? Not even to get your coaching spot squared away, get everything right with your community. That was your 'moment of choice.'"

"I just want to stop this. I don't want anyone else to get hurt. And someone has been sending me those books. I think they sent them to me for a reason."

The playful smile went away, and her gaze seemed to harden. "Yes, Naomi Sheller got around. Screwed Roger Nesbeth. Screwed Brady Latrelle. So what? You got it solved?"

I'd never heard Renee talk this way. Like Alice Nesbeth, she exuded disgust. I thought of Cantwell warning me about her. My world was crumbling around the edges. I couldn't stop it.

"Naomi Sheller broke up their homes, just like some little slut broke up mine."

Renee sipped her coffee as I absorbed this.

"I'm sorry, Renee. I didn't know."

"You wouldn't know. I don't go around talking about my life in New York, or my dead husband. I'm not one of these oversharing types, like Kimber with all her 'protector' and 'exile' silliness. I just move on."

It brought me back to the barbeque following the first game of the season.

Women can be psycho-bitches, Theresa had said.

They kill themselves, they kill their boyfriend, or their husband's mistress.

Or maybe their cheating husband.

Renee tucked her free hand into her overalls. I wondered if she had a weapon hidden away in there somewhere. "Eric Sheller let his wife screw other men, and he just moved her to a new town. She was just going to do it all over again."

I wasn't sure how to respond. "You're probably right. She seemed to have a problem."

"Like a sex addict?" Renee scoffed. "She had no morals. And neither did her husband. He was a cuck. You can't have people like that in your community. They're like a poison. I tried to drive them out of Tannersville, but they went right into Buxton. Like rodents scurrying to another nest. Into *your* neighborhood, Lainey. Doesn't that make you angry? Isn't that why you became so preoccupied with this? On some level, you knew it was immoral. Their whole situation. You sensed it."

"I think I just want to know if you're okay, Renee. If something like that happened to you, I think it would be extremely difficult to move on."

"I wouldn't be worried about me." She gestured to me. "I'd worried about your own self. About why you try so hard to fit in. About what you're still running from."

Her words stung, but I knew this wasn't about me. I didn't take it personally. I didn't have anything to hide. "You're right. It's been important to me to be accepted. You all have something I don't. You've been here longer. There's a trust."

"You need to trust yourself. That's what I think."

She reminded me of Cantwell.

"The thing about those books," Renee continued, "the ones I don't like, the women are always behaving like imbeciles. They go to the private island, they want to fit in. Their husband is cheating, they don't know what to do. The killer is coming after them, they run up into the attic."

She paused long enough for me to wonder if I had a chance to reason with her.

"Renee . . ."

"It wasn't until Naomi moved in next door to you that it really hit me. How you were in our texting group, talking about your new neighbors. I knew all about her. I knew what was going to happen to her. I knew Gary was going to propose to Cara because *she* knew he was going to. And I knew about Janine Persad. But there you were, right in the middle of it. And you showed up at the memorial. With this look on your face . . . Like you were hunting."

Her hand went deeper into her overalls, and I froze. This was it. She was going to stab me or shoot me now because she'd confessed, gotten it out of her system.

I was coiled, ready to rush her, knock her down if I had to, but she pulled a wadded tissue from her overalls and used it to blow her nose. "I never get used to the autumn," she said. "It always gets my allergies going."

When she was done, and put the used tissue back in her pocket, and my heart slowed to survivable speeds, she looked at me. "I know what you're thinking: those books were a cry for help. But I needed to give you something. The crimes were too far apart. You'd never get it. And the last book? You're the plucky heroine who won't stop until she solves the mystery. At all costs. Coaching job be damned, husband, family — you almost got killed in a car accident! And yet here you are."

"I'm here," I managed to agree, my voice no more than a trembling whisper. "And now you can do the right thing, Renee."

She seemed stuck on that, like a problem that made no sense. "The 'right thing'? Did you hear anything I just said?"

I started to respond but stopped. Nothing I said would really matter at this point. I also didn't know if I was looking at a killer or not. Had Renee followed Naomi into the woods? Cut Gary's brake lines? She was certainly capable on a physical level. She was strong. Despite her size and age, she moved quick. And her husband was dead. Did I need more?

"Let me help you," I said. "Tell me how Janine Persad is involved and let me help you. Is she still alive?"

Renee laughed mid-sip of her coffee and put her hand over her nose. When she regained her composure, she said, "That's it? 'Help me help you'? Jeez, Lainey. You're back to being the idiot woman who runs up the stairs. I know you can do better."

I started toward my car. She tracked me like a predator. "Well, then I have to go. I have a lot to do before getting the girls."

"Ah . . . the girls. That Charlotte is quite the little soccer player."

I instantly regretted mentioning her; Renee talking about Charlotte made my stomach twist.

"Yeah," I said, going with it as I made my way closer to the car. "She's my little go-getter."

"Takes after Mommy. Ambitious. Let's just hope she's less self-sabotaging than her mommy."

I bumped into the car. Moved around it without taking my eyes off Renee. Fumbled for the door handle.

She watched me from the front of the tenant house. She didn't say anything else until I opened the door. "I'd be careful," she called. "Bad brakes going around. And those rentals — well, you never can be too careful. I'd have it checked before I drove anywhere."

Shit.

Maybe she was bluffing. Could I risk it? "I'm sure it's fine," I said.

She clucked her tongue as she followed me at last. "Yeah, I don't know. Can't be too careful. Maybe you should have Brady take a look at it for you."

I followed her gaze as she looked to the driveway. Watched as a large truck came rolling in, a man behind the wheel who looked vaguely familiar.

I'd seen him before, at his garage in town. And I'd seen him right here, at this very house.

CHAPTER FORTY-SIX

Brady Latrelle parked his heavy-duty truck behind my rental. I could drive forward onto the lawn, circle around the main house, but Renee had me worried about the brakes.

Go! Go anyway!

I opened the door wider, ready to slip behind the steering wheel. But then, I didn't.

If there was any chance Renee knew where Janine Persad was, I had to find out.

Brady Latrelle's mud-splattered boot stepped onto the side runner. His other boot crunched down on the gravel. The air was thick with diesel fumes as he swung the door shut.

"Brady," Renee said, "did that old coot give you a price?"

"A hundred per ton," Brady said.

"For the grass?"

"For the alfalfa." Brady spit. "Fifty for the grass."

"Per *ton*?"

Brady shrugged.

"Jesus," Renee said. "Farming isn't what it used to be."

"It never used to be much. Now it's worse," Brady said, eyeing me.

"This is Elaine Barrister," Renee said, by way of introduction.

"I know her." Brady kept staring, trying to intimidate me and succeeding. He was two hundred pounds of thick muscle, like he chopped wood in his sleep. Or, apparently, baled hay on Renee's property.

"Lainey had a car accident just a couple days ago," Renee said. "Pulling out of her driveway — backing out — and got clipped by someone going by. I never asked you, Lainey, who was it?"

"Someone from out of town."

"They're okay?"

"Yes. No injuries to the other driver."

"Their insurance covering everything? Or did they pay out of pocket?"

I didn't answer.

"Don't rest until you get your money," Renee said. "You never know with those bastards. Lainey, do you remember Brady from the engagement party?"

I nodded.

"Wasn't much of a party," Renee said conversationally. "Just a few friends."

Not to mention an opportunity to access Gary's vintage car. Maybe to make the final cut in the brake lines, I thought.

"Do you know what happened to Janine Persad?" I asked them both. My voice sounded strange to my own ears. A voice coming from someone far away.

"Now, why would you ask that?" Renee asked. Brady had moved to her side, and they stood next to her truck.

"Because of the books you sent me."

The corners of her mouth twitched.

"She's in the barn."

"Renee," Brady said under his breath.

"It's all right. It's all right." Looking at me, she said to him, "We're going to put her in there too."

My body shut down. As if I'd awakened in REM sleep, paralyzed.

Renee tossed aside the now-empty cup of coffee as Brandy circled around behind me. Despite my immobility, I could move my eyes. I looked longingly toward the distant road as Brady took hold of my arms. He went easy, but his grip was firm.

"Why?" It was all I could manage. The only word of dozens, maybe hundreds, jostling in my brain.

Renee led the way to the barn. She picked through that large ring of keys she always carried as Brady pushed me along behind her. I was stiff, my movements awkward, but I went.

She reached the door. "What explanation would you like? And what good would it do you?" She paused, as if to say more, then used the key and pushed the door in.

His hands clamped on my arm, Brady walked me through the doorway.

The barn was spacious but had no electricity, no lights, not a lot of windows. The only light came through the empty hay loft.

An old tractor sat beneath a gray tarp. Various tools hung from the walls: spade, pitchfork, shovel. The floor was dirty and dusty, but with clear footprints leading to a seam in the ground. Renee grunted as she got down to one knee, used another key to undo the padlock, undid the lock, then set it aside.

Grunting and groaning some more, she swung open a large door and eased it down, revealing a square cut in the floor. Wooden stairs led down into darkness.

A poured foundation existed beneath the barn. Back in the day, it might've been a root cellar or moonshine store. Now something else was down there. Shut-in odors, rank with mildew, floated up.

"Nnnnn . . ." A woman's voice. A semi-conscious moan.

"Renee," I said quickly, finding my voice. "Let me help you."

"When I sent you the housekeeper book, I was thinking you'd connect to Persad because of old Mrs. Marvin. But maybe it was your friend Courtney Whitmer? She might've known about Hemlock hiring a thief."

So, Renee was after Persad for possible crimes? Not because she knew something about Naomi's murder?

"You don't have to do this. Let's talk. Please."

Renee shook her head in dismay. "You know how it goes, honey. Talk is cheap."

It gave me an idea. "You used to teach English."

"Everybody knows I taught Freshman Comp." Renee seemed unimpressed but didn't move, letting me hurry on.

"My mother taught too. She taught history just for a couple of years. She loved it." I swallowed over the rocks in my throat. "You lost your temper with a student. You got fired."

"Is this from your PI friend?"

"Why did you lose your temper?"

Renee narrowed her eyes in suspicion. "Hmm," she said, as if evaluating my line of questioning. "What are you up to there, Lainey Barrister? Is this your psychology breakthrough? Are you stalling?"

"Did you lose your temper with your husband too? Did you kill him?"

Renee squared up with me. I'd never really noticed the mole on her cheek, or the striations of color in her otherwise gray eyes. Everything was hyperreal. "No, Lainey, I didn't kill my husband. Peter got drunk, which he often did, and fell down the stairs." She turned back to the cut in the floor as if that settled it.

I heard another moan. Someone trying to speak.

Every nerve vibrated. Every cell in my body, it felt like. Turns out that's true about fear.

Renee abruptly faced me again. "Maybe I did want to get caught, you know?" She looked pleased with herself. "Did you read them all? The books?"

"Most of them."

The pleased look faltered a bit. But she seemed determined to enjoy herself. "Bonnie Harper's *The Family Next Door*. I mean, come on. Right? The main character is in a wheelchair. Or at least, you think she is. That was you. Draper's fiancé book; just so perfect, so apropos. And when I found out about Folger's new live-in health worker, when I heard she might've stolen from poor old Mrs. Marvin, well, I couldn't resist." She sized me up. "I saw potential in you, Elaine. All your fear and your neediness. But inside you . . ."

She trailed off, hearing noise from outside. We'd been talking, so the approach of a vehicle had been mostly masked. Now, as she and Brady picked up on it, the vehicle was obviously close enough to have stopped.

Renee glared at me, then at Brady. "Who is that?"

"The fuck should I know?"

A car door opened and closed. I prayed for more — a series of doors opening and closing with the arrival of the cavalry — but it was just one. Renee now seemed to be signaling Brady to put me in the hole in the floor, but he stopped before getting me halfway there.

"Hello?" The feminine voice was barely discernible. Then, louder, "Hello? Anyone here?"

Brady clamped a hand over my mouth and yanked me back deeper into the barn.

CHAPTER FORTY-SEVEN

"New York State Police," the woman outside said.

Renee hustled to close the door to the underground room. I struggled against Brady as he dragged me past tarped equipment and stacked lumber. When I bit down on his hand, he hit me on the head and I crumpled to the floor, dazed.

"Did she call the police?" Brady asked Renee. The words sounded like they came through a thick pane of glass.

The answer was yes. I had. Before I even arrived. But instead of calling Bo Smith, I'd called Investigator Cojuangco and told her everything, including what Alice Nesbeth said about Smith and Brady Latrelle being high school friends.

I should've waited for her. We were going to talk to Renee, since she seemed to know things about the Latrelle family. But I hadn't linked Renee to Brady Latrelle in my mind, so I'd gone ahead of Cojuangco. It wasn't until Cantwell's message that I was able to make the connection, but by then it was too late.

"Keep her quiet." Then Renee moved away.

Brady put his knee in my back and his hand on my neck, holding me down like cattle. My head, still concussed from the crash, ached from Brady's blow. Something hard and cold pressed against my temple. "Move and I'll kill you."

"Oh, hi." Cojuangco was in the room. "I wasn't sure where anyone was."

"Yes ma'am. Sorry, work's never done around here. What can I do for you?"

"Is Elaine Barrister here?"

"No, ma'am."

Brady's weight was crushing, making it hard to breathe. My head throbbed in time with my heartbeat. Hulking farm equipment continued to block the way between me and Cojuangco.

"She didn't stop by this morning?"

"No, ma'am. Was she supposed to?"

I thought about that. I'd never told Renee about Cojuangco coming; I hadn't even said what I wanted to talk about. She'd assumed it was about coaching.

"She asked me to meet her here," Cojuangco said. "To speak with you together. When's the last time you saw her?"

"Well, I saw her a couple of days ago, before her accident. Did you know she had a car accident?"

"I did."

"I tried to see her in the hospital, but things have just been crazy. Is she all right? Is she missing? Oh my God, did something happen to her?"

"Who else is here?" Cojuangco wasn't buying it, it seemed.

"Nobody. It's just me. What's going on?"

"Who does the Dodge Ram belong to?"

"The Dodge . . . Oh, that's mine too. My help uses it. Officer, what is going on?"

Should've run the plates, I thought at Cojuangco. But she'd just been showing up for a chat. She wouldn't have thought to run the plates of every vehicle in the driveway, my rental included.

"So, you haven't heard from her at all?"

"Ma'am, I would tell you. Just please tell me she's all right."

I tried to scream but Brady's hand blocked it. Pain blasted through my lower back as he drove his knee deeper. I thought I felt something pop, like a vertebra, and groaned.

"What was that?"

Renee took a step, it sounded like, because Cojuangco said, "Don't come any closer, Ms. De George."

There was a crash; something big toppled over. A metal clatter of smaller things — wrenches, bolts. The gunshot that followed was deafening.

Brady pushed on me one more time, so hard all the air went out of my lungs. But then it was over, and he yanked me to my feet. I thought, *This is it; this is how I die.* I saw my two girls. Delia's soulful eyes. Charlotte's infectious laugh. Just as clear as if they were standing there now; as if they knew everything, and it was going to be okay. I closed my eyes, waiting for Brady's bullet to enter my skull.

But it didn't. I expected to be dead, but I was still alive. And now there were more shots, but from elsewhere in the barn. Cracking back and forth — a shootout. Until I heard a woman scream.

And then, nothing.

* * *

A door slammed closed from the other direction, as if someone had run out the back. I didn't want to wait to find out. Getting up was excruciating; my back felt like it was on fire. I couldn't move my wrist, and I had a splitting headache. At the same time, I felt exhilarated, grateful to be alive. Slowly, using the equipment to haul myself up, I regained my feet.

Renee stood at the back door. She'd locked it with a padlock and was returning the ring of keys to her belt.

Then she walked past me, toward the front of the barn. I snuck around the equipment for a better view and saw Cojuangco lying on the floor in a widening pool of blood. I hurried to her, lurching, the pain almost blinding. She was on her side. She'd been shot in the hand, it looked like, and again in the chest. I found a weak pulse.

Renee had Brady's gun tucked into her wide back pocket. I heard a truck engine fire outside. Brady's, surely. The vehicle sounded like it blew a U-turn in the driveway and roared away.

"Jesus," Renee said. I thought she was speaking to me, just not looking at me. "What a mess." She pulled some metal cans from beneath a workbench and set them side by side. Three of them. Gasoline.

She picked the first one up, walked to one side of the barn, and started dousing everything.

I looked at the front door. I might be able to reach it before she could stop me. But even if I could move faster than she could draw and shoot — and it was doubtful in my condition — I'd be leaving behind two others.

"Renee."

"Fucking-A, Lainey," she shot back. "You really made a mess."

"Stop, Renee."

She threw aside the empty gasoline can and walked back to me so fast I thought she would take out the gun and shoot me point-blank.

"That's Brady's gun," I said quickly. "Isn't it? So, you say he shot her. I didn't see anything."

Renee's hair was wildly out of shape now. There was some kind of dirt or soot smeared on her face, blood at the corner of her mouth and on her knuckles. This woman who, for some reason, had invited me into her and Brady's criminal world.

"Just remember that I believed in you," she said.

"Tell me how I can help you. I'll do anything."

It was hard to make my vocal cords work. I wondered where Cojuangco's gun had gone. Maybe that was the one Renee was carrying, and Brady had kept his own. She'd just let him leave?

Yes. And now she's going to burn the barn with you and the inves-tigator in it and Janine Persad in the basement. She'll make up some story about warning people to stay out of the barn because of all the combustibles. And that I'd met a cop here on some wild goose chase and we'd ended up burning ourselves alive.

"You could have told me you invited her out here," Renee said. "I would've been fine with that. You didn't have to sneak around."

I tried to process her words, but a fog enveloped my brain.

"I don't think she would have found anything," Renee said. "Or maybe she would have, I don't know. Maybe everybody knows. Do you ever wonder that? If everything you think you keep hid-den, people really know about anyway? These small towns, it's life in a fishbowl. Everybody is connected to everybody else."

I thought of Courtney.

"Maybe you didn't do anything wrong," I said. "Brady killed Naomi in a rage. He killed Gary for knowing about it. Tell the police. Renee, there's a way out of this."

She straightened with pride, stiffening her neck. "Maybe I didn't kill the skinny homewrecker bitch. But I've got a kidnapped woman in my barn. That's not going to look too good."

And she started coming for me.

CHAPTER FORTY-EIGHT

Stacy Meyer. Always there, waiting there in the woods. Even after all of these years.

Crouched in the shadows, waiting for me to come through.

I'd spent years hiding my shame. That I'd been bullied, that somehow it was my fault. But I'd only been a child, confronted by the trauma of another child. Lashing out at me because of her own issues, things she'd never asked for either.

Renee's family and the Latrelles went back generations. Some of the Latrelles and their friends worked the large property for her. One night, after the day's haying was done, Brady Latrelle had been drinking with the other workers, and he talked about Naomi. How she was the most beautiful woman he'd ever slept with. How she was now with some other guy, Roger Nesbeth. How her husband, Eric, stayed with her. And what a mess it all was.

Gary had been there that night. And Renee had heard it all from the porch. It reopened old wounds for her; it hadn't been that long ago that Peter had cheated. Eric Sheller was just going to let this continue? His wife going from Brady to Roger? Who was next?

A few nights later, after a little too much to drink at the local bar, Renee scratched the word "cuck" into Eric Sheller's door.

The Shellers moved. But only up the road a-ways, to the very town where Renee coached the local soccer team. It felt like an insult. Naomi Sheller wasn't going to flash that ass of hers around

Buxton, no, no. Not after what happened in Tannersville. Not after what happened in Renee's own marriage. She wound Brady up. She described Naomi being in the arms of another man. She told him it had to end, or he'd be tortured for the rest of his life.

I found all that out later. I'd tried reasoning with Renee, but she'd kept slipping any kind of mental hold I could get on her. Layer after layer of denial and justification, until there was nothing left. Nothing I could ever understand, anyway. And between the gas fumes and my pounding head, it was getting harder and harder to think.

There wasn't much else I could do.

What happened next required every ounce of strength I had. When Renee started toward me, I stood up from Cojuangco, who was barely clinging to life. It surely looked to Renee like I was in pain, which I was. Like I wasn't a threat. So, she didn't pull her gun. And I rushed at her before she had the chance.

I shouldered into Renee De George, ramming her against what had to be a tractor under all that canvas. Grateful, let me tell you, for every extra pound of flesh on my human body.

Renee fought back once she had time to react, but I was determined, all focused adrenaline now. Her shoes even scraped across the gritty floor as I pushed, and then I reached around behind her for the gun in her pocket.

Her hand went there too. We struggled for a bit and then, somehow, it went off. I went into a protective crouch, my ears ringing. But I had it in my hand. I aimed it, standing, then backing away. She first stopped, looking scared, then probably figured I wasn't going to do anything with it. I let off a shot just to the side of her head, though, and she stopped again.

Shouting over the ringing in my ears, I told her to open the door in the floor. She started rifling through her keys.

"It's unlocked," I said. She'd been opening it up when Cojuangco arrived. She'd closed it but not locked it again.

She did as I asked.

"Janine Persad!" I shouted. "Can you hear me?"

At first, nothing. Just Renee staring at me, this maddening smirk on her face, like I'd imagined the whole thing.

"I'm here," someone said. "Please, help me."

"She's a criminal," Renee said.

"Janine, can you see the stairs? Go to the stairs and climb out." I waited.

"I'm . . . I can't. Tied up. I'm tied up."

A trickle of sweat rolled down the side of my head. My whole body shook so hard, the gun clattered. Or maybe it was my teeth. I was having a hard time seeing. My vision blurred at the edges. All those fumes . . .

"She's a criminal, and Folger is an old lech. Ask Courtney about it sometime. These are loathsome people, Lainey. All of them. Everything I did was righteous."

"Can you untie yourself?" I tried to move closer so I could see in. There were indeed stairs going down. I moved for a better angle, and . . . there. *Dear God.* Two eyes shining in the darkness. The outline of a face peering out. A woman tied at the hands and feet. What looked like food wrappers around her, puddles of excretion . . .

"Eric and Naomi were poison. Gary was no good for Cara; he had the bad gene in the family and wasn't going to change," Renee said. "Janine the klepto housekeeper. All of them clichés. I stopped them. And in the process, I helped you. I mean, look at you, Lainey. Look at you now. Holding a gun. Rescuing the poor immigrant. Like someone ripped from the pages of a novel."

My world swam. I was going to pass out. The gasoline stench was so acrid, it stung my eyes. Renee seemed affected too. Her red-ringed eyes watered. Her lips quivered in that horrible grin. And when she pulled the Zippo lighter from behind her, I knew what I had to do.

CHAPTER FORTY-NINE

I shot Renee De George. I aimed center mass and pulled the trigger. Never in my wildest dreams did I think I would ever hold a gun, let alone shoot someone. I studied criminal justice to help people, get them out of trouble, help communities avoid this kind of thing as much as they could.

Maybe some things you couldn't ever guard against. Not completely. Renee was like a storm in this endlessly hot summer, one for the books, and I shot her.

She fell back into the hole in the floor.

But not before she'd managed to toss the lighter, its flame ignited, into a gasoline-soaked pile of rags. The area immediately burst into flames.

I had no time to rest, no time to think. Putting out the fire was just instinct. The tarp on the tractor hadn't been hit with any gas yet, and I started to pull it free. It caught on several knobs and handles, and I screamed and pulled until there was a tear and the whole thing came loose. I threw it over the growing blaze to smother it. I didn't know if I even expected it to work, but it did.

The air was worse than ever, now as smoky as it was choked with fumes. I hurried to the hole in the floor and went down the stairs, my back seizing, leading with Brady's gun, aiming into the darkness. I saw Renee on the ground, unmoving. I went to Janine Persad and inspected her bindings. Not good: large zip ties, the kind that needed a special tool to break or had to be cut through. Binding her wrists and her ankles. But at least she wasn't tethered to anything. The room was an otherwise empty cellar.

I stuffed the gun into my pocket. Picked Janine Persad up and put her over my shoulder like a lumberjack. And then, somehow, I climbed the stairs.

The gun worked its way out of my pocket and fell to the ground. But now I was at the top. I still needed to get Janine outside, and Cojuangco too. I had to take my chances. But I could close the door, and I did, slamming it down on top of Renee.

Janine was okay, but she seemed groggy, as if drugged. I searched the area for something to cut with but just had no ability to discern one tool from the other. Nothing obvious — no wire cutters or heavy-duty scissors — leaped out. I picked up Janine again and carried her to the front door of the barn, where I stopped.

I thought I'd heard Brady Latrelle leave, but how could I know for sure? Best to sit Janine beside the door. I patted my pants for my phone and pulled it out. The screen was cracked, but it came to life. One bar of service here in no-man's land. I dialed 911. I told the operator where I was and what was going on.

Help was on the way.

Putting my phone away, I realized I was crying. My spine felt numb. I crawled back across the dirty floor of the huge barn until I reached Cojuangco. The fumes would suffocate her, or the flames would burn her alive, before help arrived. I'd get us all at least to the door where we could wait for the ambulance and police.

I reached Cojuangco and just remained on all fours for a moment, trying to hold on to consciousness. Something made a banging noise behind me. The cellar door opened a few inches, then fell shut. Renee was trying to push her way out. I got on top of it, pushing it back down, feeling her try to buck it open beneath me.

The animal sounds I heard made no sense at first. I realized it was her, snarling and howling like a trapped badger. She fired the gun, blowing a hole through the door inches from me. I rolled away, crying out.

I needed something to lock it with, but I had no idea what. Just something I could wedge in there . . .

I stumbled to the wall with the tools and grabbed the first thing that looked good. As I hobbled back, Renee attempted to come up out of the room again, lifting the door.

Her eyes, then her face, cleared the floor and she looked at me. I aimed the business end of the pitchfork at her and thrust out with it. She ducked, the door slapping down again. Quickly, I spun the tool around and jammed the handle through the loop in the clasp.

But it didn't fit.

I needed something heavy instead. Something I could drag over the door. The tractor was obviously out of the question, but there was a stack of 4 x 4 posts. I went after them, tossing them onto the door in the floor, feeling the tendons go in my wrist, my arms numbing next after my spine. It got so bad that by the fourth post I couldn't move, and dropped to the ground, nearly paralyzed.

I lay there, cheek to the dirty floor, as Renee tried to bust out of her prison.

The door came up, just an inch, and then dropped back down.

She rammed into it again. And again.

From my position on the floor, I could see beneath the tractor. A gun. Cojuangco's gun. Kicked or tossed away when she fought with Renee. I crawled to it, reached it.

I aimed it at the door. When Renee pushed upward again, I fired. This time, when the door slapped shut, it stayed.

I thought I heard her mumble something after that. I couldn't be sure, but it might've been, "Okay. That'll do it."

And then I heard sirens in the distance.

CHAPTER FIFTY

October

"Mom? Are you coming?"

"Be right there."

I grabbed the crutches and made my way down the hallway. Charlotte stood at the end in her Buxton Lions jersey. As she watched me work my way down the hallway, she sniffed back some mucus and wiped her nose with the back of her hand.

"Char, use a tissue, honey."

Kids were always getting sick.

"Do those hurt?"

"The crutches? No."

Well, my armpits were sore, and my wrist hurt despite the new cast, but I was too grateful to be alive to complain about any of that. "Blow your nose, honey. Come on."

We got some tissues and made our way outside. Geoff and Delia were already in the car waiting for us. "Maybe I should just leave these," I said to Geoff about the crutches. Fitting them in the back hatch was proving a logistical challenge; they were too long, sideways or longways.

"You might want them," he said.

In truth, I was a little embarrassed. It would be one thing to show up to the game, and people would know what happened, because everyone knew what had happened. But the crutches just felt too showy or something.

Then I realized I was stuck in an old pattern. My protector part was trying to keep my exile from being hurt. The fact was, I needed the crutches. My back was still healing, and so was my right knee. There was no reason to make things worse because I was worried what people might think. It was none of my business what people would think. I knew who I was.

I shut the hatch with the crutches mostly in, though they jostled about when the door closed. "Whoops," I said.

We drove to our local field, behind the school. Last game of the season. Once we arrived, and Charlotte went running off and Delia found her friends, Geoff and I talked to a few people as we made our way to a spot on the sidelines. I wasn't coaching, just spectating. Geoff carried two chairs while I carried myself. Theresa smiled at me and told me I was looking good. Kimber actually waved from the field where she was now assistant coaching. Wendy and I made eye contact, and I smiled at her. She tried a smile back that was unconvincing. But that was okay; that was her stuff. Martin had been let go from the police department, and it wasn't because of me. It was actually Smith who'd made the official complaint.

Geoff and I found a spot almost midfield and he propped up the chairs. Sitting felt good, though I had to keep my right leg stuck out at a funny angle. The kids warmed up; Charlotte ran by, looking for us. Seeing us, she brightened and waved.

"Hi, honey!" we called.

She sprinted ahead.

"She's getting so big," Geoff said. "Look at those strides. Her legs are getting longer."

Geoff hadn't been to a game all season, something we'd only realized just a few days earlier. Well, I had known it, but it hadn't really registered with Geoff yet. He was planning on being there for more stuff, he said. Whatever it was — sports, piano, teatime, all of it. Taking care of the community was important to him, but he felt like he'd been missing his own life.

I noticed Cara among the group of spectators. She caught my gaze, stood, and approached. "Hi, Mrs. Barrister," she said, sitting beside me and Geoff in the grass.

"Lainey, please," I said. "How are you doing, Cara?"

"Okay." She watched the players for a minute, like she was warming up on what to say. "Listen, Mrs. . . . Lainey. I just wanted to thank you."

"You don't have to thank me."

"Well, I want to say I'm sorry, then. I feel like I hardly know you, and you've been here for years, and you've done such a good job with this team. And everything you . . . It means a lot . . ." She wasn't able to complete the sentences because she started crying. I put my hand on her shoulder and leaned close. She reached up and put her arm around my neck. "Sorry. I didn't expect that," she said, wiping her eyes and pulling away.

"It's okay. Of course it is."

The game started. Cara eventually went back to sit with some other people. Every few minutes, someone else would stop by to talk to me and Geoff. Delia came around, asking for snacks. Charlotte almost scored a goal, but just missed. My phone rang around halftime — Cantwell — but I'd call her back. I owed Courtney a call too. I'd get to everything, in time.

Buxton won the game by two goals. You would've thought it was the World Cup the way Charlotte and the other kids charged toward each other and jumped and hugged and bounced in a circle. The kids were jubilant, the parents screaming and cheering. What an end to the season.

But as everyone shifted gears toward the after-game picnic, I wandered off alone toward the parking lot. I'd been to see

Cojuangco in the hospital already, but she was still on my mind. Doctors said she'd make a full recovery, but she had a long road ahead and lots of PT. I wanted to get better myself, so I could be there for her. I leaned my crutches against the brick wall of the school and walked into the parking lot on my own. I was stiff and uncoordinated and twice had to lean on the backs of cars.

A man walked toward me.

"Looking good," he said as he got closer.

I almost slipped and went down on my butt. Smith hurried toward me, putting a hand under my elbow and the other around my back. "Here, let me help you."

"My crutches are over there," I said.

We walked back toward the school. I asked him to help me down to the curb, forgoing my crutches for now. Smith sat beside me. "How are you feeling?"

"I'm okay." I asked about Cojuangco, but he only told me what I already knew. "I want to see her again."

"I'm sure she'd like that."

I could hear the voices and laughter of the soccer families in the field behind the school.

"Listen," Smith said. "I want to apologize to you."

"Everybody is saying sorry," I interjected. "I'm the one who went to Renee's place alone, and I put Cojuangco in danger because of that. She could have been killed."

"No, I put her in danger. And you too. I told you that blood had been found in the car. You were worried about Janine Persad. And I never told you about knowing Brady Latrelle. It wasn't quite enough for a conflict of interest, technically, but I should have stepped away from the case anyway. But please know this — there was never any moment I didn't try to get justice for Naomi or Gary because of knowing Brady."

"I believe you."

He sighed. "Thank you. And I should have taken what you said more seriously. I should have taken the books more seriously. Well, I did. I just didn't push hard enough for the forensics. Because we were finally able to trace them back to Renee De George. She used a proxy account, but we can link it to her through financial records. She'll be prosecuted to the fullest extent of the law. Brady too. They're not getting out of jail for a long time."

Over the past couple of weeks, details reached me that Brady Latrelle had followed Naomi Sheller into the woods that evening. Renee stoked his jealousy, helped turn it into something lethal, but he'd been the one to kill in cold blood. He killed Gary too. Convinced his nephew saw him that night, the blood on his hands, Brady devised a plan with Renee to make his death look like an accident. Brady was pleading guilty in exchange for life without parole.

Smith told me that Eric Sheller, on the other hand, would likely be released soon. That the lawyers were negotiating, and Eric had a court appearance the next morning. "If everything goes well," Smith said, "he'll be a free man."

"That's good."

"Finally, Lainey, you asked me about Janine Persad a couple days ago. Like I said, her family, her lawyer, they've excluded any visitors. At least until she makes a full recovery. But they did tell me to pass on their deepest gratitude to you. I think they're just . . . It's complicated. It's looking like Persad was cajoling Folger Hemlock to give her power of attorney. I'm not involved in that case — it's actually going federal — but the prosecutor is saying Persad got tired of these scams that didn't work out, or just tided her over, and wanted something more long-term. Nathan Hemlock admitted his brother — in his eighties, mind you — was 'susceptible to the charms of younger women,' and that Persad was close to getting what she wanted. He'd said as much to Renee De George after one of their board meetings. And next thing you know, Brady Latrelle shows up to snatch her. Well, he tried that first night, but you scared him off. So, then Renee herself went for it, showed right up at the house, talked to Persad, then hit her on the head and took her away in Hemlock's Kia. Like some kind of crazy, middle-aged vigilante. Brady came and picked them up, and they put Persad in the barn."

Smith's words shook me, took me back to those horrible moments. I tried to hoist myself to my feet. I wanted to get my crutches and get back to my family now. Back to the celebration.

"Jesus, I'm sorry," Smith said. "I didn't mean to dump all that on you."

He helped me to the crutches, and I got them seated under my arms. His face shone with guilt, but I could sense he still wanted to finish what he'd come here to tell me. So, I waited.

"Lainey, I just wanted to say — this is the craziest fucking case I've ever been a part of. This woman takes the cake. Goads a guy into killing his lover, helps him take out his nephew, who suspects him, then goes after a honeypot maid."

The way he said it, I suddenly burst out laughing. All the tension gathered from revisiting events dissipated.

Smith laughed too. "I mean, holy shit," he said. And we both laughed harder.

I settled, though, thinking about Renee. This former English teacher with her bizarre morality, violence, and fixation on genre tropes. On me.

I waved off any more assistance from Smith and made my way back to the field. It felt like everyone turned to watch me make my way toward the picnic table where my husband and daughters were sitting with our friends. People I knew in passing, some I knew better. As I took in their faces, I stumbled with the crutches. Somebody caught me. Multiple hands worked together to keep me up. A young guy Gary's age stood and insisted on walking beside me. A woman joined him. I let them.

This was my community.

EPILOGUE

Something woke me up. A sound? A light? Maybe both. I got out of bed slowly, remembering my injuries. It was just after midnight; I'd only been asleep for a couple of hours.

In the semidarkness, I walked to the bedroom window. Maybe my brain had triangulated the noise I'd heard, maybe it was just habit. But there across the way, a car was sitting in the Sheller driveway. I vaguely heard the engine running, and then it shut off. Three doors opened, and two loud boys got out, then ran for the house. A man's voice shushed them, called them back, told them to each take something into the house. They popped back to the car, and he handed each of them a bag. He told them, I think, to keep the volume down. "People are sleeping," he might've said.

A jangling of keys came next, and the boys struggled over who was going to open the front door. One of them did — I couldn't see who from that distance — and they went inside, dragging their bags behind them, their excited voices fading.

The man turned back for the car, dug for something himself, then came up with a clothing bag he threw over his shoulder. He closed the door and hit the key fob, and the car chirped.

Even from here, I could discern the way Eric stood, the way he walked. I'd been watching the Shellers out this window for some time now; I was trained to recognize them. Here was the man who had gone to jail for suspicion of his wife's murder, reunited with his sons at last. It had all started with a woman in the grocery store, overcome by her life. The childhood traumas Naomi had endured, the tangled web she'd weaved as a result — it had all become too much, and her husband couldn't save her. At least he was free now. At least he was home and could begin again.

Eric started toward the front door, about to follow his sons inside. But he stopped halfway, and he turned in my direction.

He was looking at my house, no question. It felt like he was looking right at me. He raised his hand in a wave, as if to say, Thank you.

I waved back.

THE END

ACKNOWLEDGMENTS

Thanks go to Stuart Dodd for his companionable encouragement. Gratitude for early readers Veronika Jordan, Michelle Green, Trena Stooksberry, and Lisa Redondo. (Veronika, you're so fast! Michelle, so thorough!) Obeisance to my editors Jodi Compton, Shannon Scott, and Matthew Grundy Haig. To Kate Ballard and Kate Lyall Grant and everyone at Joffe Books: my deepest appreciation for bringing it all together and putting it out into the world. And to my readers: the longer I do this, the more I realize it's all made possible by you. Your thoughtful reviews and heartfelt messages are sips of water in the desert.

THE JOFFE BOOKS STORY

We began in 2014 when Jasper agreed to publish his mum's much-rejected romance novel and it became a bestseller.

Since then we've grown into the largest independent publisher in the UK. We're extremely proud to publish some of the very best writers in the world, including Joy Ellis, Faith Martin, Caro Ramsay, Helen Forrester, Simon Brett and Robert Goddard. Everyone at Joffe Books loves reading and we never forget that it all begins with the magic of an author telling a story.

We are proud to publish talented first-time authors, as well as established writers whose books we love introducing to a new generation of readers.

We won Trade Publisher of the Year at the Independent Publishing Awards in 2023 and Best Publisher Award in 2024 at the People's Book Prize. We have been shortlisted for Independent Publisher of the Year at the British Book Awards for the last five years, and were shortlisted for the Diversity and Inclusivity Award at the 2022 Independent Publishing Awards. In 2023 we were shortlisted for Publisher of the Year at the RNA Industry Awards, and in 2024 we were shortlisted at the CWA Daggers for the Best Crime and Mystery Publisher.

We built this company with your help, and we love to hear from you, so please email us about absolutely anything bookish at feedback@joffebooks.com.

If you want to receive free books every Friday and hear about all our new releases, join our mailing list here: www.joffebooks.com/freebooks.

And when you tell your friends about us, just remember: it's pronounced Joffe as in coffee or toffee!